CRUISING TO MURDER

Titles by Mark McCrum

Non-fiction

HAPPY SAD LAND
NO WORRIES
THE CRAIC
CASTAWAY
ROBBIE WILLIAMS: SOMEBODY SOMEDAY
GOING DUTCH IN BEIJING
WALKING WITH THE WOUNDED

Fiction

THE FESTIVAL MURDERS *

* available from Severn House

CRUISING TO MURDER

Mark McCrum

severn
House

This first world edition published 2018
in Great Britain and the USA by
SEVERN HOUSE PUBLISHERS LTD of
Eardley House, 4 Uxbridge Street, London W8 7SY.
Trade paperback edition first published
in Great Britain and the USA 2018 by
SEVERN HOUSE PUBLISHERS LTD.

Copyright © 2018 by Mark McCrum.

British Library Cataloguing in Publication Data
A CIP catalogue record for this title is available from the British Library.

ISBN-13: 978-0-7278-8807-5 (cased)
ISBN-13: 978-1-84751-934-4 (trade paper)
ISBN-13: 978-1-78010-989-3 (e-book)

All Severn House titles are printed on acid-free paper.

Severn House Publishers support the Forest Stewardship Council™ [FSC™],
the leading international forest certification organisation.
All our titles that are printed on FSC certified paper carry the FSC logo.

MIX
Paper from
responsible sources
FSC
www.fsc.org FSC® C013056

Typeset by Palimpsest Book Production Ltd.,
Falkirk, Stirlingshire, Scotland.
Printed and bound in Great Britain by
TJ International, Padstow, Cornwall.

'It is not known precisely how often crimes occur on cruise vessels or exactly how many people have disappeared during ocean voyages because cruise line companies do not make comprehensive, crime-related data readily available to the public.'

Finding 8, Sec 2, Cruise Vessel Safety and
Security Act 2010, USA

'We have got archaic laws going back to the days of Captain Cook . . . we don't allow it to happen in the airline industry, [so] why are we allowing the lawlessness so much in the cruise industry . . .'

Mark Brimble, Australian campaigner for
cruise ship safety, recipient of the Order
of Australia medal, January 2016

'Do your little bit of good where you are. It's those little bits of good put together that overwhelm the world.'

Desmond Tutu

What had just happened? She was gasping for air, choking out saltwater, pain in her chest – oh God, such pain. A big wave slapped her from the side and now she was swallowing more. No, she wasn't going under. *Wasn't.* She struck out with her arms, strong swimmer that she was, but she could hardly move them for the stabbing agony. She had broken something hitting the water. Cracked a rib, must have done.

She remembered the sea racing up towards her: black, glittering with moonlight. She remembered screaming, at the top of her voice, all the way down.

Then nothing. She spluttered as she gulped the warm air. She tried to yell again, but she could hardly hear herself against the noisy waves. It didn't matter anyway. The ship was far away now. A little silhouette coming in and out of view, a few tiny lights showing.

How had she got here? Drunk, yes, she had been that, all evening she'd been drinking. Cocktails, wine, brandy, champagne, on and on till she tipped over, as always, into stupid oblivion. But she hadn't *fallen*, she was sure of that. She had been holding the rails, looking out at the silver path beneath the moon, when she had felt that sudden push from behind. Hoist, more like. Firm hands on her waist, flip, that thump of her head on the ship's side, and then suddenly nothing . . . but the long, terrifying plunge.

So who, who had done that to her? And why? Because she'd had her suspicions about Eve? And Rising Star? That had to be it. She should never have asked those questions. She should have said more to Don . . .

Useless speculations raced through her brain as she fought to stay on the surface, hyperventilating as she floundered in the huge swell. They would see her. *No.* They would turn back and rescue her. *No.* A lifebuoy would be dropped. *No.*

The choking had stopped. She was going down, a beautiful woman in a gold cocktail dress, sinking into the depths like a scuba diver without a BCD.

Under the water, no longer trying to breathe, she opened her eyes. The moonlight was still strong, shining through the turquoise sea from the shimmering surface above her. She was flooded with memories. Her mother, Luisa, gone when she was a little girl, just a mass of dark hair and a white dress in a green garden. Father Jorge, playing his guitar to her, ever nimble fingers, that silly little song, 'Chumba chumba cha-cha', how that had defined her life, taken it over really. And then when he was gone, so suddenly . . . boys . . . men . . . beautiful Diego, all those nights of sobbing. *Papita* in his white suit, making her laugh again.

Even under water she was crying for her lost life, salt tears into the salt sea.

So this is how I die.

ONE

Tema, Ghana. Friday 21 April.

'Oh, yes, that rotting shark, dis-*gus*-ting!' the large Englishwoman was all but shouting. Despite the rattling of the minibus, Francis couldn't help listening as she swapped stories with the two tanned American guys sitting opposite her. They were discussing unpleasant local delicacies from around the world. The shark was what they insisted on giving you in Iceland; washed down with this 'local firewater' that 'kind of took the taste away but then again didn't'.

Cue laughter. But had she ever been to Malaysia and tried Durian fruit? asked the younger American. 'Oh my *gad*, the smell of it! It's like a *gym sock*.'

'What did that guy in Taiping say, Damian?' the other replied. 'That after you'd eaten it your breath smelt like you'd been French kissing your dead grandmother.'

The Americans were chortling, but the Englishwoman wasn't to be outdone.

'You remember those widgetty grubs we were offered at Uluru, Gerald?' she said, turning to her companion, a skinny fellow with a trim grey goatee. 'So gross, weren't they?'

'We didn't eat them, Shirley,' he pointed out.

'We just *couldn't*,' she admitted. She had three, if not four chins, wobbling below a face like a pink blancmange. Trying not to stare at her, Francis found himself wondering what she might have looked like when she and Gerald were young. She had a dainty nose buried in there somewhere, and intense, rather beautiful pale blue eyes.

'*Ooh-loo-roo*,' asked Damian, 'where's that?'

'In Australia. Haven't you been? It's the most sacred Aboriginal site in the world.'

'You mean, like, Ayer's *Ruck*?'

'The Aborigines call it Uluru,' Shirley replied, a tad self-righteously, but she clearly wasn't going to spoil her fun new friendship over a matter of parochial PC. As the Americans fought back with turkey testicles in Hong Kong and deep-fried guinea pig in Argentina, Francis tuned out. Through the tinted windows, under the cloudless cobalt sky, was the here and now of Africa; to each side of the potholed coast road, stalls on the orange earth, selling everything from bananas to motorcycle tyres. *Happy Corner Shop Bar. In God We Trust Butcher.* There was one ramshackle outlet that had fifty identical Pepsi bottles for sale. Women, swathed in colourful robes, walked languorously through the late-morning heat, carrying their goods and shopping on their heads; on individual braided topknots was balanced everything from a huge white enamel bowl full of pineapples to a teetering pile of black bin bags.

Over the other side of the coach, the competitive travel-boasting had advanced from delicacies to destinations. The worn tarmac coast road had degenerated to a rutted dirt track, so Francis strained to hear over the bumping and clattering. The Americans were now enthusing about Burma: '. . . temples laid out on the plain . . . totally awesome . . . you can take a balloon at dawn.' Shirley fought back with Georgia: 'Not the American one, the Caucasus . . . stunning frescoes . . . you just walk in.' But Brad and Damian had been in Antarctica which had been amazing: '. . . Like, armies of penguins . . . you have no idea how huge the icebergs . . .'

But – oh no – Shirley had been to Chernobyl. 'They only let you in for two hours. And you have to wash all your clothes afterwards. But it's extraordinary. Incredibly spooky. Wasn't it, Gerald?'

Brad and Damian couldn't top Chernobyl, but they didn't have to, because suddenly the minibus had turned on to smooth cement and they were into Tema docks, driving past tall stacks of oblong containers in red, rust-brown, pale blue, grey – MAERSK, MOL, CGM stencilled on their corrugated sides. Assorted vessels were moored up along the quay. Gulls swooped and squawked among tall masts. The fresh, salty tang of the ocean was mixed with the industrial whiff of engine oil. At one end, dominating the rest, was the gleaming bulk of a cruise liner.

'That's our ship!' Shirley cried, stating the obvious excitedly.

The minibus came to a halt in its shadow. Francis had been told that the *Golden Adventurer* was not large. Indeed, one of its merits, the PR people back in London had stressed, was that it was comparatively nimble, could go to places that more sizeable cruise ships could not. But to Francis, as he stepped out and stood looking up at it, it seemed substantial enough, with its five long rows of windows above the waterline. Portholes in the black hull, then above the encircling red line, where every surface was a gleaming white, small, round-cornered square windows, then much bigger ones, with sliding doors and slim, flush balconies, then another layer with a surrounding walkway. Above that, tall white railings circled the open-top deck, which bristled with masts and funnels and satellite dishes.

As the new arrivals got out and gathered in a loose gaggle on the quay, a silver Mercedes drew up beside them. The front door swung open and a uniformed chauffeur sprang out, ran round and opened the left rear door, from which disgorged an elderly woman in a large and floppy straw hat, a dark-blue silk knee-length dress, navy tights and tan leather espadrille wedges. The old fellow that followed her, helped out by the chauffeur, was correspondingly dapper: blue blazer over checked grey trousers, shiny brown brogues, Panama hat. He smiled round at the waiting group and then followed his urgently beckoning partner over to the narrow gangway that led steeply up to the walkway three decks above.

At the foot of this stood a Filipino crew member in a crisp white shirt and pressed dark trousers.

'This way, please, ladies and gentlemen,' he said, grinning as he gestured upwards.

As the others stepped on to it, one by one, the gangway wobbled visibly. Big Shirley looked terrified, holding tight to the rails as she manoeuvred herself carefully to the top, where there were more smiling staff to take her hands and pull her on board. A fresh-faced blonde with her hair up stood with a circular silver tray holding flutes of champagne. Another stockier greeter, with tight brown curls and a rather tense smile, offered flannels from a neat pile. Francis took one, gratefully. It was cool on his skin, delicately scented. Sandalwood, he rather thought.

'Sparkling apple juice?' asked the blonde. 'Or a Bellini?'

Why not? It was after noon already and Francis had woken early in his unfamiliar hotel room. He took a Bellini and waited in line as the newcomers handed over their passports and were registered at a desk in a gloomy reception area with patterned blue and gold wallpaper and deep blue carpets. The elegant elderly couple – she still in the hat – were being given the royal treatment by a handsome fellow with four-stripe epaulettes on his white shirt and thick blond hair swept back from his forehead.

'So good to see you again, Mr and Mrs Forbes-*Are-lee* . . .'

His accent was almost cornily French, while Mrs Forbes-Harley was American, from somewhere on the East Coast, Francis thought; distinctly *refained* anyway.

'And you, Gregoire. How have you been keeping?'

After a minute or so of this, as Gregoire moved seamlessly on to a little old lady with a grey bun, Mrs Forbes-Harley turned round to take in Francis. Close up, her lipstick gleamed a deep maroon against the wrinkly brown crepe of the surrounding skin. Her coiffed blue-grey curls trembled as she smiled, revealing incongruous but magnificent white teeth.

'They treat you so well on this ship,' she said. 'This is our seventh time. We love it. I'm Daphne, by the way.'

'Francis,' said Francis, taking her extended hand.

'Good to meet you, Francis. And where do you hail from?'

'London.'

'London, England? Oh, we love London. Brown's Hotel in Piccadilly, d'you know it?' She pronounced it as if 'a dilly' were some kind of exotic flower. 'It's one of our favourite hidey holes.' She gestured at her companion. 'This is my husband, Henry.'

'Nice to see you again,' said the old man, vaguely. Then he focused and smiled charmingly. 'It's Tom, isn't it?'

Daphne gave Francis an apologetic moue. 'You – haven't – *met* – him, Henry,' she said slowly, as if speaking to a small child.

The old man looked taken aback. 'Don't we know each other?' He paused, as if retrieving some distant memory. 'From Antarctica?'

'No, honey. *Francis* is new on this ship. We've never seen him before.' She switched on a thousand-volt smile. 'Are you travelling on your own, Francis?'

'I am.'

He could have told her that he was a crime writer and had been invited to lecture; and that in return Goldencruise had offered him the ten days for free. But he decided to enjoy being a man of mystery, for the time being at least. What was he? Newly divorced? An inveterate single? Gay? Wealthy, obviously.

'Do please consider us to be your friends,' said Daphne.

Now Gregoire was making an announcement: about the cabins, which were, he said, in the final stages of preparation, and would be ready for occupation immediately after lunch. 'So please, feel free to go on up to the restaurant, one deck above us 'ere, which is now open.'

With remarkable speed the passengers got moving. Francis heard the rising crescendo of Shirley's laugh dwindling away down the corridor.

He stayed where he was, taking a seat on a blue velveteen banquette, sipping his Bellini, noting that the peach juice was mixed with real champagne. No half-measures in this luxury zone. Below, on the quay, a few final bits and pieces were being loaded on to the ship; square crates hauled up on tense, quivering blue nylon ropes to the open top deck above. Urgent shouts accompanied the work; but none of them, thankfully, were for Francis.

He was glad to be away; to have escaped, even if only briefly, the pressures and distractions of his life in London. Not to mention the demise of his latest relationship, with the stimulating, sexy, but in the end impossibly solipsistic Chloe G—. What had happened to him? The temporary fame that had settled on him after he, a mere B-list crime writer, had solved the 'litfest murders' of Mold-on-Wold had led him to a strange place. For an autumn and a spring, he had found himself lionized. In public, there were requests to appear on TV and radio shows, to contribute his thoughts to this or that desperate rag: *Of what quality in yourself are you most proud? What advice do you have for an aspiring writer? Has your colour ever held you back? Wine or beer? Steak or sushi?* In private, there were invitations to little dinners in London suburbs, where he was often seated next to a suitable 'single' female, generally equally put out to be so obviously matchmade. On the couple of occasions he had followed up these thoughtful introductions of his married friends, he had found that things were not as simple as they seemed and there was a present or past attachment lurking. Chloe had been one such. In her late thirties, allegedly looking for someone to settle down with but in reality hung up on another, older man who had messed her around for years. In the end it had been easier not to try and compete; to back out and put a stop to intimacy and its complications. At least for a while. Back to lonely but straightforward celibacy.

* * *

After ten minutes or so, Francis got to his feet and followed the others through, out of the reception area and into a central landing from where circular stairs went up and down. He passed a young man with a bushy blond beard peering into a cupboard with a torch. Up one floor at the entrance to the restaurant, a maître'd in black tie was waiting to receive him. Another Filipino, another clean white smile. *James* said the name tag on his lapel.

'Good afternoon, sir. Please, take a seat.' James gestured through to the swathe of empty tables. There were bigger windows up here, mirrors on the walls and a lighter colour scheme, cream and gold, so it was altogether brighter. Shirley and Gerald and the two American guys were lunching together, but Francis didn't feel ready to butt into such gregarious hilarity. He walked over and found a table in one corner, with a view out in two directions: to the quays and containers and assorted masts of the docked ships one way; and then, to the other, beyond a distant breakwater, the open sea. He took out his notebook and settled in for some quiet thinking time.

But now James was upon him, beaming. A couple of yards behind stood a tall, red-faced gentleman with thick white hair and a matching moustache. He seemed to be twitching slightly.

'Would you like company, sir?' James asked.

To refuse would surely be churlish.

'Of course,' Francis replied. 'Why not?'

He smiled up at his new acquaintance, who grunted loudly as he bent to take a seat at a right angle from him. Klaus was his name and he was from Hamburg, Germany. A surgeon, though now retired. 'I must apologize in advance for my school English,' he said.

'Please don't. I have no German at all.'

'In the world as it is, you have no need to.' Klaus chuckled as he picked up the menu. Now was Francis having wine? Good. Was he familiar at all with German wines? No? So perhaps he would allow Klaus to choose?

There were, Klaus said, after he had tasted the Spätlese and they had clinked glasses, in his opinion three stages of an individual's life. The first, until about twenty-five, thirty even, was learning. The second, from thirty to maybe sixty, was working. And the third, which some unimaginative persons called retirement, was living. 'At last,' he grinned, 'you have got shot of your responsibilities. You have, if you have been at all clever, accumulated some nest egg or so. So now you have the freedom to do what you have always wanted.'

In this living phase Klaus was now in, he loved to travel. Sometimes his wife came with him; quite often she stayed behind in Hamburg. Klaus liked it either way, though each was different. 'When I cruise with Helga, it is all very nice, but we sit together at meals, and we have a drink after dinner in the bar before retiring to our cabin. When I am on my own, I get to know strangers. I explore. I am more, how-to-say, adventurous.'

He really did say 'how-to-say' and his th's were z's, like some character from a bad sitcom. Under the friendly surface, there was something, in the look from his cool grey eyes, if not menacing, at least controlling. You got the sense that Klaus was not a man who was used to being thwarted.

So had Francis ever been on a cruise before? he asked. No? OK, so perhaps he should explain that there were cruises and cruises. On a standard cruise around the Med, you would find all types, and perhaps all ages too. Such things were starter cruises. Then there were the huge American leisure ships, ten, twenty times the size of this, with passenger numbers in the thousands, which went from island to island in the Caribbean.

'Horrible,' said Klaus, grimacing. 'Thankfully, I have never been on one.'

And then there was this kind of cruise, which was, how-to-say, top-end, but also for the more experienced cruiser, the traveller, if you like. Had Francis ever heard of the Century Club? No? To be a member you had to have visited over one hundred different countries. Not just states, or subdivisions of countries, like Wales or Scotland, but proper separate nations.

'And have you got your hundred?' Francis asked.

'No. I am not concerned with such nonsense. But there are plenty who are. And if you take this particular trip, the whole way from Cape Town to Dakar, you would be able to add at least twelve to your list. So you will find some who are here just for that.'

'How many countries have you been to?'

Klaus sat back. 'Sixty, maybe seventy. But then I do not have an obsession with stamps in my passport. What is the point of going to Monaco for two hours just to get the stamp? What do you learn? No, it is all very stupid.'

Klaus had travelled with the Goldencruise group before, he explained. To the Antarctic, another how-to-say adventurous location. And then before that along the north coast of Australia. 'The Kimberley, they call it, after one of your British colonial administrators. A very wild area. Plenty of crocodiles but no people. There were some Aborigines there once, but those convicts poisoned most of them.' He laughed, challengingly, but Francis wasn't going to rise to this sort of provocative non-PC; he always preferred to listen and let people reveal themselves.

As their starters arrived, there were loud shouts from below as moorings were untied; then a wobble as the ship moved away from the quay and out into the harbour.

'At last we are sailing,' said Klaus, raising his glass again.

It felt good to be on the move, the port receding as the view from the windows changed to the open blue of sea and sky. They passed fishing boats heading out beyond the long stone breakwater, each with its halo of circling white birds.

At the welcome drinks that evening, Francis wore a cream linen suit. He had bought it on a whim in a January sale and never quite found the right occasion to wear it at home. Now, he felt, it came into its own. He looked round at the dressed-up groups of guests gathered in the wood-panelled Panorama Lounge. They were mostly from what Klaus would have called the 'living' third of life: white-haired, bald, turkey-necked, liver-spotted. The best plastic surgeons in the world couldn't totally turn back the clock, though valiant attempts had been made here and there.

Francis wondered if he had the nerve to go and chat to one of the exceptions: a tall, middle-aged Asian guy with shoulder-length dark hair, magnificently turned out in a crimson and gold salwar kameez, who was standing next to a portly white fellow in a double-breasted Prince of Wales check. He decided he didn't quite, not yet, then found himself exchanging smiles with the dark-haired young woman he had noticed during the afternoon's mandatory safety briefing up on the top deck, when the guests had been shown their emergency muster stations and how to put on their lifejackets (as well as being warned to keep their blinds down at night because of the 'slight risk' of piracy). Her name was Sadie and her older companion was not her mother, as Francis had imagined, but her *ant.* Aunt Marion's husband Saul had had to drop out of the cruise at the very last moment but fortunately Sadie was working in South Africa for nine months so had been able to fly up and take his place.

'My husband the workaholic,' Marion grumbled, flashing chunky diamonds as her bony fingers seized a smoked salmon tartlet from a passing tray. 'I only wish he knew what he was missing out on.'

When dinner was called, Marion invited Francis to join them. Head waiter James put the trio on a table for six and then brought three singles over. First, the old lady with the grey bun who Francis had seen at check-in, all sparkly and smiley now in an eau-de-Nil top criss-crossed with threads of silver; she was English too, it turned out, and her name was Eve. Then a pink-cheeked American with a head as shiny as a billiard ball – Joe. And finally, crisp in a navy blazer with brass buttons, Klaus. He took the last place between Marion and Sadie. Having introduced himself to Sadie, he gave Francis a man-to-man nod which pretty much said, *A very attractive woman I see. You are the younger man. All yours for now.* He then turned politely to the aunt.

So Francis settled in with Sadie. Her missing uncle Saul was some big-shot on Wall Street and – she rolled her lovely brown eyes – he was always doing this. Aunt Marion only forgave him because he earned such pots of money. It was obscene, to be honest, how much he pulled in. Not that she, Sadie, usually got the benefit of his holiday no-shows. But because she was in Cape Town *anyways* it made sense. She was working for the Peace Corps on an education project down there. It was in this township, Khayelitsha, which was like this huge sprawling area of shacks that most whites never saw, except when they flew over it into the airport. Some of the classrooms were actually in ship's containers. 'Like the ones we saw in dock back there? You wouldn't believe the poverty?' She had that sing-song rising inflection more usual with Australians or Californians than East Coast Americans.

The starters arrived. Roasted goat's cheese with herb salad for Sadie; steamed monkfish medallions for Francis. Accepting another top-up of Chenin Blanc, Sadie started telling Francis about her South African boyfriend, Louis, who was like the most exciting guy in the Cape Town NGO sector; but then, she giggled, it was only Cape Town. She couldn't really imagine him being her boyfriend in New York. In fact, to be totally honest, she was wondering what to do about him.

With the arrival of the *intermezzo*, Klaus swung round and joined in. 'Did I hear you two talking about the Peace Corps?' he asked and he was off, starting with the interesting info that George W. Bush had, counterintuitively, actually doubled its size during his so-called war on terror. Francis was aware that on his left Eve had been dropped by the bald American and was eating her curried cream of clam soup by herself. So he left Klaus and Sadie to it and turned to her, introducing himself by offering her a glass of wine.

'Thank you, but I won't,' she said. 'I gave it up *many* years ago.'

Eve had thoughtful green eyes above a puckered, amused mouth. She lived, yes, in the UK, in a little town called Malmesbury – did Francis know it? Just north of the M4 near Bath. Her husband, Alfred, had passed away seven years ago and after that she hadn't seen the point of sitting around at home thinking about their life together, so she'd decided to do something completely different. She went on a cruise, just a little one, up to the Norwegian fjords. 'And then I got a taste for it, and there was no stopping me. Now I do three or four a year.'

'I'm impressed,' said Francis.

'So you should be!' She laughed. 'I've been all over. The South Seas. That was extraordinary. All these tiny islands with vast tracts of ocean between them. You feel wonderfully remote. Then I went to Greenland last summer, and I loved that so much I followed it up with Antarctica at Christmas. Got to see these places while you've got the chance, don't you think? You wouldn't believe the colours you get in the icebergs. And the wildlife is quite magnificent. Polar bears in the north, penguins down south. Such funny little creatures. Like so many pompous Rotarians heading off for a black tie dinner. To see them out there in the wild is such a joy.'

Next year she had signed up to do the Russian Far East and Indonesia. 'I've always wanted to visit Kamchatka, ever since I played Risk as a child. And it may sound silly, but I've a hankering to see Komodo dragons.' She loved Goldencruise. 'They do this very nice thing where the ships aren't too big, so you can get to know the other passengers. And the staff and crew. They become your friends too, believe it or not.'

'I see,' said Francis.

'You don't believe me, do you? Poor, lonely, deluded creature, you're thinking. Imagining the staff are her friends.' Eve's eyes twinkled. 'But sometimes, Francis, people tell an old bird like me things they can't tell anyone else.'

'Such as?'

'Personal things. Troubles they might have at home. That sort of stuff. You know, I like those sorts of confidences. It makes me feel useful again. And if you travel with the same ship, you see the same people. Lovely Gregoire, waiting to greet you with a kiss at the top of the gangway when you arrive. It somehow makes you feel safe . . .'

The funny thing was, she went on, that she had never travelled at all until she was seventy. In her middle age she had looked after her elderly mother for years. 'I was a carer, basically, though we didn't call it that in those days. Not a lot of fun, looking back. Mummy got needier and needier, until it came to a point where I gladly would have smothered her. And I missed out on children. Which was a shame. Then, when Mummy finally shuffled off her mortal coil, I met darling Alfred, at a bridge night, and my life changed again. He was a lovely man, but not a traveller in the leisure sense. He spent so much time going round the world for business that he was happiest on the golf course back home when he had time off.'

Somehow it didn't seem polite to ask where the money had come from: Mummy, or Alfred? Had Alfred been the charming adventurer, latching on to a lonely middle-aged woman with inherited wealth? Or quite the reverse?

'I realize I'm very fortunate,' Eve said. 'To be as old as I am and still to have my health and sanity. So many don't, do they? Living in la-la land, unable to recognize their friends and relatives. Ghastly. And yes, to be comfortably off with it. But when you get to my age you realize you can't change the way the world works. I give to charity, of course; but then I also make the most of things, because if I don't, who's going to? And when I do finally pop off there'll be some very happy donkeys in Somerset.'

A blackberry and apple sorbet arrived. Then, with the main courses, the conversation became general. It emerged that the bald American was a soldier; *Colonel* Joe, no less.

'Did you see action?' Sadie asked; a trifle mischievously, Francis thought.

'Nothing like the boys do these days.' Colonel Joe paused, then puffed out his barrel chest. 'No, ma'am, I was more what they called a Cold Warrior.'

Francis caught Sadie's eye for a second; her lips quivered, but there was no open laughter. Colonel Joe was serious, as he was, too, about the risk of piracy, which had been rather *scooted over*, he thought, during the safety briefing earlier. Over half the world's attacks took place, he said, either off the coast of Somalia or in the Gulf of Guinea, which is where they were right now.

'This adds a certain how-to-say frisson to our dinner, does it not?' said Klaus.

'It would be more than a freakin' frisson if any of these guys got on board,' said the colonel. 'They're famous for their ruthlessness.'

'Stop it, you two, you're frightening me,' said Eve. 'Goldencruise surely wouldn't take a risk with this sort of thing, would they?'

'That expedition leader guy did say they had made preparations,' said Sadie.

'Preparations!' scoffed Colonel Joe. 'But cruise ships are not allowed to dock if they're carrying weapons, so I don't know what they'd do if there really was an attack.'

'They have search lights,' said Klaus, authoritatively. 'Very powerful ones. And loudspeakers. And water hoses and such.'

'Loudspeakers,' scoffed Colonel Joe. '"Will you please remove your Kalashnikovs from the ship."' He mimicked a tannoy announcement and then laughed. 'I don't see a bunch of war-hardened n— Africans taking much notice of that.' He had swerved off the N-word just in time. Presumably for my benefit, Francis thought.

After the meal, Francis accepted Sadie and Marion's suggestion of a digestif in the Panorama Lounge. Klaus was close behind them, adding himself to the group by asking what people would like to drink. This was a somewhat bogus way in, as everyone knew the cruise was all-inclusive, so it wasn't as if he were standing a round.

There was a pianist in black tie tinkling away in the corner, a pint-sized Filipino doing shmaltzy covers of popular classics, but not many from the dining room had come up this first evening of the second leg. The fabulously dressed Asian and his portly chum were there, drinking up at the bar with another odd couple: a short, tanned old fellow with suspiciously jet-black hair straggling down over the collar of his blue Hawaiian shirt and a much younger woman whose glowing caramel skin was set off beautifully by a tight silver lamé dress. They were all laughing extra-loudly, as if at a sequence of private jokes.

In Francis's little group, Klaus rather dominated the conversation, revealing yet another area of expertise: where to find Club Class flights on the cheap.

'Excuse me,' said Sadie. 'I'm just going for a walk on deck. Clear my head. Would you like to join me, Francis?'

How could he refuse? As he got to his feet Klaus gave him a sophisticated look: that of a man whose dominance of the conversation has been usurped by half the listeners leaving, but who is determined not to show that he minds, even a little; added to that, the ill-disguised envy of an older man who watches a younger one being invited away for who knows what reason by an attractive woman.

'Mind how you go,' he said, raising his whisky glass and giving Francis a wink. 'Remember – no lights. No torches, not even smart-phones.' He cackled, proprietorially.

One floor up, on deck six, Francis held open the double doors. A whoosh of night air greeted them, warmer and more humid than the air-conditioned interior. At this level a gangway ran right around the ship, passing the steel wall that enclosed the theatre and then, ahead of that, up by the bow, the big, curved-glass windows of the Observation Lounge, all blinds down tonight. At the stern was an open area of deck with another bar, though that, too, was dark and closed.

'Shall we go up to the top deck?' said Sadie. Francis followed the swish of her cocktail dress as she climbed the clanging steel steps. Above, they found the open space of deck seven, the two big lifeboats on either side dark silhouettes against the brilliant night sky.

Sadie all but ran to the stern, where she grasped the white railings.

'Sorry,' she said, after a moment, turning, smiling. 'My *ant* was doing my head in down there.'

'I thought it was Klaus who was being the bore.'

'Oh, yeah, he was, for sure.' She giggled. 'But it's just the way she sits there and takes it, all twinkly-eyed, expressing interest in something she has no interest in *at all*. She's loaded. Why would she give a toss about cheap flights? She and Saul always fly First. When he joins her, which he doesn't, because he's usually having an affair. Really, everybody knows except her, it's tragic. But I mean, why does she even bother to pretend to be one of the real-traveller gang? It's so phoney.'

'She's just being polite, surely.'

'Oh, sure she is. I'm sorry. I shouldn't be getting annoyed by her at this stage of the holiday. She's been very kind, asking me along. It's just, like, we're sharing a cabin and, I don't know how she does it, she manages to get right on my last nerve within about an hour of me first seeing her. Anyways, this is better.' She let out a long, powerful sigh. 'Just look at that.'

Below them, beyond the deserted tables of the darkened deck six bar, the white wake of the ship bubbled away in a flat, narrowing line into the blue-black night. To the side, the sheer drop down to the ocean was dizzying.

'You wouldn't want to fall in there, would you?' she said.

Francis shivered and held the rails tightly too, his old vertigo kicking in. 'You wouldn't,' he agreed.

Sadie flung her profile upwards. She had a lovely retroussé nose above those frankly rather sensual lips. 'Check these stars,' she said, turning. 'So bright out here, you feel you could reach out and touch them.' She sighed. 'That's the thing I like most about Africa. The night sky. And the sunsets,' she added.

'And the space,' said Francis. 'Just the vastness of it.'

'You've been to this continent before?'

'I lived here. Some years ago.'

'You never mentioned that.'

'Nobody asked me.'

'Even when Klaus was telling us about his great expedition to the tree where Stanley met Livingstone.'

'Yes, well, there is a virtue in not sharing everything, don't you think?'

'I'd say.' She turned and gave him a long, approving look. 'You're very English, you know that.'

'Shall I take that as a compliment?'

She laughed. 'You should. That's exactly the sort of thing I mean. "Shall I take that as a compliment?"' she repeated, in a poor imitation of his accent. 'Very Downton Abbey. So where were you in Africa? What were you doing?'

'Something a bit like you, I suppose. Helping out in a school in Swaziland. It was only for six months. After I left college.'

'When was that?'

'A while ago.'

Francis was vain enough not to want to say how much of a while. But without dating his experience, he gave Sadie the gist of it. How, too, he had hoped to identify with the heritage of his Botswanan birth father, but had soon realized that what he had in common with the kids he was teaching had nothing to do with skin colour. Indeed, the whole experience had made him realize just how British he was.

When they went back down to the bar, half an hour later, Klaus and Marion had gone off to bed.

'Separately, I hope,' laughed Sadie.

The glamorous Asian and the old white guy with the suspect hair were the only ones left at the bar. His shapely younger partner, if that's what she was, was out on the little circular dance floor, twirling round and round to the music on her own. She looked sad, and not entirely sober, stumbling a little on some of her turns.

'Lively scene,' said Sadie. 'You want a nightcap?'

'Maybe I'll pass on that.' Francis yawned. 'There's an early start tomorrow.'

'Yes, Togo, exciting. A bit of real Africa.'

They went out together past the library and down two decks to discover they were sleeping on the same corridor.

'I'm right opposite you,' Sadie said, inserting her keycard in the wall slot with a giggle.

'See you in the morning,' Francis replied.

'If those pirates keep away.' She winked.

He fell asleep to the soft rolling motion of the ship; the low hum of the distant engine; the gentle rustle of the sea on the hull. He imagined what it might be like, making love to a woman, in this bed, with these soothing sounds in the background. But no. That was absolutely not what he'd come for.

TWO

Lomé, Togo. Saturday 22 April.

As the guests teetered slowly down the wobbling gangway at nine a.m. the following morning, a posse of dancers was waiting for them on the quay, the low sun casting their long shadows across the grey, oil-streaked oblong cobbles. The women were in crimson bikini tops, their fleshy upper bodies criss-crossed with strings of white shells, long wraparound red skirts above blue flip-flops below. The men beside them wore matching red shorts, half obscured by ankle-length skirts of hempen rope. To the beat of a group of seated drummers they were all boogying together in that rhythmic, hip-swirling movement that Africans call 'toyi-toyi'.

Three or four were more outlandishly dressed. One wore silver boots beneath baggy, blue, floral-patterned trousers. Layered over these was a wide skirt of oval hoops covered with a gold and orange peacock-feather design, each with a border of glittering turquoise. Over his – or was it her? – face was a black mask, with white eye sockets and a long 'beard' of shiny gold fabric. Above that, a flat, wide-brimmed hat, hung with orange tassels, was crowned with a ring of carved ebony mannequins. The other outfits were equally bizarre and splendid.

Now from one side into the centre of the circle came two more figures, raised up high on wooden stilts, to which their legs were tightly bound with rope. Their faces were masked too. One had white sockets for eyes and mouth; the other was an elephant man, with a dangling yellow trunk where his mouth should be. Turning towards the shuffling whiteys, they waved their black-gloved hands in studiedly slow motion. If this were a welcome, Francis thought, it was a decidedly ghoulish one.

Cameras were nevertheless out en masse to record this first flavour of exotic Togo. Fit, bronzed Damian had a lens as long as a paparazzo's; he was scurrying and crouching all over the quay to get the shot he wanted.

Beyond stood a smiling line of expedition staff: six fit-looking guys and a glam, gym-toned blonde, all in khaki. Their lanky leader, Viktor, was another German, his long grey-brown hair tied back in a neat ponytail. '*Gu-u-ten Mo-orgen!*' he cried, echoing the call with which he had woken the ship's company over the tannoy at seven a.m. Now his arm was stretched genially out towards two waiting coaches. Francis watched Klaus step up into the almost-full first one, then he discreetly took his place in the second. Towards the back he found Eve sitting alone by a window.

'May I?' he asked, indicating the seat opposite.

'Of course. Aren't they wonderful?' she said, nodding at the dancers. 'You can see why I like to go on cruises. We never get this sort of thing in Malmesbury.'

Two open-backed Jeeps accompanied the coaches as they drove up from the port and into the wide, dusty streets of Lomé. They were manned with beefy guys in black shirts and flat caps which read POLICE in bold white letters; they had guns at their waists and were carrying batons like hefty black baseball bats. As their blue lights flashed and sirens blared, the near-stationary traffic grudgingly opened to let them through. Only in Africa, thought Francis, do tourists get the presidential treatment.

From the front of the coach a skinny, high-cheekboned local guide, Didier, gave the guests a running commentary on the sights of the capital, which seemed to be mainly a number of huge and gleaming new buildings erected by the Chinese. In between, he kept up a stream of facts: the average life expectancy in Togo – sixty-one for women, sixty for men; the forty different ethnic groups; the official language of French, the main local languages of Kotokoli and Ewé. 'And now,' he said, 'I shall teach you a few important words of Ewé. When I greet you on the road I say, "Woezo!" To which you must always reply, "Yo!"'

This went down well with the guests, with a particularly loud 'Yo!' coming from big Shirley, who was up the front of the coach with her goateed husband squashed in beside her.

'Some people just love getting into these native customs, don't they?' said Eve, raising her eyebrows. 'You almost get the feeling that they prefer them to their own.'

As the city dwindled away into dense green bush, Didier's stream of information was replaced by a more lyrical commentary. 'Now we leave Lomé, you will see our landscape here in Togo is very beautiful. Green, green, green. I will stop talking now and leave you in peace to contemplate the nature.'

He was silent for all of a minute before an amplified low humming filled the coach. 'And there on your right,' he continued, 'a mango tree.' There was another short break, then he had brought the microphone back to his lips for more soft singing. Then: 'These trees with big leaves, we call them Tik.'

'Very chatty, isn't he?' said Eve.

Way out in the countryside, the buses came to a halt by an empty field. Before the guests were allowed to disembark, Viktor introduced his colleague Leo, the only black face on the expedition team, who was from Nigeria and a herpetologist, if people knew what that was.

'An expert on herpes,' came an Australian voice.

'Funnily enough, no,' said Leo.

'Snakes!' shouted Shirley.

'Correct.' Leo smiled broadly. 'Snakes. Now the good news is that most African snakes are not aggressive. But you will still need to take care, especially if you leave the village and wander off into the bush. Sometimes you will find puff adders sleeping in the sun, and they can look exactly like small sticks. Should you tread on one, it would almost certainly bite. The venom is very slow acting, and we do of course carry the antivenom serums for the common varieties of West African snake with us in the field, but obviously it's all much better if everyone is careful.'

'Goodness!' said Eve, when he'd finished. 'What a continent this is! If the Yellow Fever doesn't get you, the snakes will. Luckily I've got my little Saint Christopher with me.' She tugged at a gold medal on a slender chain around her neck. 'He's always looked after me. From the South Seas to the icebergs of the Antarctic.'

Out in the field two rows of women were waiting for them. They wore colourful headscarves, uniformly pink blouses and long patterned cloths for skirts, and danced and sang as they rattled orange gourds in front of them. Each gourd was wrapped in an elaborate criss-cross weave of coloured beads and buttons, which spoke all-too eloquently of the difference in lifestyle between these lean dark faces and muscled bodies, and the flabby white figures who passed between them, grinning sheepishly beneath their designer shades.

Beyond this welcoming gauntlet was the 'typical Ewé village' that the glossy itinerary had promised: round huts of clay brick with thick, overhanging thatch – *rondavels* as the South Africans call them. Dotted here and there were more modern breezeblock buildings with roofs of corrugated iron.

Under an open shelter sat a weaver at an old-fashioned loom working patiently on a length of cloth with a gorgeous parallelogram pattern of orange, black and green. He was soon surrounded by clicking cameras; everyone trying to get the shot that didn't include other white visitors.

With Didier leading, there was a move towards the schoolhouse, where four rows of children had lined up to sing 'Frère Jacques'. Little golden-palmed hands clapped obediently as their teacher looked on, smiling solemnly as he clutched his big stick. Brad knelt to one side as Damian snapped away.

Eventually the expedition staff rounded up their charges and led them over to an area where a presentation was to be made to the village chief, who was sitting under a large, shady tree with a white enamel mug full of wild flowers on a rickety table in front of him. He was a gentle-looking fellow, wearing a navy-blue fez decorated with a golden star and crescent moon. You'd rather be up before him for some transgression, Francis thought, than the dead-eyed thug seated to his right, in the black hat with the broad white band, who was 'the village head man'. Other men sat on benches immediately behind, with a crowd of teenaged boys and women standing silently behind them.

It was Henry and Daphne Forbes-Harley (today in a stylish cream cloche hat) who were formally handing over the ship's gift, which lay waiting on a table to one side. This was a collection of useful items for the village school: pencils, masking tape, pads, biros.

'Total value probably thirty dollars.' Francis turned to see Sadie right behind him. She was looking, if possible, even better than he remembered, in a loose green top and tight white jeans.

'Presumably,' he replied in a low voice, as Daphne burbled on graciously in the background, 'some actual cash has also changed hands.'

'You reckon? I wouldn't be so sure.'

Across the clearing, the chief smiled and replied with a few words in Ewé, which Didier translated into English. The chief very much hoped, he said, that the honoured guests had enjoyed what they had seen. They were very welcome in his village, and his people were very grateful for the gifts they had brought. 'And maybe, too,' Didier added, in words that now seemed to be his own, 'what you have seen is that what you have, with all your possessions, does not in fact reflect the level of happiness so much. As you see, they are content here with very little. So now the children are going to show you how they are happy from the heart.'

'Art?' said Henry, loudly, looking round at the villagers with a troubled expression. In his white topee, khaki shorts and long socks in brown brogues, he looked like a relic of Empire, Cecil Rhodes inspecting the troops. 'Where?'

'From the *heart*, darling,' Daphne replied, grabbing his arm as he meandered off towards the huts.

'Oh.' He smiled round at Francis. 'I thought they said "art". I thought we were going to see some primitive acrylics or something.'

'Henry!'

'That might have been nice. Don't you think, Tom?'

As Francis smiled, and there was a gentle titter around the clearing, the beautiful children opened their lungs again, in Ewé this time.

'Sweet,' said Sadie. 'Though if one of them gets sick from malaria, or Dengue or Lassi fever, they may not be so happy from the heart then. The healthcare in this country is not good. There's something like one doctor to every thirty thousand people.'

'Is that right?'

''Fraid so: a) they don't have the facilities to train any more up and b) a lot of them go abroad to practise. To Europe and the US, if they can. Or else they train abroad and don't come home. Why would they?'

The coaches made their way off the flat green plain and up a narrow, winding road through thick jungle. This was more like the Africa of imagination, with deep green foliage still dripping and steaming from the night's rainfall. High on a hilltop, they arrived at a second typical village, which reminded Francis of one of the little places in the mountains of Provence, with tall, shady trees around a central square, though you would never have found dancers like this in the south of France, toyi-toying barefoot in bikini tops and long skirts, their ebony shoulders and backs painted with elaborate patterns of white spots. Market stalls ran out along the roadside, where traders were selling scarves and hats and Mandela shirts and masks and carved wooden figures of tribesmen and elephants and kudu and all the other typical African souvenirs. The visitors were not ashamed to bargain, indeed many seemed to regard it as their duty to beat these impoverished people down to the lowest possible price.

'How much does this cost you to make?' Colonel Joe was asking a gaunt woman with sunken bloodshot eyes, who was selling colourful necklaces and bracelets. 'No, don't tell me how much you *want*, just tell me straight, how much does it *cost you to make*? You get the beads *wholesale*, right?'

He turned away from her with a confident grin. 'I was taught how to do this in a souk in Morocco,' he told Francis. 'You basically divide the asking price by ten, and then work up from that. Never show you like the merchandise. It's all a game. They basically only respect you if you're prepared to play along.'

Eve had bought a pair of tall, kissing lovers in shiny ebony. She had paid the asking price. 'It seems rude not to,' she told Francis. 'They're going to fit beautifully in my little travel cabinet back home. I have stuff from all around the world, you know, and I'm constantly adding to it. One day it will be quite a collection.'

On the far side of the square was a barn-like building with a corrugated-iron gable roof but no walls, where rows of chairs and long wooden tables had been laid out. Oval steel catering dishes were piled high with chicken on skewers, sliced avocadoes, quartered egg on halved tomatoes, rice, chips, green salad, baguettes. There was even a dish of rather orange-looking prawns.

As Francis stood in line with Eve, Klaus approached. He was wearing a colourful scarf and holding up a silver hip flask he'd removed from his bulky khaki shoulder bag. He took a swig and wiped his lips with the back of his hand.

'*Visky?*' he offered. 'In Africa I always do this. Before and after you eat, believe me, it is wise. Look at that – prawns, delicious, but how far are we from the sea up here? In this heat? I swear by *visky sandvich*. It has never let me down.'

'I'm fine, thank you,' said Eve; she had already helped herself to the seafood and clearly wasn't going to be put off her choice.

'Before is more important,' said Klaus, waving his flask at Francis. 'Are you certain you want to risk those?' he added to Eve.

'I'm sure Goldencruise have vetted everything thoroughly,' she replied tersely. 'They look fine to me.'

'I see you bought a scarf,' Francis said, to change the subject.

Klaus ran it between his fingers. 'The least I could do. I appreciate that these guys are how-to-say con artists. The scarves are made in China most likely, like all the smart new buildings in Lomé.' He laughed loudly at his own joke. 'But there's no harm in a little redistribution of wealth, is there? What's fifty dollars to me? I would pay much more than this in Hamburg. And here I have a souvenir. And when I get home and decide I don't like it after all, I have a Christmas present for my daughter-in-law.'

Discover Africa's voodoo past, during a mysterious and memorable ceremony in a typical Ewé shrine, the itinerary had promised, and after lunch the coach was full of jovially nervous anticipation. 'Voodoo, oh my!' called one American voice from a seat just in front of Francis. 'I do hope we're going to make it back to the ship.'

'But you must not be afraid of voodoo,' Didier replied, in his gentle sing-song voice. 'Hollywood has made it into this frightening idea, but it is really just a word from our local language of Ewé. It means "sacred".' The religion of voodoo, he added, was followed by some fifty-five per cent of Togo's population.

Nor was the shrine in some dark and spooky clearing in the jungle, but at the back of a pink breezeblock bungalow in a nondescript suburban district of Lomé. After the bulky, white-robed priest had thrown water from a brimming calabash on to the parched red earth 'to welcome down the ancestors', he led the visitors along a narrow passage to a backyard part-covered with a flat roof of dried reeds. A chiaroscuro of sunshine and shadow fell on the male drummers seated round the central dirt floor, where women were already dancing, wailing high notes over the deeper chants of the men. But this was something altogether more intense and purposeful than the carefree toyi-toying of earlier, as the participants, hunched over, sunk themselves into a group trance. Two or three at the centre had faces contorted with real or imagined pain. Others swayed around them, pouring water on them, rubbing their necks and backs with talcum powder, guiding them as they stumbled one by one through the multicoloured curtain of plastic strips at the door of the shrine, a whitewashed building with a glassless open window crossed with thick steel bars.

Francis sat next to Eve, who fluttered a hand back and forth in front of her flushed face.

'So . . . *hot*, isn't it?' she said.

'Are you OK?'

'I'm fine.' She smiled stoically. 'But I do rather wish that I'd bought one of those pretty fans at the market.' She nodded towards the priest, who was watching from a bench to one side, a benign smile creasing his chubby face. 'He seems very relaxed about all these poor ladies, doesn't he? Oh, well, perhaps it's just their tradition. Not for us to interfere.'

Now some of the dancers were encouraging their guests to join in. The few takers were all female: a blonde American in a white skirt, orange blouse and huge sunglasses, who had the air of one who had been a cheerleader in her distant youth; then, to Francis's surprise, Sadie, moving her hips and shoulders in a not unconvincing imitation of the easy African way; and finally – Praise the Lord!   Shirley, chubby white arms out in front of her as she kangarooed adventurously across the floor. She was laughing loudly at her own attempts to toyi-toyi; but then, suddenly, she wasn't laughing, losing herself in the beat of the music, face down, grimacing like one of the women who had vanished through the door of the shrine. As the locals saw her expression change, they darted around her like little fish, tugging up her big white blouse and rubbing talc into the skin of her back, then pouring water over the thin curls on top of her head. So it was hard to tell, when she finally lifted her face again, whether the gleaming moisture on her cheeks was water or tears. Pulling herself upright, she looked round at her audience with a blank stare, shook herself like a big dog and made her way off the floor, supported by three helpers.

As the guests arrived back at the ship that evening, the hawkers were out on the quay in force. If you hadn't already bought your Togoan necklace, carving or Mandela shirt, now was your chance. Beyond, by the steel gate to the gangway, stood a row of crew in crisp white shirts, purple waistcoats and black bow ties, holding out a banner which read *Welcome Home*.

'That was quite a day,' said Eve, as she stepped on to the solid surface of deck three. 'I'm looking forward to a little lie down now.'

'Will we see you at dinner?' asked Francis.

'I might just watch a film and have some soup in my cabin. Can't manage the full bells and whistles every night.'

They walked together past Reception and along the narrow corridor, lined with its tightly sealed cabin doors.

'Here I am,' said Eve, as she reached 314.

'I'm just one along,' said Francis.

'How nice,' said Eve, touching his arm as she met his eye. 'It's reassuring to have you there.' Francis looked down at the wrinkled V of her neck and felt a wave of affection for her. Without thinking, he leaned forward and gave her a hug.

'I'll see you tomorrow morning,' she said, waving as she backed into her cabin, 'unless I get a sudden second wind.'

There was just enough time to shower and change before evening cocktails in the theatre. As if they hadn't seen enough dancing already today, the guests were treated to a final display, introduced by the ever-enthusiastic Viktor. Though there were even more elaborate masks and costumes than at the breakfast-time parade, this performance seemed somehow tamer, the contained touristic entertainment it was. But then, at the drum-beaten climax, a cloud of dry ice was released, tipped from a bucket at one side by hotel director Gregoire, his handsome profile in silhouette against the billowing white. For a minute or two there was a tangible sense of mystery as the lights dimmed and the eerie masked creatures shimmered through the ersatz mist.

Then, with a few coughs from the audience, the magic was gone. The lights came up, dinner was announced and the dancers were bundled off down the gangway, gleaming and pungent with the sweat of their exertions. There were yells from the dockside as the moorings were untied. The ship wobbled, and the guests shuffled upstairs for another very European repast.

THREE

Day at Sea. Sunday 23 April.

Francis woke feeling relaxed. It was a day at sea, so there was no wake-up call for the guests this morning, just a leisurely shower and a stroll upstairs to the breakfast room where a sumptuous buffet was laid out. Along from the fine spread of cereals, mueslis, exotic fresh fruit and the deep silver dishes of bacon, sausages, tomatoes, mushrooms, scrambled egg et al, two more Filipinas in chef's hats were grinning away behind an omelette station.

'Yes, sir, what can I get you?' they parrotted. 'Cheese omelette, ham omelette, omelette with everything?'

Francis paused for barely a second. 'Omelette with everything, please,' he said.

'We will bring it, sir.'

At seven thirty a.m. the place was half empty, so he was able to find a table with a porthole view over the sunny ocean outside. There was even a newspaper to read, the *Golden Adventurer News*, a one-page digest of recent world events with a touch of local colour thrown in. How much easier life would be, he thought, devouring it in a minute, if this were the sum total of the news he was given at home instead of the incessant feed of papers, radio, TV, websites, tweets and Facebook shares with which he cluttered up his day, allowing himself to empathize with situations and causes he would never be able to do anything directly about.

Glancing at his mobile, he realized that he had become Facebook friends with Sadie last night. After dinner at different group tables, they had gone up to the bar together and sat with their drinks near the little circular dance floor, where the chic younger companion of the old man with straggly hair was no longer alone, instead being waltzed around expertly by none other than gorgeous Gregoire.

'Is that a service he offers all the ladies, d'you think?' Sadie asked.

'Dancing lessons?'

'Let's hope it stops at that.'

'Hubby looks like a dog whose bone has been taken away.'

'Perhaps it has. They're an odd couple, aren't they? Bostonians. He's some kind of magazine publishing tycoon and she's his long-term Puerto Rican girlfriend.'

'How did you find that out?'

Sadie tapped her nose. 'I keep my ears to the ground. And that beautifully dressed Asian guy is a famous designer, did you know that?'

'I didn't.'

'Like, seriously, the John Galliano of Mumbai or something. Among other things he does loads of the outfits for Bollywood.'

'Well, well. And his sinister friend?'

'A bit scary looking, isn't he? If you ask me, he's the money. Or maybe the emotional rock. Or both – a handy package.'

Francis laughed. 'You have been busy.'

Sadie shrugged. 'And guess what? You know Shirley?'

'The large English lady . . .'

'Who you find annoying.'

'Is it that obvious?'

'Er, yes. And I kinda take your point. She is a bit up herself sometimes. But I was chatting to her over dinner and in fact she's rather amazing. She's been a nurse all her life, looking after sick children, and now she's got terminal cancer.'

'You're joking.'

'I'm not. How unfair is that? You're not to tell anyone this, but she and Gerald have pretty much blown their life savings coming on this trip. She's finished treatment and it's not looking good. They can't tell her how long she's got, apparently, but it may be just months. So she's going for it, doing the stuff she always wanted to do, which I think is rather cool. She was making us laugh, saying that every time she finishes a tube of toothpaste she celebrates, because that means she's survived a few more weeks.'

As Francis met Sadie's eye, she rested her hand on his arm. It sent a tingle right through him, and for a moment, flushed with wine and whisky, he had found himself wondering if this were an invitation – and, if so, whether he should take it up. A fling on the ocean wave – how liberating and romantic! Especially after all the hassle he'd had with Chloe. But though such a release might be fun, he was old and experienced enough to know that it might also not be; and if it wasn't, how would he ever get away? In any case, hadn't he promised himself a break from emotional complications? Demands that he couldn't fulfil. No, in the sober light of morning he was glad that their intimacy was still just virtual.

Relishing his freedom, he lingered over his breakfast, watching the Filipino waiter in the cream jacket as he seated new arrivals and took their orders. *John* the badge on his lapel read. 'Is that really your name? John?' asked the American couple at the next-door table, as he brought them poached eggs.

'Yes, madam,' he replied with a patient smile, 'John since 1972.'

Back in his cabin, Francis found his bed had already been made. A rabbit, folded from a flannel, squatted on his pillow. He unpacked his laptop and found a place for it on the narrow desk below the mirror. Booting it up, he opened his journal file and typed the day's date. Once he'd done his daily entry (like prayer for him), Francis's plan was to spend the morning doing some serious planning for his next project, which was not – please don't tell his publisher! – another murder mystery featuring his series hero George Braithwaite, retired professor of forensic science, and his feisty wife Martha, but a new departure into non-fiction, his long-planned memoir of adoption. It was something he had been skirting around for years but now felt he could put off no longer. To delve into those deep and troubling feelings that it would be so much easier not to examine, starting with the moment he had realized, at the age of six, that it was biologically impossible for a little brown boy to be the child of two white parents. 'Daddy, are you really my daddy?' he had asked, in a line that had gone down in family mythology. A joke, but not actually a joke; and it was that tricky area that he wanted at last to explore.

First things first. Francis typed in the glamorous dateline – *Golden Adventurer. At sea somewhere off Ghana. 23 April.* But as his fingers hovered over the keyboard, he heard, quite unmistakeably, a scream. Next door, it sounded like, in Eve's cabin. He jumped to his feet and ran out of the room.

The door to 314 was half open. Francis slid in, pulling it carefully to behind him. Hentie, the deck three butler, was standing immobile by the bed, her charcoal-uniformed back to him. She was the tense-looking young woman who had handed out the cold flannels as they had arrived, but Francis had spoken to her only once, when she had called on him to show him round his cabin on the first afternoon. In front of her, Eve was tucked up soundly, asleep it looked like at first glance.

'What's going on?' Francis asked.

Hentie turned. 'Oh God,' she said blankly, in her thick Afrikaans accent. 'She's dead. Out cold. I just touched her.' She shuddered.

Francis stepped closer. Eve lay, head on the pillow, eyes closed, horribly still.

'Are you sure?' he asked. 'Did you take a pulse?'

'I didn't need to. She's cold. Hard.'

Francis nodded. 'Rigor mortis. That means she's been gone for a while.' He moved to lift the covers and see for himself.

'No!' cried Hentie. 'No, leave her.'

'OK,' he said quietly, backing off.

'Really. You shouldn't be here.' Hentie was shaking her head, her hands visibly trembling. 'She was fine last night,' she said. 'I brought her soup. She was watching TV.'

'So why did you come in this morning?'

'Unless there's a *Do Not Disturb*, we always call on our single passengers at breakfast time. Just to see they're all right.'

'I see.' That routine had certainly paid off today, Francis thought.

'You shouldn't be here,' Hentie repeated.

'I heard your scream.'

'I shouldn't have screamed.'

'But you did. It's perfectly natural, Hentie.' Francis used her first name deliberately; if he was going to stay, trust needed to be established fast.

'Oh my God, man, you *should not* be here.'

'It's fine. You won't be in trouble. Now you should get the doctor, don't you think?'

'Yes.'

'I'll wait here,' Francis said.

'I must inform the captain too.'

Hentie looked panicked. Almost as if this were her fault; which, unless she was a very accomplished actress indeed, it clearly wasn't.

'You do that,' Francis said. 'But get the doctor first. He needs to verify this death. Certify it,' Francis corrected himself.

'It's a she.'

'OK. But go. I'll be here.'

Hentie headed off. As she reached the corridor, she turned. 'Don't you think you should just go? It would make it so much easier for me.'

'It's fine,' Francis replied. 'I'll explain. You're perfectly within your rights to scream when you find a dead body in one of your cabins. And I'm perfectly within mine to come and see what's going on.'

'I'd rather you went.'

'No. Someone should stay with her. Anyway, I'm not going to cover up what I heard.'

Hentie turned and walked off. Francis followed her and made sure the door was pushed to.

Someone should stay with her. An entirely bogus reason, they both knew that. So what had possessed him to insist? Curiosity. Just like the last time.

He looked slowly round the cabin. It was identical to his, even down to the bland abstracts on the walls. Through the half-open cupboard door in the corridor he could see a stack of evening dresses. The empty soup bowl was still by the bed. So for all her attentiveness, Hentie had not been back last night.

Further over on the white counterpane was a paperback. *Mindfulness: A Practical Guide to Finding Peace in a Frantic World.* It had a little green cloth bookmark about halfway in, on which was written, in gold, *by words the mind is winged – Aristophanes.* Francis turned his gaze slowly towards Eve. Her mouth was no longer dancing with wry amusement at the foibles of the world; it was just a thin, lifeless line in a downward curve. Well, whatever had happened, she had found peace now. A stroke, was it, or would that have made for a more traumatic expression? Was it possible just to pass away like this? When only yesterday she had seemed so alive. He had barely known her, but looking at these abandoned features, tears welled up. There would be no trips to Komodo or Kamchatka for her now. St Christopher had failed her. Oh well, she knew nothing about it. Rest in Peace, Eve. She was back with Alfred, playing celestial golf.

He paced slowly round the room, giving it, despite himself, the Braithwaite treatment. There was really nothing to remark on. Eve's clothes were all tidied away, just one pair of slightly scuffed white trainers neatly paired in the corner by the minibar, on which sat a sharp knife, an uncut lemon and an empty champagne bucket. Next to it, folded, was a copy of yesterday's *Golden Adventurer News*.

'OK, let's see what's happened here,' came a woman's voice down the corridor. It was an efficient, controlled, medical voice, bordering on the patronizing, even with a body that was no longer alive to be patronized.

The doctor appeared: not only was she female, she was young and good looking with it. A Filipina with bobbed dark hair in a figure-hugging white coat.

'Good morning,' she said brightly.

'Good morning,' Francis replied.

'I understand from Hentie that you heard her screaming.'

'Yes. I'm in the next-door cabin. I thought I'd better stay here until you arrived.'

The doctor nodded. 'That's fine. Hentie's gone up to the bridge to inform the captain. I expect he'll be down in a minute. I'm sure he will decide . . .'

She trailed off, though 'what to do about you' was clearly implied. She approached the bed slowly, then paused and took out a pair of transparent plastic gloves from the pocket of her coat.

'Yes,' she said quietly, slipping them on. 'No longer with us, I'm afraid.' She turned to Francis. 'Almost looks as if she's sleeping, doesn't she? Poor Eve.'

'You knew her?'

'Oh yes, we all know Eve. She's a regular. Much loved by the staff, partly on account of her generous tips. And one of those people who never complains, even when they're ill.'

'So what's happened?' Francis asked. 'I was out on an excursion with her yesterday and she seemed absolutely fine.' He suddenly remembered the orange prawns in the second village; but no, if Klaus had been right, and something was wrong with them, she'd have been violently sick, surely. They wouldn't have killed her. Would they?

The doctor shrugged. 'She's old. Could be anything, I'm afraid. A stroke. Or myocardial infarction – that's a heart attack. Sometimes people of this age just slip away.'

The doctor pulled back the duvet. Eve was in a thin white nightie, which did little to conceal her otherwise naked body. The saggy, lined flesh, peppered all over with brown liver spots, was something of a contrast to the neatly clad figure he had chatted to at dinner and on the coach.

'I'm guessing she was in her mid to late eighties,' the doctor said. She reached out her gloved forefinger and touched Eve's upper left arm, then followed up with a second gentle poke to the flesh below the neck.

'Stiff already,' she said.

'Rigor mortis,' said Francis.

'Exactly.' She smiled. 'Are you, perhaps, a reader of crime fiction?'

'I write it actually.'

This surprised the doctor. 'Really?'

'That's why I'm here on the ship. I'm lecturing on the history of the genre.'

'I must try and come. I don't get a chance to read as much as I'd like, but that's one of my favourite things, when I've got time off . . .'

As she talked she was continuing with her checks. Francis noticed that even though Eve was clearly dead, the doctor took her pulse.

'That's routine,' she said, spotting his interest.

'I'm Francis, by the way,' he said. 'Francis Meadowes.'

'Alyssa Lagip.'

They exchanged a slightly awkward nod.

Having poked and prodded a little more, Dr Lagip pulled back one of the eyelids and examined the eyeball.

'Hm. Interesting.'

She pushed back the lid, which slid shut like a doll's, and studied the other eye. From her pocket she took out a black notebook and a pen and made a note.

Just as Francis was about to ask her what was so interesting, the cabin door swung open and there was the sound of voices. It was Hentie, accompanied by the captain, a fellow officer with four stripe epaulettes, Viktor, and the blonde expedition staffer.

'Close door, please,' said the captain. He was a beefy fellow with a rather rough red face and thick black hair, cropped short. Hentie, at the back, must have done what he asked, as Francis heard the click. The little posse reached the centre of the cabin and stopped.

The captain nodded at Francis but said nothing; it's just a matter of time, he thought, before he asks me to leave.

Dr Lagip turned. 'Captain,' she said, with a smile.

'So,' he replied, after a few long moments studying Eve in silence. 'We have Operation Rising Star.'

'I'm afraid so,' said the doctor.

'We're not having much luck on this ship, are we? So what happened to this one?'

'It's not entirely clear. But I would like to request a post-mortem, sir. As soon as possible.'

The captain didn't answer this question. Instead he turned to Francis, fixing him with startling blue eyes. 'Hentie tells me you heard her scream when she discovered this body?'

'Yes, Captain.' Francis had toyed with 'sir', before deciding to copy the doctor. 'I'm in the cabin next door.'

'This is in a way unfortunate. But I suppose you are here now.'

'Yes.'

The captain said nothing for a few moments, his brow creased in thought. Then: 'We like to keep this sort of thing quiet. Not deliberate deception, you understand. But obviously it spoils cruise for other guests if they are thinking one of them has died. If people ask about missing person, we generally say that they are ill, confined to cabin.'

'I understand,' said Francis. 'You can trust me to be discreet. As you may or may not know, Goldencruise has invited me here to lecture—'

'Yes,' said the captain, cutting him off. 'I am aware of your status. And also your story. You will probably find yourself at my table one evening for dinner, along with a selection of other distinguished guests, and then you can tell us all how you write your books. And also, maybe, about how you solved famous murder at English music festival.'

'Literary festival,' Francis corrected, feeling a little absurd.

But the captain had already turned away. 'So how immediate must post-mortem be, Doctor?' he asked.

'As immediate as possible. There are hospitals in Takoradi.'

'Can't it wait for Dakar?'

'Not really, Captain, no.'

'Why not?'

'Because we should establish a definite cause of death. As soon as possible.'

'What are you saying?' The captain looked slowly round the group. 'That there is some uncertainty here?'

Dr Lagip gestured towards the body, immobile at the centre of the bed, with its horrid little downturned grimace. 'Eve was old,' she said. 'In her mid eighties, I am guessing. It is perfectly consistent with her age that she should have suffered a heart attack or stroke and died suddenly in her sleep. But I don't know. There is something about this that doesn't feel quite right to me.'

'How do you mean?'

'Her eyes are a little bloodshot. Of course, it may be nothing, but then again . . .'

'Then again what, Doctor?'

'Such a symptom would be consistent with, for example, suffocation.'

'You think somebody suffocated her?' The expression on the captain's heavy-set features was one of astonishment. 'Really? Who?'

'I have no idea. I'm not even saying that it's likely. Just that I would like to be sure. Another possibility is some kind of toxin.'

'Toxin! Are you serious?'

'It is a possibility. There are several small hospitals in Takoradi, sir. A post-mortem could easily be arranged.'

'I appreciate that,' said the captain, exchanging a look with his fellow officer. 'But even if you are not questioning cause of death, authorities will have to be involved with removal of body – if they allow it at all. So we have problem. African police, swarming all over my ship, searching for God knows what. Not a pretty thought. When did she die? Have you established that?'

'Rigor mortis has set in,' the doctor replied. 'So at least six hours ago. Probably longer.'

'And who else has seen her? Apart from butler?'

'Hentie?' asked the doctor, looking over at her.

'I don't know,' Hentie replied. 'Nobody, I would think. Her door was locked.'

'And when did you last see her?' the captain asked.

'I brought her supper last night, sir. At around seven o'clock.'

'You didn't come back to clear away?'

'No, sir.'

'Why not?'

'It was only a bowl of soup, sir. She was watching a film . . . I thought she would want to sleep, sir . . .'

Hentie was as flustered as the captain was displeased.

'I shall be speaking to hotel director about this,' he said. 'You know routine. But you were first to see her this morning?'

'Yes, sir.'

'At what time?'

'Eight thirty, sir.'

The captain nodded. 'So if this woman died last night, some time after seven o'clock, who's to say she even died in international waters? Technically speaking, we might have to sail back to Togo. To allow another bunch of – of – chaotic idiots on board.'

'With due respect, Captain,' said Viktor, turning towards his staffer for support, 'the police in Togo were extremely helpful and professional. As Carmen will agree.'

The blonde nodded. 'They were,' she said; her accent was Australian.

'Giving your two coaches escort,' said the captain, 'through crowded city. In return for fat bribe. Of course, they are helpful. That's what they do. Most of time. But investigating possible murder. Of wealthy white person. On luxurious ship such as this. It's recipe for disaster. They could keep us in port for days. And even then not allow body off. Come on. We all understand what we're talking about here.'

'Of course I understand, Captain,' said Viktor, though the set expression on his features said otherwise.

'Sorry to offend your PC sensibilities,' said the captain, 'but this is my experience. Of this continent. You saw yourself what happened in Libreville.'

'With respect, sir, that was an entirely different situation. And Gabon is a different country.'

'Africa,' said the captain, with a shrug. He looked towards Francis, then over at his fellow officer again, whose lips registered a slight, supportive smile.

'Who does have jurisdiction in a matter like this?' Francis asked, into the awkward silence. 'I mean, just for the sake of argument, what would happen if the death occurred while you were in international waters?'

The captain said nothing and for a moment Francis thought he had overstepped the mark. But: 'It's grey area,' he said eventually. 'If death actually happens, physically, in territorial waters of particular country, like man overboard, then yes, we must inform that country and expect them to be involved. But death on board ship, in middle of ocean, it doesn't come up. Wherever we are, we normally keep body in morgue, take it off at next appropriate port, and then in due course report death to police in Nassau.'

'In Nassau!' said Francis. 'Why Nassau?'

'Vessel is registered in Bahamas. Deaths on board are technically concern of Bahamas Maritime Authority.'

Despite the tense atmosphere, Francis was on the brink of laughing out loud. 'So strictly speaking,' he said, 'if Dr Lagip has a concern about what happened to Eve, it should be investigated by a detective from the Bahamas?'

'It's not something I've encountered before,' said the captain. 'But yes.'

'But you just said you've had deaths on board before?'

'Of course. It goes with demographic. But nothing ever,' he slowed down and looked hard at the doctor, 'considered suspicious. Not on my watch.'

'Eve here is a British citizen,' Francis went on. 'What about the UK police? Shouldn't they send someone out?' He turned towards the doctor. 'If you're really concerned?'

'Why would they be interested?' said the captain. 'We are well away from UK. There is no consulate for high seas, I'm afraid.' He paused and looked round the assembled party. 'My problem here is that this situation is avoidable. Your suggestion that cause of death was not natural is based on what, Doctor? Bloodshot eyes? Can I really jeopardize entire cruise for bloodshot eyes?'

There was silence.

'Viktor?'

The expedition leader shrugged. 'I will obviously go along with your decision, sir,' he replied, tight-lipped.

'If Dr Lagip wants to have a post-mortem,' Francis suggested, 'couldn't you organize one under the radar, as it were? Just get the body delivered discreetly to a hospital and checked out without informing the police.'

'And how is body going to be "delivered discreetly" to hospital

in small port in Ghana?' asked the captain. 'Where everybody knows
everybody. When we have removed bodies before, it is usually done,
discreetly, yes, while guests are on day tour. Local authorities in
such a case are aware, because generally body is being shipped
home. So all is fine. But are you likely to conceal from authorities
ambulance leaving biggest ship to come into port in weeks?' He
turned towards Francis. 'You've seen what it's like in these places.
Every hawker in town is on quay. Do you imagine police are not
also noticing everything that is going on?' Now his gaze rested on
Alyssa. 'Really, Doctor. This is silly. An old woman has died. Very
sad. Why can't we leave it at that?'

'We can,' said the doctor, her mouth tightening. 'But I cannot sign
the death certificate, I'm afraid. And I would like it registered in the
logbook that I had these concerns. In case anything else happens.'

'Anything else happens . . .' the captain repeated slowly. 'What
are you saying?'

'I don't know,' said the doctor. 'This is why I would like to be
sure . . .'

The captain drew in his breath. 'We have impasse,' he said,
after a moment. 'But then again, this is my ship. So I can insist
that body remains in morgue till Dakar.'

'You can,' said Dr Lagip. 'But then you would have no doctor.
I cannot allow myself to be compromised in this way. This isn't
just my reputation at stake here. It's a matter of professional ethics.'

There was silence at this sudden blast. After ten long seconds
Francis decided to take a chance; for what, really, other than a
satiation of curiosity, did he have to lose? He had stumbled into
this situation by accident; he was quite happy to be asked to stumble
out again. 'So there's really no way,' he said quietly, 'that you can
put your worries to rest without a post-mortem, Doctor?'

'No. As I said, I don't have the equipment on board to check
for toxins. And in any case I'd like a second opinion before I sign
the death certificate.'

'So how long do these toxin tests take?' Francis continued.
'I mean, surely they're not immediate.'

Dr Lagip held out both her hands in a gesture of controlled
frustration. 'Of course not. It might take days, weeks even, to get
a full set of results. I'm not trying to stop the cruise. Just so long
as the body gets properly medically examined I'll be happy.'

Her clear brown eyes were flawless in their sincerity.

'I see,' said Francis, turning towards the captain. 'Is there, perhaps, another way forward here . . .'

At a quarter to one, Francis headed up to the open-air restaurant – the Whirlpool Grill – at the back of deck six. There was a tiny plunge pool at the centre, surrounded by slatted wooden tables for four or six. Each had a large white parasol at its centre, up and flapping lightly in the brisk sea breeze. All but one table in the corner was already taken, with groups of guests enjoying beers, cocktails, hamburgers, minute steaks, fish and chips, salads. The more elaborate lunch menu of many courses was not served out here, but that suited Francis fine. A beer and a burger with a view over the ocean was just the ticket; he hurried over and staked his claim at the last available table.

But no sooner had he sat down and been served a beer in a glass frosted with condensation than he was aware of a shadow falling on him.

'The open sea!' said Klaus. 'Nothing like it. May I join you?'

'Of course,' said Francis, putting down his book, doing his best to manage a smile.

'I would have left you in peace, but this is the last table.'

'It's a popular place.'

'Which is why I came up early,' said Klaus. 'And are you feeling OK this morning?'

'Fine, thank you.'

Klaus ordered two drinks from a hovering waiter: a beer and a whisky. 'You see, I am sticking to *visky sandvich*, even on board ship. You can never be too careful. Especially at the moment.'

What was he talking about? Francis gave him a puzzled look.

'Yes, it is a day at sea, and people are relaxing in their cabins,' Klaus said. 'But I have noticed quite a few are missing. I have not this morning seen, for example, the glamorous Indian and his, er, friend.'

'No?'

'Nor the large English lady and her husband. Nor the merry widow who ate those fluorescent prawns at lunchtime yesterday.' He raised his bushy white eyebrows theatrically. 'I can only hope she is OK.'

Francis hoped his face didn't give him away. 'I'm sure she's fine,' he replied.

'But it's not a mystery.' Klaus leant forward confidentially. 'I notice there are suddenly those antiseptic hand gel dispensers everywhere. That is a sign. They are worried about the norovirus. If an epidemic takes hold it could stop the ship from docking. Even at the next port, Takoradi. And then everything goes to pieces. Because not only can they not stick to the itinerary, but there are problems with deliveries of fresh produce and so on.'

'Is that so?' said Francis innocently.

'I have also seen the doctor. Do you know her? A surprisingly young woman of Far Eastern appearance. Filipina, I should guess. You might wonder to look at her whether she's even passed her exams. But she is looking worried today. Brows crinkled. Something is going on.'

'Yes?'

'She is preoccupied. Definitely. You are the writer. I am surprised you have not noticed this. She will have confined these cases to cabin, and they will have been sent a strict letter from the captain, forbidding them from leaving, under pain of being put off at the next port. That is normal. But can she stop the sickness spreading? That is the question.

'Do you know the code they have for illness on board these cruise ships? Operation Bright Star. If you hear that over the tannoy one time, that means a seriously sick passenger. And if you hear' – Klaus tapped his long nose with his forefinger – 'Operation Rising Star, do you know what that is?'

Francis shrugged; he had guessed, from what the captain had said in Eve's cabin, but he didn't know.

'A death,' Klaus said, leaning closer. 'If there are no relatives, they keep that sort of incident very quiet, just remove the body down to the morgue below decks.'

'I see,' said Francis.

'It holds three bodies. There was one cruise I heard about,' Klaus continued, 'where they had so many deaths on board that the morgue was full and they had to start using the freezers in the kitchen to store the corpses. The only thing the guests knew about it was that they were suddenly all offered tuna for dinner. Tuna special, eh!'

FOUR

Takoradi, Ghana. Monday 24 April.

The African sun was a giant shining disc, too bright still to look at for more than a second, its lower circumference now just kissing the brilliantly backlit clouds above the dark horizon. The ship's engines were throbbing. Up on deck six, the Whirlpool Bar was packed with passengers, standing with cocktails looking down one way at the stacked-up containers of Takoradi port, the other at the fishing boats chugging out past the long breakwater to the open sea, each with its attendant flock of gulls. The whole scene was bathed in a glorious evening light: enhancing the orange and pink of cocktails in bulbous goblets, the scarlet and maroon slashes of lipstick on wrinkled faces, the shiny black of dark glasses, the twinkle of jewellery, emeralds and rubies and sapphires and diamonds, nothing too showy, not really. Just that one oversized one, glinting in that caramel cleavage, showcased by a dress of shimmering gold.

She was smiling, the Puerto Rican, and her scruffy senior partner was grinning devotedly beside her, a change from his furious expression last night, when her tipsy dancing with a variety of partners had reached new heights. Today had been an interesting day, out at historic Elmina Fort, where you could not help but be moved by the slimy green walls of the Male Slave Dungeon and the Female Slave Dungeon and the heavy metal 'Door of No Return' which led directly out to the rocks above the sea, where once gangplanks would have been laid, up to the ships where more had usually died than survived on the dreaded 'Atlantic crossing'. There had, the latest local guide had told them, been up to 600 slaves waiting for transit crowded into those cells. One tiny barred chamber had a grim skull and crossbones above the door. This was the punishment cell, for any brave spirits who dared to put up resistance.

On a whitewashed wall a marble inscription read:

As the German barked with laughter, his drinks arrived. He knocked the whisky back in one. 'Down your hatch, as you say in UK.' He looked back at the hovering waiter. 'A Scottish beefburger for me, please. And you, Francis. Are you eating?'

Francis's peace had been destroyed, but there was a certain wry amusement to be had from the German's misconceptions. It was not for Francis to enlighten him about what had happened to poor Eve, the urgent meeting that had taken place in her cabin and the agreement that had finally been reached: that the ship would dock in Takoradi as usual; that while the guests were out on their scheduled excursion to the famous slaving fort at Elmina, an unmarked van would be arranged to take Eve's body to the hospital; and that Dr Lagip would accompany it, any talk of a post-mortem or reasons for that being kept in strict confidence. With the sincere hope, among all parties, that this would avoid the unwelcome attentions of the Ghanaian authorities.

IN EVERLASTING MEMORY
OF THE ANGUISH OF OUR ANCESTORS
MAY THOSE WHO DIED REST IN PEACE
MAY THOSE WHO RETURN FIND THEIR ROOTS
MAY HUMANITY NEVER AGAIN PERPETUATE
SUCH INJUSTICE AGAINST HUMANITY
WE THE LIVING VOW TO UPHOLD THIS

The carved letters were infilled with black, but a part of that had peeled away, leaving some words harder to read than others: ANGUISH, ROOTS, LIVING. Fading already!

'That guide was a bit bad-tempered, though, wasn't he?' Candy from Chicago was saying to English Shirley, as they stood with their partners by the ship's rail, looking out to sea, cocktails in hand. Candy had been the cheerleader woman in that voodoo dance in Lomé, and was still dressed young, tonight in a tight frock as pink as her name.

'Wouldn't you be,' Shirley replied, 'repeating that terrible story of injustice, over and over, day after day. Especially if you're black yourself.'

'Sure, I get that,' Candy replied. 'But the guide didn't have to take it out on us. I got the sense that he resented us somehow.'

'Because we were white and obviously well off,' chipped in her husband Bruce, whose puce face was adorned with a skinny white moustache.

'Did you feel that, Gerald?' Shirley asked.

Her other half managed a smile. His hands were trembling, Francis noticed. Out of nerves, being put on the spot by his wife, or did he have the shakes habitually?

'I see what you mean,' he replied. 'He could perhaps have been a bit more . . .'

'A bit more what?' said Shirley, aggressively.

'Upbeat, maybe.'

'Exactly,' said Bruce. 'You know, I almost got the sense that he felt he was doing us a favour, showing us around. I mean, tourism has got to be that place's greatest asset. What else have they got? A few fishing boats. I don't personally think they should be cocking a snook at the people who are paying their wages.'

'So – what?' said Shirley. 'He should adjust his attitude and become a grinning Uncle Tom, just to please us?'

'I didn't use that phrase and I'm not saying that.'

'What *are* you saying?'

'I'm agreeing with Candy. The experience could have been better. And yes, I did think there was some poor attitude there. Look, we're twenty-first-century tourists, not nineteenth-century slavemasters.'

'We're descended from them.'

'Are we? I don't think I am. My ancestors came to the US from Ireland a hundred years ago. I don't remember hearing much about the Irish Slave Trade. In any case, even if I were descended, so what? This is history. I was talking to a German fellow last night, very interesting, who was telling me that the African leaders themselves were just as much involved with all this slavery business as the Europeans and Americans.'

'Encouraged by the Europeans and Americans,' said Shirley. 'Come *on*. There would have been no transatlantic slave trade without the demand from wealthy whites.'

'They weren't all wealthy, that's just the point,' said Bruce, his voice rising towards anger. 'And they weren't all white. Some of their new masters probably needed those slaves *because* they weren't wealthy.'

Shirley was laughing. 'That's an interesting point of view,' she said, looking round and rolling her eyes. 'We're not going to agree about this, I'm afraid.'

'What do you think, Francis?' asked Bruce.

Francis had been standing to one side, half listening to this sudden, alcohol-fuelled barney, half looking out over the gunwale at the sunset. The sun had turned a deep red, staining its surrounding blanket of grey as if with blood from a wound; above, the scattered clouds were picked out against the green-yellow sky in a deep flamingo pink. Was he being oversensitive in thinking that this entreaty from his latest shipboard acquaintance had something to do with his colour? *You may not be African, or even properly black, but you are at least brown-skinned, so your opinion on this subject has some validity.*

'I found the fort very interesting,' he replied. 'I take the point about the guide, he did have a bit of a grouchy attitude, but then again, perhaps he was having a bad day, perhaps we were just unlucky.'

'Attitude!' cried Shirley. 'His ancestors were shackled and led down those steps, left to rot and die on the slave ships, and you're talking about attitude. I'd have that attitude if that were me.'

They were interrupted by the announcement over the tannoy of the day's round-up and briefing, down in the theatre. Francis eased away from the two couples and stood back, watching them join, separately, the shuffling queue heading downstairs. The guests were very dutiful, it had to be said. Almost all of them went down every night to hear Viktor's studiedly irreverent recap of the day's events, and his look forward to what was on the agenda for tomorrow; which was, as it happened, another two days at sea, as the ship steamed past the huge territories of Cote D'Ivoire and Liberia, none of whose ports had been deemed suitable, apparently, for a visit by the adventurous First Worlders.

Just before he followed the others inside Francis took a last glance across the deck and spotted a familiar silhouette against the spectacular backdrop. Dr Lagip with a cocktail. He sauntered over to join her.

'Amazing sky, isn't it?'

'Oh, hello,' she replied with a smile. 'How are you?'

'Good, thanks. Is it cheeky of me to ask how your day went?'

'Fine, thanks. And yours?'

She was a bit of a tease, this one. Which was not to say he wasn't enjoying her considered flippancy.

'Interesting. I went out with the rest of the punters and had a look round Elmina Fort.'

'Slaves and guilt?'

'Exactly. Lots of thoughtful conversations on the coach on the way back. Not to mention just now here on deck.'

'I would have loved to have seen it. It's the second time I've had to miss. Next time, perhaps.'

'This is becoming quite a popular route, isn't it?'

'The more seasoned travellers love Africa. It titillates them. Takes them beyond the standard sights most cruises do. Makes them feel like explorers, even if they are explorers who return for a four-course meal every night.' She giggled. 'Then again, you only need one disaster to put a stop to it all.'

'A pirate attack?'

'For example. Or something happening in the interior.'

'An ambushed coach or something?'

'I personally think that's unlikely. The Africans are incredibly keen to make this kind of high-end tourism work. Look at the escorts they give us. I know this is a doctor's point of view, but I'd say it'd be more likely to be an outbreak of some new disease. Ebola, Zika, you never know quite what's round the corner on this continent . . .'

Francis nodded, thinking of his daily prophylactic dose of anti-malarial Malerone, not to mention the injections he had had to have, Yellow Fever among others; all the guests would have done the same, for this adventure in insalubrious parts. 'So what are you drinking?' he asked.

'Singapore gin sling.'

'Want another?'

'This is probably enough.' She met his eyes. 'Oh, go on then. After the day I've had.'

Francis waved for the waiter.

'Are you going to tell me about that?' he said.

'I suppose I could.'

Eve's body had been removed from the ship an hour or so after the punters had left for Elmina Fort. In an unmarked van, as Francis had suggested. Dr Lagip had accompanied it, and there had been no difficult questions asked by the authorities. They had gone to the European Hospital in the harbour zone, rather than the regional hospital or – she raised her eyebrows – the Police Hospital.

The supervisor was, as it turned out, an Australian. He had been happy for things to be discreet, so an autopsy was now under way. Samples would be sent for forensic toxicology testing. Dr Lagip had done her duty.

'You said that that might take a while?'

'This isn't a TV show unfortunately. It could be six weeks before we've got the full report. Longer if the samples have to go to Europe.'

'The cruise will be long over by then.'

'Yes. But I'll get the basic autopsy report by email tomorrow, and as for the rest of it, everything's been done in the right way. You know, I wasn't setting out to be unreasonable. I just couldn't cope with the fact that the captain was trying to strongarm me into leaving this body in the so-called morgue till we got to Dakar. I don't think he quite understood where that leaves me professionally.'

'Why so-called morgue?'

'There isn't one. They just put the bodies in the meat freezer. Don't tell them I told you.'

Francis nodded. So Klaus only knew so much. 'For what it's worth,' he said, 'I admired your stand.'

'Thank you.' She looked down, her dark eyelashes fluttering like trapped insects.

'Different nationalities have different ways of doing things,' Francis said.

'They certainly do.'

'Am I interrupting?'

It was Sadie, in a tight purple dress, holding some creamy-yellow confection; a maraschino cherry, a wedge of pineapple and a pink cocktail umbrella clung to the rim of her glass.

'Not interested in Viktor's briefing?' asked Francis.

'I really don't need to be reminded about what I already saw, and the next two days are at sea, so I'm not too interested in Viktor's take on that. Lectures and things, isn't it?'

'You can come to mine, if you like.'

'What's that about?'

'"A Short History of Crime Writing", it's called.'

'I'm hoping to go,' said Dr Lagip.

'Sorry to change the subject,' Sadie interrupted, 'but I was just wondering about Eve. I haven't seen her for over two days now and I was really surprised she'd miss the slavery trip. She was so interested in the subject. Is she ill or something?'

Dr Lagip's face, as she turned slowly towards Francis, gave nothing away. 'You'll excuse me,' she said curtly. 'I am expected at the briefing.'

'So what was *that* about?' breathed Sadie, after she'd gone. Her long crimson-varnished fingers settled lightly on his wrist. 'Come on, Francis. What do you know? Eve's got the dreaded norovirus? She's at death's door?'

'I'm not sure I can say.'

'Oh, go on!' From below there came shouts as moorings were untied from bollards, then the ship began easing away from the quay.

'What's going on?' said Sadie. 'If it's some big secret I'm not going to tell anyone.'

'If I tell you, you'll have to swear to keep it to yourself. Not even share with Aunty.'

'I just had a big row with her, so I'm not in a sharing mood.'

'Your second guess was correct.'

'She's at death's door?'

'Worse.'

'Worse . . . what?' Sadie was studying Francis's face. 'Not actually . . .?'

Francis nodded.

'*Dead?* You're not serious?'

''Fraid so. The body was taken off today while we were at Elmina.'

'Oh my God! What happened?'

'Old age, probably. The doctor's not being too specific. I'm not sure she really knows.'

'But she seemed so well. Old, I grant you, but in great shape. I can't believe that she's—'

'Well, she is.'

'That's terrible. I feel so sad now. She was telling me about all the other cruises she wanted to go on, all the places she was looking forward to seeing.'

The bell was ringing for dinner.

Sadie turned away, tears in her eyes. 'I'm not sure I can face sitting down for a meal after what you've just told me.'

'I'm sorry too, Sadie. But also hungry. All that sightseeing has given me an appetite.'

Sadie smiled wanly. 'You shallow man.'

'Honest, perhaps.'

'Can we just sit together then? You and me at a table for two? I don't think I can bear to make small talk with any more of these people.'

Afterwards they repaired to the Panorama Lounge. With Elmina Fort behind them, and the prospect of two days at sea, there was quite a crowd in tonight. Hangovers could be slept off in the morning. The first (optional) engagement at eleven a.m. was a lecture on sustainable fishing by one of the expedition staff, the bearded Australian marine biologist whose name was Mike. To the accompaniment of the pianist's cheesy playlist, people were letting rip. Every now and then sporadic singing broke out. 'Danny Boy' was sung to applause by a white-haired gentleman with oddly black eyebrows.

There was a lot of loud laughter from a group right by the bar: the Indian designer and his portly companion were back with the Bostonian couple again, and now joined by Shirley and Gerald too.

But then their good spirits seemed suddenly to have soured.

'*Don't* treat me like a child,' the Puerto Rican was shouting at her hung-dog partner, who even in wedges was some inches shorter than her.

'Lauren, honey,' he was saying, 'I only said that *maybe* you should think twice . . .'

'You think I can't make my own financial decisions.'

'You don't know who these people are . . .'

The old man's voice dropped as he picked up on the hush in the bar. There were no such qualms for her. She raised a finger.

'I *do* know who they are. As it happens. And guess what? It's none of your freakin' business anyways.'

As if by magic, hotel director Gregoire had appeared and led Lauren out on to the little dance floor. The pair stood out effortlessly against the older couples, so much younger and more energetic. Even Carmen and Leo, now out of boring khaki and into floral African shirts, couldn't keep up. At one point, breaking into a stylish rock and roll routine, the French/Puerto Rican combo garnered applause from across the bar.

Now Klaus was here too, clutching a brandy, asking if he might join them. He had some interesting facts about stowaways, who were, he said, a particular curse of Takoradi. They crept on to oil tankers, cargo ships, all sorts, and hid till they docked in Europe.

'And sometimes the crew knows perfectly well they are there.' He chuckled. 'I noticed the expedition team searching the ship very carefully this evening. Before we left. These migrants are very good at hiding, if Europe is the prize.'

'But the cruise ends at Dakar,' said Francis.

'And then the ship continues straight on to Lisbon.'

'Are you seriously suggesting a stowaway would try and hide out for the duration of two cruises?'

'Three weeks. It's nothing for these people. I don't suppose you remember the story of Kingsley Ofusu?'

They didn't, so Klaus told them. Ofusu was a Ghanaian who
had worked on the docks in Takoradi, back in 1992. He'd had
ambitions to get to Europe and train as an engineer, so he stowed
away with seven others on a ship loaded with cocoa. Sneaking on
at night, they had hidden themselves in the hold, only to discover
yet another stowaway who had already boarded the ship, at Doula
in Cameroon.

After six days, one of the nine managed to break the water
container they had all been drinking from. They became so thirsty
that one of them crept out into the corridors to look for a replace-
ment. At this point he was discovered by a member of the crew.

'And then their troubles really began,' Klaus continued. 'Because
the crew found all of them and confiscated their money and locked
them into the tiny compartment where the anchor chain was stored,
without food or water. After three days they took them out of there,
in groups of two or three. They told them they were going to put
them in a comfortable cabin. Instead' – Klaus's eyes shone – 'they
killed them. One by one. They beat them to a pulp with an iron bar
and then shot them, before dumping them overboard.

'Kingsley Ofusu was the last to be taken out, with another fellow.
As the crew came for them, they saw blood on these men's clothes
and realized what had happened, so they tried to break away.
Ofusu's companion was shot, but he managed to escape and hide
deep in the bowels of the ship. Incredibly, the crew failed to find
him until they docked at Le Havre in France, when he escaped
again and made his way to a police station. The crew were arrested
and under the good ministrations, how-to-say, of the French police,
four of them confessed. All six of them were tried. Five were found
guilty and went to jail. What nationality do you think these pleasant
people were?'

'I have no idea,' said Sadie.

'Ukranian. Like our charming captain.'

As Klaus fixed them with a knowing look, there was more
commotion across the bar.

'I am *nart listening*, Donald!' Lauren was shouting. 'If I wanna
dance with somebody I will dance with them. What are you saying?
That I can only dance with you. Maybe I'm sick of dancing with
you . . .'

'Lauren, please, people are watch—'

'I don't care if people are watching. Anyway, you dance like a donkey, you pig.'

It was clear, even before this non-sequitur, that she was drunk again. She turned back to him.

'I could walk out tomorrow, you know that.'

'Honey, please . . .'

'Don't "honey" me. How can I be your honey when you can't even get it up, you useless old dipshit?'

'Lauren, *stop* it . . .' He moved towards her and took her upper arm.

'Get off me!'

The courtly Indian had stepped into the breach.

'Come on, Lauren, please, if I may—'

'No, you may not!' she cried. She wasn't so drunk that she didn't realize this wasn't her husband. 'This is between me and Don.' Then she looked slowly round the bar, picked up on all the watching eyes and made for the exit, clacking out noisily across the dance floor in her high heels, her stacked cleavage wobbling as she went, leaving the silenced drinkers to slowly piece their conversations back together again; or not, given that here was something wonderful for everyone to start offering gossipy speculations about. The air was thick with 'Did you see?' and 'Oh my *gard*!' and 'If looks could *kill*!'

'How much older would you say he is,' Francis heard, from the group of nodding skulls in the next bay, '*thirdee* years, *fordee*?'

'She could be his daughter.'

'His *grand*-daughter, more like.'

'Ha ha ha! Not quite.'

'Abso-*lute*-ly quite.'

Up at the bar, the old man was still very much present, head shaking stoically as he gulped a glass of brandy with his two friends.

'Oh dear,' said Sadie, making a face.

'They have some unresolved issues between them, I think,' said Klaus, getting to his feet.

'So it would seem,' Francis agreed; he did nothing to encourage him to stay.

In the background the pianist's hands moved rapidly over the keyboard. The tinkling chords rose and fell and the little man sang on, in his proud, strong, Americanized Filipino voice.

FIVE

Day at Sea. Tuesday 25 April.

Francis was woken by a hideous groaning. Not of a stowaway, in a cupboard in his cabin; nor of some stricken old lady, being beaten to a pulp with an iron bar through the wall in another cabin; nor even of a group of drunken guests making their way down the corridor, but of the entire ship. Some terrible strain was being put on the fabric of the hull and he could hear it moaning in protest, feel the vibrations coming up through the floor to shake his bed.

He lay there for a minute or so, still half-asleep, wondering if he were dreaming. Then he sat up, leant across and clicked on the bedside light. It was 3.26 a.m.

He was not dreaming. The pictures on the wall were shaking too.

He rolled out of bed and pulled a pair of jeans and a jersey top over his pyjamas. He located his keycard on the coffee table and headed off into the corridor. The deck three Reception desk was closed for the night. He ran up three floors and let himself out through the heavy metal door on to deck six. At the stern, the water in the little spa pool was splashing up over the pale blue plastic surround and on to the scrubbed wooden decking. Now he could see what was going on. The ship was turning. A huge arc was marked in white on the dark surface of the sea. Francis became aware of figures above, leaning over the railings, scouring the choppy waves with powerful torches. He clattered up the metal steps to deck seven.

'What's going on?' he asked a crew member in a brown boilersuit, who was standing to the stern of one of the lifeboats, which made a shadowy bulk against the brilliantly starry sky.

'Man overboard. Captain is turning the ship.'

Man overboard! How on earth had that happened? Was it passenger – or crew? And what possible chance did they have of finding someone in this vast, black ocean, even if they did manage to get back to the exact point they had been when he'd gone over?

Francis looked up to see a familiar figure approaching across the deck. Klaus was looking remarkably relaxed in a purple track-suit with white go-faster stripes, matched with a pair of well-worn trainers. Round his neck hung a powerful pair of binoculars.

'A terrible accident, it seems,' he said.

'D'you have any idea who it is?' Francis asked.

'The young wife of the old man, who made such a scene in the bar earlier.'

'Oh my God . . .'

'Yes, indeed, "Oh my God". They will be exceedingly lucky to find her now, given that she must have been drunk when she went over.'

'And what if they don't?'

Klaus's eyebrows twitched meaningfully. 'They keep moving,' he replied. 'These aren't the waters of the United Kingdom or Italy or Miami, where you can scramble a helicopter in minutes. This is the Gulf of Guinea. There is no supportive rescue service for hundreds of miles. Thousands, maybe. If you ask me, the captain has only turned to obey protocols, not because he hopes to find this woman. He has to make the appearance of trying. If only for his records.'

'What happened?'

'Nobody is saying. I'm not sure they know. Perhaps she'd had enough of a life of arguing in public.'

'Suicide? You don't really think so?'

'Or a little feminine protest that went too far. But it's not easy to fall off a ship like this. You don't just slip through these railings, do you?'

'Unless you're very drunk.'

'You would still need to climb over. Unless of course you had some help.' Klaus met Francis's gaze with those alert grey eyes of his. 'By the way, I was sorry to hear about the merry *vidow*.'

'What did you hear?'

'That she left us. At Takoradi. In a box.'

'Who told you that?'

Klaus looked pleased with himself. 'I have my sources. I had started to suspect it wasn't food poisoning. Or even the norovirus.

That sort of thing is usually over in a couple of days. She leaves a fortune perhaps?'

'I don't know about that.'

'You don't take four cruises a year unless you have very substantial money. Or perhaps you are a distinguished how-to-say freeloader like yourself.'

Francis was fairly sure that Klaus knew the difference between a freelancer and a freeloader, but he wasn't going to rise to the old man's egregious sense of humour. They stood side by side at the railing, watching as the ship completed a wide semicircle, then slowed and maintained its course for several minutes, returning the way it had come. Klaus had pulled his field glasses up to eye level and was keeping a close watch. The other men with binoculars were all standing on the port side of the ship, scanning the dark sea. There were a number in uniform, together with a group of the expedition staff, gathered in a huddle round tall Viktor.

Now a huge searchlight was switched on, its beam reaching down to make a bright track over the water. It swept back and forth, back and forth, but there was nothing to see but the crests of the waves. There were no waving arms, no bobbing head, no body.

After about half an hour the ship seemed to have stopped entirely. There was a lot of frantic hurrying to and fro, up and down stairs and into hidden doorways. The searchlight continued to scour the empty surface of the sea.

'So,' said Klaus, wandering back over to join him. 'The party is over, I fear. For her at any rate.'

'Surely they'll wait till it's light?'

'They may. To keep face. But they are not going to find her now. She is on her way to David Jones's lock-up, as you say in England. Perhaps accompanied by a shark. I'm sorry to say there will be nothing more to see. I'm going back to my cabin.'

Francis surfaced slowly. He was aware of the brilliant sunlight on his curtains; then that something was wrong; then, with a jolt, he remembered. Man – or rather woman – overboard. He shuddered at the thought of it, unable to put out of his mind the circumstances of his own wife's death, twenty years before. A shocking holiday accident on the Nile, when the felucca he and Kate had been sailing in had flipped over during a terrifying desert storm. He had survived, despite losing consciousness, but Kate hadn't made it. The image of her naked body, washed up on the stony brown mud, still haunted him and his recurrent nightmares; in the life he had, as opposed to the life he might have had – should have had, he sometimes thought, before his better self took hold of him and told him that self-pity was not allowed, for Kate's sake, if nothing else. She who would never have countenanced such indulgence.

When Viktor's wake-up call came, it was not the cheery, sing-song '*Gu-u-ten Mo-orgen!*' they had been used to previously. Just a clipped English 'Good morning', followed by an announcement that because of an incident that had happened during the night the first lecture at eleven o'clock had been cancelled and there would instead be a mandatory briefing in the theatre. 'In the meantime,' Viktor concluded, 'I hope you will enjoy your breakfast.'

Francis took his omelette-with-everything out to the open area at the back of deck six, where the sun was already, at seven forty-five a.m., shining a brilliant yellow-gold on the slatted tables. John-since-1972 was as smiley and solicitous as ever, as if nothing untoward had happened. 'Can I get you anything else, sir? More tea? Another croissant? Some jam?'

Francis had been back in his cabin only ten minutes before there was a knock at the door. He opened it to find himself face-to-face with the blonde expedition staffer, Carmen.

'Hello,' he said, a trifle awkwardly.

'Francis,' she began.

'Yes.'

'We didn't get introduced properly yesterday. I'm Carmen, one of the expedition team.'

'I'm aware of that.'

'Viktor sends his apologies, he's very busy this morning.'

'I imagine.'

'He was wondering if you might be able to join us in the captain's office on the bridge.'

'Is this to do with the man overboard?'

'I wasn't sure how much you were aware. The staff are under instructions not to talk about it.'

'I was out there last night in the small hours. Up on deck seven when the ship was turning.'

'I see,' Carmen replied. 'In any case, the captain is keen to have you present at our discussion. Would you be OK to come?'

'Right now?'

'If that's OK.'

At the end of a short corridor, through a connecting door, the bridge was revealed as a quiet, orderly space, flooded with light from a long curve of floor-to-ceiling windows that looked directly down over an empty section of deck to the ocean ahead. In the centre was a huge console full of knobs and dials and gearstick type devices around a monitor that was presumably the main navigation control. Two long desks stretched away on either side. An officer in a white shirt sat at one, looking intently at a screen. Another officer with powerful binoculars was standing in the centre of the window at the front, a silhouette scanning the blue ocean beyond. Surely they weren't still hoping to find her now?

The captain was in a little office to one side. Francis found the same small group as before, minus Dr Lagip. Both the captain and Viktor looked drained, as well they might after such a night.

'Thank you for joining us,' the captain said to Francis, as the burly four-stripe officer pulled the door firmly to behind them. 'Your contribution was useful last time. Indeed, it resolved difficult situation for me.'

'I was glad to help.'

'You know everyone, I think.' He gestured towards the four-stripe. 'Alexei Ninishivili, our First Officer and Head of Security.'

Francis and Alexei exchanged a nod.

'And so,' the captain continued, taking his seat, yawning extravagantly then placing his big, hairy hands face down on the table, 'I think we are all apprised of latest incident. Shortly after two a.m. last night we lost woman overboard. She fell from deck seven, it seems, from sun deck/viewing area towards stern. Alarm was raised by engineer who was running routine check up on port lifeboat.

'First he was aware of situation was person below him, in gold evening dress, screaming as she flew past deck five and then straight down into sea below. He immediately threw down lifeline and safety ring and ran to get help from bridge. Because it was small hours, there was longer delay than there would have been in daylight, as we only have basic night watch up at that time. Any questions so far?'

'He just saw her flying down, screaming?' Francis asked. 'There was nobody else around?'

'So he said.'

'And you believe him?'

'I have no reason not to. He is trustworthy guy.'

'And you don't have any automatic systems in place for spotting a man overboard? Or CCTV or anything?'

'No. This is only small ship. And you must understand, this MOB situation is extremely rare, even with those huge liners that carry five thousand passengers.'

'I see.'

'So,' the captain continued, 'we took immediate action and executed standard Williamson turn, but at speed we were going this didn't start until we were several nautical miles beyond spot where incident occurred. Having turned, we tracked back to position that was our best guess of where this woman went over. We brought ship to standstill and used all resources to check surface of ocean. But even with searchlights, we saw nothing. I can't say I was hopeful of success, but nonetheless I waited until first light at five thirty a.m. Still nothing, so after further hour of looking, I gave order to abandon search. Unless they are picked up very quickly, I'm afraid chances of finding someone in remote waters such as these are very small.'

'Is there no one else who can help?' Francis asked. 'Other ships, coastguards?'

'I have obviously put out an Attention All Shipping, with estimated coordinates of incident. But there are not so many ships round here. A few African fishing boats, but many of them don't have radios, so they wouldn't hear. Illegal Chinese ones will not want to get involved. So what else am I to do? Summon Liberian navy?'

'Is there one?'

The captain laughed. 'Actually, there is coast guard officer based at US Embassy in Monrovia. But we are three hundred miles from there. The nearest port in Cote d'Ivoire is Abidjan, but they have nothing other than those kind of inflatables you would use in port or very near to port.'

'So this engineer who reported the incident,' asked Francis. 'Did he see how or why the body went over?'

'He said not. He heard scream, then he saw body falling down, splash, into ocean. It was only by chance that he was there at all. Normally these routine checks take place by daylight.'

'So why was he out there at two in the morning then?'

'He thought he had forgotten to do something. One of important safety procedures.'

'Is that likely?' Francis asked, eyeballing the captain.

'I know this man,' the captain replied. 'He's very conscientious. It's typical that he would have double-checked. It's not as if he was sleeping otherwise. He was anyway on night shift.'

'OK.' Francis nodded. 'So nobody really knows what happened?'

'No.'

'And yet the decks and stairways are well-protected by guard rails. You would be unlikely to slip and fall by accident.'

'No,' said the captain. 'On other hand, this is ship. Far out at sea. If you wish to climb over railings or jump from deck there is nothing stopping you.'

'So what are you all thinking?' Francis asked. 'That this was a suicide?' He looked slowly round: at the captain, the first officer, Viktor and Carmen. They were all silent, as if unable to voice the thought that was surely now on all their minds. 'Or even,' he continued, 'foul play? Related perhaps to Eve's death?'

'I don't personally think "foul play",' said the captain. He gave a slight twist to the phrase, as if he found this very English coinage quaint. 'Suicide?' He shrugged in disbelief. 'She was, I heard, drunk earlier in evening and arguing in bar with husband.'

'Yes,' said Francis. 'Not for the first time. They were becoming a bit of an after-dinner cabaret act. One of those couples who have deep-seated issues that keep bubbling over.'

'Or perhaps,' said the captain, 'they enjoyed arguing. It is kind of foreplay maybe.'

'It didn't look much like foreplay to me,' said Francis. Despite the sombre mood, there was laughter from the group. Even First Officer Alexei managed a smile.

'Foreplay,' he said gruffly. 'Then foul play.'

'Whatever cause of death,' said the captain, ignoring this, 'there is nothing we can do about it now. This woman is gone. I am obliged to report her missing, which we have done. But action to find her has been taken and proved unsuccessful, so we don't technically have to do anything further.'

'And who else do you report to?' asked Francis. 'The Bermudan police again?'

'The Bahamas Maritime Authority, yes. We are in international waters here. Those are our protocols.'

'I still find it incredible,' Francis said, 'that you don't have to tell the US authorities, for example, or the FBI, that one of their citizens has gone missing. It seems like a giant loophole. If I was someone who wanted to bump off their partner, I'd look seriously into the cruise option. It doesn't seem to have too many downsides.'

'I thought things had changed in the US,' said Carmen. 'Wasn't there a law passed saying you had to report all deaths on board ship to the FBI?'

'And sexual assaults, yes,' said the captain. 'Since 2010, there are new rules. But only on vessels that embark or disembark at ports in US. These ships also must have onboard video surveillance. Deck rails have to be certain height. One of crew has to be trained as detective . . .'

'You're joking,' said Francis.

'No, that is now serious requirement. But this new law was designed for those big ships that go round Caribbean with 4000 on board. If you're under 250 passengers, as we are, it doesn't apply. Even if you are leaving US port. And US is still only country that bothers.'

'So you wouldn't be expecting any enquiries from outside law-enforcement agencies?'

The captain looked across at the first officer again. 'No, we would not be expecting that. Would we, Alexei?'

'No, sir.'

'No Bahamian policeman turning up at Freetown?' Francis asked.

The first officer chuckled grimly. 'They have enough to worry about on their own island.'

'Amazing,' said Francis. He still didn't quite believe them; he would have to do some Internet research when he got back to his cabin. 'So what about this poor woman's husband? How is he?'

'In his cabin,' said Carmen. 'Under sedation. He was up on deck last night after she fell off. He was part of the search.'

'And nobody thinks he might have had anything to do with it?'

'What are you suggesting?' asked Viktor.

'I'm not suggesting anything,' Francis replied. 'I'm just asking. Because he and his partner were arguing earlier. And then she vanishes off the side of the ship.'

'He's one with money,' said the captain. 'It would only be suspicious other way round.'

'This is true,' said Francis. 'But then again, if she were dependent on him in that way, there's always the possibility that he wanted to be rid of her. Or maybe she knew some dark secret that he didn't want disclosed.'

'Doesn't seem very likely to me,' said Viktor, 'if you saw the way he looked at her. He loved her, I think.'

'Even when she was dancing with the handsome hotel director?' said Francis. 'As she was last night.'

'Maybe there were jealousy issues,' said Carmen.

'It would be interesting to know what he thought about all that,' said Francis.

'D'you want to go and talk to him?' asked the captain. 'Maybe you could go along too, Carmen. And then both report your findings back to us.'

All eyes were on Carmen. For a moment, Francis thought she was going to turn this offer down. But it was clear that even if she'd wanted to, she couldn't. 'Sure,' she said. 'I'll accompany.'

'As long as you don't stop my ship, I am happy,' said the captain. 'My bosses require me to stick to schedule and deliver my passengers safely to Dakar on the twenty-ninth of April.'

'OK,' said Francis. 'Now I don't want to be alarmist, but to go back to our discussion on Sunday morning, if someone on board was responsible for Eve's death, this could be his second victim.'

'Or hers,' said the first officer.

'Indeed,' Francis agreed. 'Though manhandling someone as young and fit as Lauren over the railings would require a strength not in evidence in most of the ladies on the ship that I've seen.'

'Or most of the men, for that matter,' said Carmen.

Despite the tense atmosphere, there was laughter.

'But what do drunken Puerto Rican and genteel English lady have in common?' asked the captain. 'It doesn't make sense to me.'

'It doesn't seem to. Does it?' Francis agreed. 'But then again, they were both on the ship. Eve has been on cruises before. So, by all accounts, have this American couple. You can't rule out the possibility of a link. Both Don and Eve's husband Alfred were successful businessmen. Alfred did a lot of work in the US. Maybe one or both of them did someone down, years ago. Someone who's been waiting all this time for revenge.'

'I think this is your writer's brain making up stories here,' the captain said.

Francis shrugged. 'Maybe it was just as simple as that Lauren knew what had happened to Eve.'

'In which case she would have said something.'

'To whom?'

'To us, of course.'

'Are you sure about that?'

'If you're suggesting she found out about a murder, she would hardly have kept that to herself.'

'You think?' said Francis. 'I'm not sure it's a given. She might only have told her partner. Or be biding her time.'

'That is unlikely,' the captain replied dismissively. 'It seems to me that what we have here is old woman who got sick of norovirus, completely normal, I'm afraid, on cruise like this, and then, very sadly, passed away, probably from unrelated cause. Our ship's doctor had some suspicions about this, because old woman was supposedly healthy and there were no obvious indications of stroke or heart attack. But she was of good age, over eighty. These things happen. I went along with doctor's protest, because to be frank I can't be searching for new doctor in mid cruise and she is competent. But we've not heard anything back from Takoradi lab. No urgent call to tell us that, yes, after all, she had strychnine in her blood. Or even rat poison, which we keep on the ship. And then last night, terrible accident. Woman who has been seen by everybody to be drunk and unhappy falls from top deck. Why? Maybe she'd had enough. Maybe she made mistake. Maybe she thought someone would rescue her. I don't know. But I think we are looking at two separate situations here.'

'I'm not so sure,' said Francis.

'So what do you want me to do?' asked the captain, looking over at his first officer for support. 'Put passengers on alert for possible killer in their midst? I don't think that would create best atmosphere, especially as we now have two days at sea before we stop at Freetown.'

'Can we talk to this engineer?' Francis asked. 'Who saw Lauren fall.'

The captain seemed taken aback, though it was hardly an unreasonable request. 'He is sleeping now,' he replied. 'I would rather not wake him until next shift.'

'Which is when?'

'Noon. Or four o'clock. I will check. He's not going anywhere,' he added. He turned towards Viktor. 'But now we must concentrate on briefing to passengers, which starts in thirty minutes in Panorama Lounge. At very least we can try and make sure that no one else falls off ship. And who knows, we may get more witness accounts of what happened to this unfortunate woman last night.'

SIX

After the passenger briefing, Francis made his way with Carmen down to Don's cabin on deck four. The Bostonian couple had not been in the cheapest rooms, down on deck three, but then again, they had not been in the grander suites with balconies up on deck five, and certainly not in the staterooms of deck six.

The old man was in bed, in pyjamas and dressing gown, looking groggy. The sedation Dr Lagip had given him was light, she had told them privately at the Panorama Lounge briefing, so he would be perfectly able to talk. She had dosed him up enough to calm him, that was all.

In daylight, the skin of Don's face was baggier and more parchmenty than it had seemed in the flattering evening light of the bar. Even with – particularly with – that shiny black hair, he looked his age, and that was something over seventy, Carmen had found out from the passenger records.

'Don,' said Carmen, as they stood at the foot of the bed. 'This is Francis Meadowes, who is trying to help us piece together what happened to Lauren last night.'

The old man took in his visitor, then stared out through his porthole at the empty sea.

'So what are you?' he asked, eventually. 'Some kind of police officer?'

'No,' Francis replied gently. 'For what it's worth, I write crime novels.'

There was a mirthless gurgle. 'Crime novels! So, because you can construct a plot, you think you can untangle this real-life horror, do you?'

'Not necessarily.' Francis looked over at Carmen, who gave him an encouraging nod. 'But I was asked to help, by the captain, and the leader of the expedition team, Viktor, so here I am.'

'And what do they think?' Don asked. 'That I threw Lauren overboard in some mad fit of jealousy? They all saw that stupid fight, didn't they?'

'I don't think anyone has any idea what happened,' Francis replied. 'We know she was, perhaps, rather inebriated last night . . .'

'*Rather inebriated*.' Don mimicked Francis's English accent. 'She was soused, not to put too fine a point on it. You saw her. Me, I can have a couple of cocktails, bit of wine with dinner, maybe a bourbon or two afterwards. That's enough. But once Lauren opened the sluices, there was no stopping her. Of course, a ship like this is the very worst place to have brought her. Free booze everywhere, all day long. It's an alcoholic's wet dream.'

'So what do you think happened last night?' Francis asked.

Don looked over at him, but it was a blank sort of look, filmy, not quite engaging. 'I have no idea. I guess it's possible she fell off. But then again . . .'

'Then again what?'

'I don't think so.' He shook his head. 'I don't see it.'

'So where were you?' Francis asked. 'When it happened?'

'Here, I guess. I went to bed. After she left the bar, I followed her down. We carried on arguing for a bit. But fighting like that never quite had the appeal for Lauren if there wasn't an audience. She liked insulting me in public. Telling me I was a useless old man, that only she would look at me now.'

'And what did you say in private?'

'I agreed with her. Told her she had a point. Told her, as I always did, that if she didn't like the situation she could leave. That just made her even angrier.'

'So you weren't married?'

For a moment Francis wondered if he'd pushed it too far. There was a powerfully beady glint in the old man's demeanour; despite the hippyish exterior, you could imagine him putting the fear of God into his employees if he needed to.

'No,' he replied. 'That was at the root of it all, I guess. She didn't just want big diamonds on her earlobes. She wanted them on her finger too.'

'And you didn't want to put one there?'

Don sighed. 'I've been married before. Twice. Maybe it works for some people, but it didn't for me. I didn't want to go down that route again. Having a freakin' sexual partner who's suddenly telling me how to run my businesses, what to do with my investments. Jesus! I built up my own fortune. I made some bad decisions along the way, but they were my decisions, so I lived with them. I also made some very good decisions.'

'I see,' said Francis. 'Though presumably there is a middle way where you remain in charge of the business and your wife only has a say on the domestic side of things.'

Don laughed. 'You married?'

'I was. A long time ago.' Francis didn't elaborate.

'See. In my experience there's always mission creep. One moment it's, "Let's change the carpets in the house," the next it's, "Why are we still hanging on to such and such a company?" She was a sharp operator, Lauren, don't get me wrong. And thorough, too. Boy, was she thorough. She'd double-check everything. That was part of the problem, to be honest.'

'So was that what you were arguing about last night?' Francis asked. 'Business? I heard her talking about "financial decisions" at one point.'

'Did you?' Don gave him a sharp look, then turned away.

Francis waited. Best to let him say what he wanted to say, in his own time.

'She had a thing about charity,' Don continued, after a pause. 'She wanted to give my money away all the time. To this or that worthy cause. Orphans of the rainforest. War children of Sudan. Aboriginals of the Australian desert. You name it. I always told her that charity begins at home. And ends at home, too, in my book. I'd say, "But sweetheart, maybe giving money to those little orphans of the rainforest isn't the best way to help them. Maybe if you give them money the first thing they'll do is buy a car and drive *out* of the freakin' rainforest." But she never saw it that way. We had it and they didn't. We had a duty to help.'

'So what are you saying?' Francis said. 'Your argument was about a charity donation?'

'What I'm saying, young man, is what I just said. And that's all I'm going to say on that subject.'

From the settled line of his mouth, it clearly was. Next to him, Carmen made a 'whatever' face.

'So after you left the bar last night,' Francis continued, 'you came down here, and carried on arguing for a while . . .'

'For a while,' Don repeated.

'And then what happened?'

'Lauren went off. Said she was going upstairs for another drink. I didn't stop her. When she's in that sort of mood, it's best just to let her go.'

'And she didn't come back?'

'That was no surprise to me. She would often wander off for half the night, then come back when it suited her. My attitude was to say nothing. Because if I said jack shit that would only provoke her. And we'd be back to: "So what right have you got to control me? When there's nothing between us."'

'So what did you think she got up to when she went off like this?'

'I have no idea.'

'Didn't you care?'

'Of course I cared!'

Don's tone and his angry look made Francis step back. He glanced over at Carmen, who raised her eyebrows a fraction. Eventually, in his very gentlest tone, he asked, 'So when did they tell you she'd fallen off the ship?'

Don didn't answer. For a few long seconds, Francis thought the interview had run its course. Then there was the sound of the old man shifting himself on the pillows and that gravelly voice started up again.

'One of the expedition staff called me around two thirty,' he said. 'Just as the ship was turning. Told me that there was a man over-board situation. That they thought it was Lauren. I got dressed straightaway. Went up on deck seven with my field glasses. It was hopeless. Even if she'd survived the fall, how would we have seen her? It's a huge ocean. They did their best. Worked out the likely coordinates of where she'd gone over. Hung around till daybreak. But when they came to tell me they were abandoning the search I didn't put up an objection.'

'Which one of the expedition staff was that?' asked Francis. 'Did they actually knock on your door?'

'Yeah, I went up with him. That Australian fellow with the beard.'

'Mike,' said Carmen.

'I guess. I'd warned her about this stupid behaviour before. Stumbling around the ship in the night. Drunk. In high heels. "One day you'll fall off," I told her. She'd already fallen down a flight of stairs. On this very same ship. When we were in Antarctica last Christmas. Banged her head, but amazingly no more damage was done.'

Yet another pair who had been in Antarctica, Francis thought. 'So is this what you think?' he asked. 'That she fell off?'

'You think I pushed her?'

'Maybe somebody else did.'

'Who? Gregoire. I don't think so. She was only ever any good to him while she was alive.'

'What does that mean?'

'Work it out for yourself.'

Francis let him sit in silence for a good half minute or so. Then: 'She was a bit younger than you, I think,' he said.

'You think?' Don laughed bitterly. 'Of course she was! That was one of her arguments. "I'm thirty years younger than you, why don't you marry me? How can you expect me to behave myself, *Papita*, if you won't marry me?"' Don mimicked her voice so well it seemed for a moment as if she were in the room. 'That's what she called me. *Papita*. It means "sugar daddy". It was a joke when we were younger.'

'So what are you saying?' Francis asked. 'That she was unfaithful?'

'That *bastard*,' Don muttered. 'You know, they're not supposed to have any relations *whatsoever* with the passengers. The staff. On pain of dismissal. And of course, they claim they don't. But . . .'

'You think he did? Gregoire?'

'You want to know?'

'Whatever you want to tell me.'

When Don spoke, it was in a quiet, almost defeated voice. 'The truth is I have no idea. She certainly used him to wind me up. "I'll go and see Gregoire," she'd say. And then return hours later. One day I went looking for her. Guess where I found her? In the library, reading a book. So, I don't know.' He turned back to look up at Francis. 'But yes, as I'm sure you noticed, she loved to flirt with him. Publicly. Dancing like that. Although, to be fair, she danced like that with everyone. Except me,' he added sadly.

'I see,' said Francis.

'OK, yes, that's what we were arguing about. In the bar and down here. I really thought she had been with him this time. She denied it. But you're right, there has been history. She's done it before. With the younger guys. There was a purser, in Australia, when we did a cruise along the Kimberley coast a year or so ago. And a gaucho in Chile, that was on dry land, in the Torres del Paine National Park. It's always a way of forcing my hand. Marry me, and I'll never cheat on you again. But why was I to believe that? Once she got her hands on my dough, she could do what she likes . . .'

'And if she didn't fall off?' Francis asked.

'If she didn't fall off – what?'

'How did she end up going over? It doesn't sound as if she were suicidal. Unless she was making a gesture to force your hand?'

'Suicide, no. Not in that way. Even though she was a lush, she loved life too much. Dancing, drinking, spending money, keeping up with her charity projects. I don't see it. No.'

'I don't suppose there's anyone on the ship you could class . . . as an enemy of hers? Or of yours?'

Don shook his head. 'No.'

'What about friends?'

'Friends? On here? I guess we've made a few. Shipboard buddies. You know the kind of thing. You drink every night and then at the end of the cruise you swap emails and vow you're going to get together some time, somewhere, God knows where. But you never do. Unless you happen to end up on the same ship again. I quite like it, actually. You can say what you like, knowing you're unlikely to see those people ever again.'

'I saw you were quite matey with that Indian fashion designer guy.'

'Sebastian de Souza. He's good fun. And talented too. You seen his designs?'

'No.'

'Something else. Lauren loved them. And him too. She even bought a couple of things of his. After the last cruise we were on together. In Antarctica.'

When they'd finished with Don, Carmen accompanied Francis to his cabin. They ordered coffee, which Hentie brought in on a lacquered tray, complete with a plate of homemade biscuits. They sat opposite each other in the sunshine that streamed in through the porthole. Francis had switched on his laptop and was checking something on Google. He made a few notes in his floppy black Smythson notebook, then looked up and smiled at his companion.

'Doing some research?' she asked.

'Yes, this and that.'

'Share?'

'If it ever becomes relevant.' He had been checking out the ship's itinerary over the last eight months, but he wasn't going to tell Carmen that; not yet anyway. There hadn't been just one cruise to Antarctica last autumn, he'd discovered, but several back to back. Two included the Falkland Islands on the itinerary, the others not; the last had been over Christmas and New Year. 'I guess we should talk to Gregoire next,' he said, meeting her eye. 'Him and then the engineer who saw Lauren fall.'

'Yes. Though the captain did say—'

'I know. I really can't see why we shouldn't wake him, though. He's an important part of the jigsaw.'

'What the captain says goes, I'm afraid. His word is law. But let's definitely talk to Gregoire, even though I'm guessing he'll deny that anything happened between them. As Don said, he'd lose his job if anyone could prove something had gone on.'

'What d'you think?'

'Actually, unlikely. He's ambitious, that man. I mean, it's fun, in the evenings, for him to flirt with the wives and partners, particularly the younger ones. But I don't think he'd ever get involved. If he wants some recreation, there's opportunities for him below stairs . . .'

'You know about someone?' Francis asked.

'No. I don't take a huge interest in all that kind of thing. But, yes, it happens . . .'

'Surely you must have some idea of what's going on? There's presumably a crew bar. Gossip.'

'I'm not really one of the gossipers, mate. Got my work cut out helping Viktor make sure the expeditions run smoothly.'

Carmen made a call on the cabin phone and fifteen minutes later the handsome hotel director was with them. And he *was* handsome, Francis thought, with his wavy blond hair and classic chiselled features. His eyes were an appropriate sea-blue; his nose just the perfect size for his face; his lips thin enough to give him a slight sexy meanness, without looking sinister; his jaw strong, without being lantern. He was fit and muscly, without looking like some gym freak. His stomach was washboard flat. The corny French accent could only help. For all his alleged flirtation, was he actually gay? He looked almost too perfect to be heterosexual.

He sat before them on the little sunny couch and seemed quite happy to answer Francis's questions. This was such an extraordinary tragedy, he said. He could *'ardly* believe it. Why, only last evening, he had had the honour of a dance with Lauren, after dinner, up in the Panorama Lounge. And she was such a fine dancer, too. With all that Latina passion.

'Did you ever get the feeling that her partner minded you dancing together?' Francis asked.

'Don? But of course 'e didn't. He loved to sit there with 'is bourbon and see 'er move. With anybody. Not just me. She 'ad a great dance with Sebastian, too, last night.'

'Why didn't Don take her out himself?'

''E did. Some evenings. But you know, 'e's older, maybe 'e preferred to watch.'

'Quite a lot older.'

'Of course.'

'Did you think it was a shame that a much younger woman like Lauren was spending her time with someone who could have been her father?'

Gregoire laughed. 'This is 'ardly an unusual story on the cruise ships. 'Ave you not been on one before?'

'No,' said Francis.

'Carmen will tell you: you get all sorts. And you quickly discover that money creates its own . . . liaisons.'

'So you think it really was just money that kept them together?'

'Life is never that simple, is it? But maybe it brought them together. Maybe it stopped them from parting. But they were fond of each other, too. You could see that, in the way she looked at 'im. But why wouldn't she like 'im? 'E's a nice guy. Funny guy. She was fond of 'im. Loved 'im, yes. I would say so.'

'You know he was jealous of you?'

Gregoire looked taken aback. 'Of me? Why? Because I 'ad a few dances with her? I don't think so.' He looked down at his beautifully polished black shoes, gleaming in the sunshine against the deep blue of the carpet. 'I was doing my job.'

'But maybe you were doing your job more assiduously with her than with some of the other wives and partners?'

'This is unfair. Lauren asked to dance with me. What is the 'otel manager supposed to say to a passenger, a regular passenger, one who 'as sailed with *Golden Adventurer* before and may very likely come again? "No"? I don't think my bosses would be very 'appy if that was my reaction. Would they, Carmen?'

'Probably not.'

'Of course it was my pleasure to dance with 'er, just as it was my pleasure to dance with Mrs Forbes-*Arl-ee*, who is in 'er eighties and cannot move so easily across the floor.'

'And you had one of those pleasurable dances with Lauren last night?'

'As you know.'

'And then?'

'I had a quick drink with them, 'er and Don, and Mr Sebastian and some others, and then I went back to my office.'

'So you weren't there when Lauren and Don started rowing?' asked Francis.

'No.'

'Did you become aware, during the course of the rest of the evening, that she and Don had had a noisy – and public – argument in the bar?'

'No.'

'About you?'

'No.'

'Are you sure about that?'

'Yes.' Gregoire turned sideways to look at Carmen. 'Carmen, I told the captain I am 'appy to help in this matter. But some of these questions are too personal. There was *nothing* between me and Lauren.' He shook his head petulantly and looked back at Francis. 'Really nothing.'

'Don thought there was,' said Francis.

Gregoire shrugged. ''E can think what he likes. I'm afraid 'e is a jealous old man. As I know to my cost, it's a type.'

'You're not married, are you, Gregoire?'

'No.'

'May I ask: d'you have a partner?'

'Please, this is my private life. What are you trying to suggest?'

'I'm sorry,' said Francis. 'I don't mean to be intrusive, I was just trying to get a picture. Not so much of what you wanted, but of what Lauren's expectations might have been.'

'Lauren's expectations were that she enjoyed my company. Particularly on the dance floor. There was nothing more to it than that.'

'Thank you,' said Francis, clasping his hands together and smiling at him in a final sort of way.

'Is that all?' Gregoire said.

Francis looked over at Carmen for confirmation. 'For the moment, yes. By the way,' he added, as the hotel director got up to go, 'I enjoyed your little show the other evening. With the Togoan forest creatures, dancing in the mist. Beautiful.'

'Ah, well.' Gregoire shrugged and smiled. 'It is a bit of fun. The guests love it, as you saw.'

'Tell me. Do you have to get the dry ice in the port you're in, Lomé or wherever, or does it keep?'

Gregoire looked puzzled, as if wondering where this question was leading. 'It doesn't keep for long, so we just get it sometimes when we can. For shows like that one. Or to reduce the mosquitos. And sometimes the doctor is using it, to keep the snakebite antivenoms cool out on expeditions.'

'To reduce the mosquitoes? How d'you mean?'

'It's a bit of fun, really. Those nasty little insects think that the sublimated carbon dioxide, that mist, is 'uman breath, so they cluster round it. So you can 'ave a champagne bucket full of dry ice to one side of the bar, it is like a 'undred people breathing out at the same time. And so, if we are in port, we can make sure that there are no mosquitos during cocktail hour.'

'Well, well. I had no idea.'

'All part of the service, as they say.' Gregoire grinned. 'This top-end luxury, it is a serious business.'

'Interestingly cagey about his private life,' Francis said, when he'd gone. 'Perhaps he is gay.'

'It's not a vibe I get from him.'

'So he flirts with you too?'

'No, it's just the way he is. Maybe he's one of those ones who has a woman in every port. And another back home in France as well. But him being cagey, as you put it, is fair enough. He doesn't know you. You're not an official detective. He's not under oath. Why should he talk?'

'Why indeed?' Francis agreed. 'So what did you think? That there had been something between him and Lauren?'

'I don't know. Initially I thought not. But when you asked him about the argument, he lost patience, didn't he? As if maybe something had been going on.'

'It was quite a strong reaction for someone who has nothing to hide.'

'Why did you ask about the dry ice?' Carmen asked.

'I was just intrigued,' Francis fibbed. 'At the lengths they go to to give the guests a good time. But that's fascinating about the mosquitoes. Did you know that?'

'It's not something I get involved in, mate. All that health and hygiene stuff. Leo deals with that side of things. If the doctor doesn't come out on an expedition, he's always the one who looks after the antivenoms.'

'Which get taken out every time?'

'Of course. Can you imagine? If a guest did get bitten by a snake, way out in the jungle, and there was no antivenom available. Oh my God!' Carmen shook her head. 'Some of these snakes can finish you off in a matter of minutes. We take it all pretty seriously, mate, I can tell you.'

'So what now?' Francis asked. 'The engineer?'

'If we can. I'll need to check with the captain . . .'

'I really think we should talk to him as soon as possible.'

Carmen nodded. She would have to go up to the bridge, she said; she didn't think she was likely to persuade the captain over the phone. But when she returned, ten minutes later, it was with a thumbs down and a grimace. 'As I thought,' she said, shaking her head. 'He's not going to let us wake him.'

'Why not, exactly?'

'The man was up all night. The captain wants him fresh for his next shift. He doesn't think there's any urgency about the interview. As he says, he's not going anywhere.'

'I suppose not,' said Francis, though he felt uneasy about the refusal. Surely the captain could see that this eyewitness's evidence was crucial? 'You don't think we can change his mind?'

''Fraid not.'

From Carmen's expression, it was clear Francis wasn't going to get around her loyalty to her boss either. 'In that case,' he said, 'I suppose it might be worth talking to the others Don and Lauren were friendly with. The fashion designer and his boyfriend, for starters.'

SEVEN

Sebastian de Souza and his partner Kurt had a stateroom, no less, up on the top deck, with a fine view out over the bow of the ship and a sunny balcony from which to enjoy it. Carmen had called them up, via their butler, so she and Francis were expected. Sebastian was looking particularly fine this morning, in a baggy yellow shirt, crimson jodphurs and a pair of slippers that would have done justice to some prince from the Arabian Nights: maroon velvet with long, upward-curling toes.

'Come in, come in!' he said. 'We're just having morning coffee on the balcony. Will you join us? Please excuse the mess.'

There were colourful African fabrics draped over every available surface. Carvings too: tall, bare-breasted ebony women; men with spears and drums; couples embracing, lips pressed together; a little boat load, two men paddling forward while two women in hats sat looking back.

'We love buying these things,' said Sebastian, looking proudly round. 'It's such an opportunity in these remote places. When I get back to Bombay I am going to start on an African-inspired collection.' He took one of the brighter cloths between finger and thumb and held it up. 'Look at these colours. Even in India, we would never put these purples and yellows and greens together in quite this way. And yet it works entirely, don't you think?'

He showed them out on to the balcony, where Kurt was sitting in the sunshine reading the *Wall Street Journal*; he was more simply dressed than when he'd appeared in the public spaces, in an untucked white shirt and baggy khaki shorts.

'You have met my partner, Kurt.'

The portly one nodded silently, his thin lips an expressionless line within the neat white beard.

Sebastian sat down next to him and gestured to his guests to follow suit. 'Now tell me, what is this all about? We took breakfast as usual in our room this morning, and then we skipped the briefing.

We really can't be bothered trotting down every time they change their minds about something.'

'I'm afraid it was more significant than that,' said Francis. 'There was a man overboard last night.'

'You're not serious!' Sebastian's eyes bulged. 'You are serious,' he said, as he registered their expressions. 'Who? Do we know him?'

'It was a her,' said Carmen. 'And you do know her, yes. Lauren, Don's partner. Who you were drinking with in the bar earlier.'

'Lauren! No . . . How absolutely appalling. What happened?'

'Nobody quite knows. But she somehow managed to fall off deck seven.'

'Fall off!' said Sebastian. 'How on earth?'

'She was quite drunk, by all accounts.'

'But still . . . you'd have to be pie-eyed to go over those railings.'

'It was very early in the morning,' Carmen continued. 'It was quite by chance that one of the night shift engineers spotted her.'

'So that explains that strange shuddering,' Sebastian said, turning towards Kurt. 'We did think the captain was changing course rather dramatically.'

'He was. One hundred and eighty degrees. They turned and went back to the exact point she'd gone over.'

'But they didn't find her? This is terrible. Have you spoken to Don?'

'Yes,' said Carmen. 'We've just been with him.'

'He must be distraught.'

'He's in shock.'

'We should go and see him, Kurt.' Sebastian looked over at his partner, whose features remained impassive; then back at Francis and Carmen with a look that was gracious bordering on grand. 'Thank you for letting us know. Why didn't they tell us what the briefing was about? We'd have been there. Obviously.'

'That was kind of the point of it,' said Carmen. 'To break the news in a controlled way.'

'I understand, yes,' Sebastian said. 'I had no idea,' he muttered.

'Before we leave you,' Francis asked, 'may I just ask you how you found them last night?'

'Found them?'

'Don and Lauren. How they seemed to you. In the bar. When you were all drinking together . . .'

'Oh, I see. You've already said it, haven't you? She was drunk. Drunker last night than I've seen her all week. And whereas before she was happy drunk, dancing, laughing, being funny, last night she had tipped over, as she does sometimes. Into something sadder. And darker. They had an argument, you probably knew that. It was pretty public.'

'Did you understand what it was about?'

'She has . . . ongoing . . . issues with him, shall we put it like that?'

'She wanted to marry him and he wasn't interested,' said Francis. 'Wasn't that it in a nutshell?'

'No,' said Sebastian. 'Not that way around. *He* wanted to marry *her*.'

Carmen looked as surprised as Francis.

'That's not what he told us,' he said. 'He said she was after his money and he didn't want to lose control of his businesses.'

Sebastian laughed. 'But he has no money! She's the one with the money. She's an heiress, didn't you know that? Her daddy wrote that song, you know, "Chumba Chumba Cha-Cha". From the seventies.'

'*Chumba chumba cha-cha,*' sang Carmen, '*I knew it was gonna be you-ou.*'

'That's the one. Think how many millions of times that piece of nonsense has been played over the years. Every time you hear it on the radio, in a plane, in an orchestral version in a lift, God knows, *kerching*, it's another royalty payment for Lauren. She's an only child. Her papa died when she was a teenager. Flipped out on his success and drugs. She'd already lost her mother. So it's all hers.'

'I thought Don had a magazine empire,' Francis said, realizing as he did so that he hadn't checked Sadie's information, not even with the man himself.

'At some point I think he did,' Sebastian said. 'But there's not much left now. She pretty much supports the couple of rags he's still got going. There was a disastrous foray into local TV, I do know that.'

'He's told you all this?'

'Yes. We know them quite well. We were on a cruise with them last Christmas.'

'In Antarctica?' Francis asked.

'It was, yes. Along with quite a few of the others here, as it happens.'

'Such as?'

Sebastian looked over at his partner. 'Can you remember, Kurt? Daphne and Henry, for sure. Eve, the English widow. That boring old American colonel who's never seen action – what's his name?'

'Joe,' said Kurt. It was the first word Francis had heard him speak. His voice was deep and resonant, like the lower notes of a church organ.

'They were all on that trip, weren't they?' Sebastian added and Kurt nodded.

Francis turned to Carmen. 'Is that normal?'

'What?'

'To get a cluster of guests like that? Going from one cruise to another.'

'Yes . . . no . . . I don't know,' she said. 'I'd have to check the records.'

'I don't think there's any great mystery,' Sebastian said. 'We all love Goldencruise. Both the Antarctic and this are exciting itineraries. More so than the normal paddle around the Mediterranean bath tub.'

'But this ship did several Antarctic cruises last winter,' Francis said. 'Yet you were all on the same one . . .'

'The Christmas one. Maybe it's as simple as that. For us folk without families. And I know the colonel wanted to see the Falklands. Like Kurt here. Not all the itineraries include that. Port Stanley and South Georgia, those war places.'

'I see,' said Francis. 'So on that cruise Don told you his life story?'

'In dribs and drabs. As you do. We're bar flies, us two. We needed to have something to talk about as the glaciers were drifting past. But yes, if you want to know, he was upset. About the way things are. He wants – wanted, I should say – to support Lauren. Or at least to be her equal financially. And things have just gone from bad to worse for him. He's quite desperate about it, in fact.'

'So she paid for the cruises?'

'I hadn't thought about it, but I suppose she does – did.' Sadness flickered over the designer's handsome features.

'Why, exactly, did she stick around?' Francis asked.

'How do you mean?'

'Well, he is that much older, isn't he? So if she had the money . . . I mean, no offence to him, but when you see them together you do rather assume, don't you?'

'Just goes to show that you should never make assumptions,' said Sebastian.

'Yes, but still . . .'

'As I said, her father died young. Maybe Don is the classic father figure. And there is of course another possibility.'

'Which is?'

'Perhaps she loved him. Did that thought occur to you?'

His sudden scorn made Francis feel almost ashamed. Maybe his take on all this was too cynical. Rich people had feelings too. 'I think we need to talk to him again,' he said to Carmen.

'I think we do.'

She got to her feet and Francis followed.

'I don't think he's got anything to do with her going overboard, if that's what you're thinking,' said Sebastian. 'For all their arguing, he doted on her. You only had to see the way he looked at her, or watched her dancing.'

'With the hotel director, Gregoire, for example.'

'Him, yes. Or me. Or Brad and Damian. She loved boogying with them too.'

'The gay . . .' Francis said and immediately felt stupid.

'Couple, yes. The *other* gay couple,' Sebastian replied tartly. 'There are actually three on board. You might not have identified the third.'

Francis thought for a moment, but he was stumped. 'I'm not sure I have,' he said.

'Carmen?'

The Australian shook her head. 'I really have no idea. It's not something I particularly notice.'

'Then that will have to remain my secret,' said Sebastian, turning archly from one of them to the other, raising an eyebrow.

'I thought for a moment you were going to say Klaus,' said Carmen. 'And Colonel Joe.'

Sebastian laughed. 'Colonel Joe is almost certainly as queer as a coot. Never married. Loves male-bonding activities. Goes to the gym every morning, religiously. Is pretty much glued to baseball and wrestling in the TV lounge. I'm not so sure about Klaus.'

Don was still in bed.

'Now what d'you want?' he said grumpily, turning his head away from the window.

'Sorry to disturb you again,' said Francis. 'But there's something we need to clear up.'

'You two are the self-appointed ship's detectives now, are you?'

'The captain needs to find out what might have happened to Lauren,' said Francis. 'He's obliged to report her disappearance, not just to the ship's owners and the Bahamian Police Authority, but to the FBI. There was a law passed recently that means that if there's an American citizen overboard, they have to look into it too. So I wouldn't be at all surprised if there was someone to meet us when we get to Freetown the day after tomorrow.'

'The FBI, huh. And what power do they have out here? Can they keep all these wealthy international citizens on board in the port of a foreign country until they're satisfied they've got answers? Or is this just a box-ticking operation?'

'I don't know what authority they have,' said Francis. 'But for the moment we're doing our best to find out what happened.'

'How very public-spirited of you. So how can I help you now?' His tone was disdainful, but Francis wasn't to be deterred.

'As we understand it,' he said, 'the story you had about Lauren wanting to marry you wasn't true.'

'Who said that?'

Francis repeated what Sebastian had told them, not mentioning his name.

'So you've been speaking to my personal bankers, have you?'

'No.'

'I didn't think so. This sounds rather like something I told Sebastian once, late one night when we were boozing together. There is some truth in it, but it's not the whole truth.'

'Then why did you tell him?'

'Perhaps I have a penchant for exaggerating. You forget that I began life as a journalist. Before I was sensible enough to realize where the money was in the magazine world.'

'But it's true that Lauren had money? Her father was a songwriter, I believe.'

'That piece of crap kept her afloat, yeah. Gave her a little independence. But if Sebastian told you it made her rich enough to sponsor both of us on regular luxury cruises he was sadly misinformed.'

'And you? You still have—?'

'I don't see how my personal net worth is any of your damn business.'

'Let's be blunt, Don. If Lauren did have the money, and you were – are – the beneficiary of her will, marriage or no marriage, then there's no way out of the conclusion that this terrible event would benefit you. Substantially. Maybe critically.'

Don looked back down at his hands, twisted together above the blue eiderdown. 'As always in these cases, it's the partner who's in the frame. Regardless of any feelings they might them-selves have . . .'

'Don, I appreciate that this is all very shocking for you. I certainly don't want to cast unwarranted suspicion. But we need to establish the facts, if only to help you.'

'Perhaps you could explain exactly how this helps me?'

'If you could tell us, for example, that there was no will in existence between Lauren and yourself. Or that we've got things wrong about your business. That obviously takes away a motive that anyone who is looking into this is otherwise going to see, whether it's me and Carmen here or some FBI agent currently on his way to Freetown.'

'You have knowledge of this FBI agent, do you?'

'I'm afraid I'm not allowed to say.' Francis looked over at Carmen, who held his gaze steadily.

'And if he does turn up, this agent . . .'

'When he turns up . . .'

'He's going to want to go through all this again? Or is he going to be happy to accept your view of things?'

'I have no idea.'

'I do. He'll want to do his own investigation. So maybe I should just wait until I have to answer to the freakin' professionals.'

Don's gaze was now firmly focused on the ocean. His mouth
was set.

'And that's all you're going to say?'

Don turned. 'Who exactly are you? As I understand it, some
Brit who was invited on the ship to lecture about crime novels.
It's none of your business how Lauren and I were situated financially.
Or anything else, for that matter.'

EIGHT

I f Don wasn't going to talk about his relationship with Lauren, it certainly wasn't stopping the rest of the guests. As Francis headed downstairs and waited in the short queue for the buffet lunch, snippets of speculation came flying past his ears. 'Probably did it to shut her up' . . . 'They'd been rowing earlier in the bar' . . . 'More than once' . . . 'It wasn't about dancing, it was about money' . . . 'One *heck* of a flirt, no doubt about that . . .'

Francis sensed the excitement, but very clearly, just underneath that, the fear: of what had happened and could so easily happen again. The wide, choppy ocean around them no longer seemed so reassuring. To him, too. He was suddenly very aware that he was stuck on a large floating metal box which might very well contain a man or woman who had killed twice and most likely would not hesitate to kill a third time to protect themselves.

His eavesdropping was curtailed by Carmen, who had popped down to her cabin for five minutes, and had now returned with a fresh layer of crimson lipstick.

'Everyone,' she said, 'but everyone, is talking about Lauren.'

'Why wouldn't they be? Big news for our little ecosystem. No one's going to be looking at that two-page round-up of world news today.'

'People are scared.'

'Of course they are. Until it's established exactly how and why Lauren went overboard, and whether there was anyone else involved, it's bound to make you look over your shoulder a little. Especially if you're not as young and strong as you once were.'

'And none of them even *know* about Eve,' said Carmen, her voice dropping to a near whisper.

'Indeed.'

'So what did you make of Don?'

'Maintaining his right to silence?'

'Does that make him more or less guilty?'

'Hard to tell,' said Francis. 'He's clearly stubborn.'

'But then again, he has a perfect right not to talk about his relationship. He's only just lost Lauren.'

'Though if there was nothing in Sebastian's story, it would be easy enough to refute it. Before he decided to shut up he more or less admitted there was some truth there, didn't he?'

'I'm sorry the FBI agent backfired,' Carmen said. 'I was rather enjoying him. Or was it her? But actually that did put the wind up him. On reflection, he might decide to spill the beans after all.'

They had reached the front of the queue, so the next couple of minutes were spent choosing from a wide and tempting array of lunch dishes. Francis restricted himself to two small helpings: Thai chicken curry and boeuf bourgignon, with a mound of plain rice in between.

'Couldn't choose, mate?' said Carmen, grinning at his selection as she joined him at the table for two in the corner which John-since-1972 had just finished relaying. 'I always end up putting on weight on these trips, even though I'm out half the days leading expeditions.' She plunged knife and fork into a plate heaped with cold meats and salad.

'So what's the plan?' she asked. 'Report back to the captain?'

'I guess we have to admit that we've got as far as we can for the moment with Don. What about the other couple who were drinking with them last night? Shirley and her partner.'

'Hello, stranger.' Francis looked up to see Sadie, right by their table, almost in silhouette against the bright light from the portholes opposite.

'Sadie, hi. You know Carmen?'

'Only from the expeditions. Hi.' Sadie acknowledged her with barely a glance. 'Where've you been, Francis?'

'Doing a bit of work in my cabin.'

'Uh-huh.' She didn't look convinced. 'So what d'you make of all this?'

'The man overboard situation?'

'Woman overboard situation. Of course.'

'We were just discussing it.'

'Pretty spooky, huh? Especially when you consider everything else that's been going on.'

'Yes,' Francis replied. He didn't want to get into a three-way conversation about Eve right now. Nor, particularly, for Carmen to know that he'd shared this secret with Sadie.

'I'm going to have to catch up with you a bit later, Sadie,' he said. 'Carmen and I were just . . .'

Sadie held up two flat palms in a gesture of bogus supplication. 'Sure, whatever. Come and join me for a coffee when you've finished. I'm going to be up in the Whirlpool Bar. There's something else I urgently need to talk to you about.'

'I'll find you,' Francis said. 'How's your aunt, by the way?'

'Completely freaked out about what happened last night. I don't think she'd realized that you can fall off a ship. And that if you do your chances of being picked up are not so great. She had an idea that if anyone ever went over, a crew member would chuck a life ring after them, the ship would be stopped, Zodiacs launched, and hey ho, they'd be pulled back on board again in time for evening cocktails.'

'Wow!' said Carmen, after Sadie had gone, weaving her way between the tables towards the door out to deck five. 'That was some display of passive-aggression.'

Francis smiled. 'She did seem a bit intense, didn't she?'

'I'd say.'

When Francis and Carmen had finished eating they returned to the bridge to report their findings to the captain. They were joined by First Officer Alexei and Viktor, who was particularly intrigued by Sebastian's version of the Don and Lauren story.

'So you think it's true?' he asked. 'That she was the one with the money?'

'We don't know,' Francis replied. 'Do we, Carmen?'

'Maybe the truth lies somewhere between the two,' she said. 'But surely the "Chumba Chumba Cha-Cha" story must be kosha. Why would you make up something like that?'

A smile crossed the captain's swarthy features. '"Chumba Chumba Cha-Cha",' he repeated, in a sing-song manner. 'Now that was tune I used to like dancing to when I was young. In Ukraine it was big hit.'

'Whether the song made Lauren as rich as Sebastian suggested,' Francis said, 'I've no idea. But Don is being stubborn for a reason. It may be as simple as pride. Perhaps he doesn't want people to know that his business empire has failed.'

'It's not good enough,' said Viktor. 'If he really has no money, he had a clear motive. Assuming, of course, that he's a beneficiary of her will. You need to go back to him. Be tougher. I am happy to come with you, if you like.'

'Thank you,' said Francis. 'For the moment, we'll keep the double act going. We've still got to talk to the others who were drinking with Don and Lauren last night. The English couple.'

'Fat lady with thin husband?' said the captain. 'She is quite something.'

'She is,' Viktor agreed. 'You should have seen her doing the voodoo dance in Togo.'

'Between ourselves,' said Francis, 'I found out something interesting about her. She has terminal cancer. Just a few months to live. This is probably her last ever trip.'

The four others were silent at this, as if embarrassed at their own flippancy.

'I am sorry to hear that,' said Viktor. Then: 'Are you saying that this is in some way significant?'

'No,' Francis replied. 'Why would it be?'

'She has nothing to lose?' Carmen suggested.

'This is no surprise to me,' the captain said. 'We often get these cases on these cruises. People dream all their lives long about doing something like this, then suddenly they've got six months to go, so they blow their savings and do it. You know, in strange way, it makes me feel good about job I do. That people want this experience so bad.'

Both Viktor and the captain agreed that talking to Shirley and her husband about Don would be a good thing to do. Despite what Carmen had said earlier, Francis asked again about interviewing the engineer.

'I thought we had spoken about this,' the captain replied tersely. 'He was up all night and has to go straight back to work later. He is safety officer, so I don't want him in bad shape. His next shift starts at four p.m. We will wake him for interview shortly before that. Say three thirty. Alexei, you take charge of that; you can bring him up to bridge. Until then he sleeps.'

'OK,' said Francis. There was little point pressing this; it was only a couple of hours to wait.

All the necessary authorities, the captain went on, had now been alerted to the missing person situation.

'So we can expect a policeman from the Bahamian Police Authority to meet us on the dock at Freetown?' said Francis.

For all his Ukranian reserve, the captain had a sense of humour. 'As you say in UK,' he said with a smile, '"If pigs could fly".'

'It still seems extraordinary to me,' Francis replied. 'When you've actually lost someone overboard. May I ask: have you experienced an MOB situation before?'

The captain nodded. 'Yes. Not with *Golden Adventurer*, though. And I wasn't captain of that vessel, I was first officer. In that case it was clearly suicide. Woman left note. Her marriage had broken down. Her only son had died in motorcycle accident. She had terminal disease, like this Englishwoman we were talking about. She had come on cruise alone. She drank bottle of whisky and downed pills before she jumped. Sad story. But these things happen.'

'So did you find her then? To know all that . . .'

'We did find her, yes. But too late to save her.'

'And which part of the world was that?'

'The Med. Standard antiquities cruise. She went overboard as we were approaching Malta. Coastguard sent out helicopter, which spotted body.'

Francis nodded thoughtfully. 'So what happens now?' he asked.

'We stick to itinerary,' the captain replied.

'A day at sea today . . .'

'And tomorrow too, while we pass Cote d'Ivoire and Liberia.'

'Not known for their visitor attractions,' said Viktor.

This brought a chuckle from the captain.

'Then a day out in Freetown,' Viktor continued. 'A nice morning on Banana Island. An afternoon on one of the islands of the Bijagos Archipelago in Guinea-Bissau. A day's birdwatching in the Gambia. Finally into port at Dakar.'

'And what happens to Don in all these places?' asked Francis.

'We keep eye on him,' said the captain. 'Unless you come up with definite evidence that he had something to do with his partner's death, in which case I will confine him to cabin.'

'And that will be enough?'

'Of course. We can lock him in, if necessary. We even have little jail on board. Next to morgue. But no, nobody wants ship to become floating investigation. This is one of reasons I have asked you to help. Because you are not member of crew and I can, I hope, trust you to be discreet.'

'And the others?'

'What?'

'Reasons?'

The captain broke into an almost embarrassed smile. 'Your previous experience. At English festival.'

'I see,' Francis said. He looked round the room at the impassive face of Alexei, and the slightly less controlled features of Viktor and Carmen. It was clear that the captain didn't need to outline what might occur if that trust was broken. Might he confine Francis to cabin too? Or even lock him in the jail? He decided to place a little marker in the sand.

'I am under no obligation to continue with these enquiries,' he said.

'Of course not,' said the captain. 'But you are curious, no? And there is perhaps professional interest here?'

Francis caught Carmen's eye. The captain had understood him all too well; and in his blunt way, he was a skilful negotiator.

Shirley and her husband were not in their cabin on deck three; Hentie had not seen them since before lunch. Francis and Carmen checked in a variety of public spaces: the glassed-in Observation Lounge at the front of deck six, the empty theatre just behind, the Whirlpool Bar at the stern of that deck, the Panorama Lounge on deck five, the restaurant on deck four, the adjacent library and games room, even the reception area and boutique back on deck three.

'Unless they've gone overboard too there's only one place left they can be,' said Carmen, leading briskly towards the stairs.

Sure enough, they found the couple up on the sun deck at the rear of deck seven. Shirley was spread out on a lounger, with only a capacious blue one-piece, a straw hat and a pair of Chanel sunglasses to cover her; while Gerald, a yard or two away in the shade of a square white pillar, was sitting upright on a chair doing a crossword. He looked beadily over his rimless specs as Francis and Carmen approached.

'Sorry to disturb you both in the middle of a quiet afternoon,' Francis said. 'Is there any chance of a word in confidence? We're trying to gather some information on the woman who went overboard last night, and we believe you were some of the last people to speak to her.'

Shirley put her Kindle aside and sat up, her lounger creaking ominously.

'And what exactly is your role?' she asked coolly. 'I don't even know you, I don't think.'

'I'm sorry. Francis Meadowes is my name. We spoke briefly during cocktails on deck last night . . .'

'Oh yes,' said Shirley. 'You didn't approve of the attitude of the guides at Elmina Fort.'

'I'm not quite sure . . .' Francis began, then thought the better of it. There was no point picking a fight with a key witness, was there? 'You were arguing that point with the couple from Chicago, I think.'

'Bruce and Candy. The rednecks, we call them. Their attitudes are *in*-credible. With a capital "I". If I'd seen a movie with them in it I would have said they were not believable characters. But there they are. Mr Sports Jock and his dumb blonde cheerleader wife. You should hear Brad and Damian on the subject – our gay American friends. Have you met them? Brad's a dead ringer for George Clooney.' Francis nodded and Shirley smiled. 'So you're trying to establish what happened to poor Lauren?'

'In a word, yes.'

'And why you exactly?'

'The captain,' Carmen cut in, 'and Alexei, our security officer, have asked Francis for help, since he has some expertise in this area.'

'So – what?' said Shirley. 'Are you an off-duty policeman or something?'

Francis looked over at Carmen. As she explained about what Francis did and his involvement in the Mold-on-Wold murders, Shirley's attitude visibly changed. 'That literary festival business?' she asked.

'Yes,' said Francis.

'Interesting. I'd like to talk to you about that some time. The famous literary critic who was killed was two-timing his wife, wasn't that it?'

'Three-timing his non-wife,' Francis corrected. 'I'd be happy to fill you in, once we've got some answers to this shocking situation.'

'It is shocking,' Shirley agreed. 'We were just saying that, weren't we, Gerald?'

Her husband nodded.

'As you say,' she went on, 'I think we were some of the last people to speak to her. We had a drink with them in the bar – good heavens, was it only last night? It feels like a week ago. Poor Lauren. She could be such fun. Before she got too tipsy. I realize she had her difficulties with Don, but . . .'

'So what did you know of those?' asked Francis, squatting down beside her. It was more comfortable out of the glare, though still impossible to read the expression in Shirley's eyes behind the gleaming panes of her dark glasses.

'Not *much* more than anyone else,' she replied. 'But we witnessed them rowing a couple of times, didn't we, Gerald?'

'I was there,' said Francis. 'Both times. Did you get a sense of what it was all about?'

'Money,' said Shirley. 'And maybe commitment. They weren't married . . .'

'We'd been told that.'

'I think . . . maybe that was an issue for her . . .'

Francis outlined the story that Don had told them, and then Sebastian's version. 'D'you have any idea which is true?' he asked.

Shirley looked over at Gerald. 'God, what a terrible thing. I just assumed he had the money. Didn't you, lovey?'

'I did.'

'Shows how wrong you can be. These patriarchal structures are so common, we don't even consider the alternative. I guess if that's what he told Sebastian, it probably is true. Sebastian can be a bit naughty, but I don't think he'd make something like that up.'

'There did seem also,' Francis went on, 'to be a measure of jealousy on Don's part. Particularly about the hotel director—'

'Gorgeous Gregoire,' Shirley completed. 'We all noticed that. Lauren liked him, no doubt about that.'

'He was much closer to her in age,' said Gerald.

'D'you know what?' said Shirley, loudly, almost as if she had to interrupt, or at least overlay this spousal intrusion. 'Whatever Don imagined, there was nothing in it. He and Lauren may have argued when she got drunk, but she was devoted to him. Really. You could see it. So what did Don say?'

'He thought there might have been something going on. From what he told us, there had been situations like this in the past.'

'"Like this"? What d'you mean?'

'Serious flirting,' said Francis. 'And, he said, actual infidelity.'

'This isn't just the fantasy of a frustrated old man?' said Shirley.

They sat discussing the relationship for a little longer. But it seemed clear that neither Shirley nor her partner had much actual knowledge. They had got to know Don and Lauren only over these past few days. They had had dinner with them once, in the company of others. But there had been no sharing of life stories, such as Sebastian claimed to have had with Don in the Antarctic. Eventually Francis got to his feet and thanked them.

'We'll keep you posted,' he said as he backed away. 'Sorry to have disturbed your afternoon.'

'We were glad to be of help,' said Shirley, taking off her sunglasses. 'I can't believe it's happened to be honest.' As she looked up at him he saw anxiety in her eyes. 'You do think we're safe on this ship?'

'Of course,' Francis lied. 'The sad truth is,' he went on, 'that Lauren may have just stumbled and fallen off. She was very drunk by all accounts.'

'It still all seems very odd to me,' said Shirley.

'So what do we think?' Francis asked Carmen, as they walked back down deck seven. The bow at this upper level was inaccessible, taken up with a bristling forest – or more correctly, perhaps, a copse – of masts around a huge, central white ball (which presumably relayed signals and other information down to the bridge two decks below). But at the stern, beyond the squat little structure that housed the fitness centre and adjacent spa, there was nothing between the two big lifeboats, slung up high on each side, but decking and railings, overlooking the deck six grill area, and beyond that the wake of the ship stretching out in that narrowing band of frothing white towards the distant horizon.

'I think we think, mate,' she replied, 'that we have no idea.'

She was grasping the railings with both hands as she turned to

smile at him, her cropped blonde hair fluffed up by the breeze off
the sea. Looking at her well-bronzed skin close up in this bright
sunlight, he wondered how old she was. She was very toned; soignée
and toned, with well-defined muscles in her upper arms. Attractive,
but not, strangely, to him; the awful truth was that he preferred
highly strung, lily-white Sadie.

'What about the gay guys, Brad and Damian?' he asked. 'D'you
think they might have something useful to say about the Don
and Lauren set-up? I saw them all chatting together in the bar
at least once.'

'I suppose it wouldn't do us any harm to talk to them.'

'Meanwhile, as Viktor said, if Lauren had the money and Don
didn't, and there's a will, he suddenly has a solid motive. We know
he was angry with her because of what he thought she'd got up to
with Gregoire. Would that combination be enough to tip him into
a moment of madness? He may be old, but he looks strong enough
to have given her a shove. Especially if she were caught unawares.'

'And was drunk with it.'

'And was drunk with it,' Francis repeated thoughtfully.

'What about Gregoire?' asked Carmen.

'As a suspect? I can't see why he'd want to get rid of Lauren. If
she had the money . . .'

'Unless Don was right and something *had* happened between
them. And Lauren, drunk and angry with her lover too, had threat-
ened to expose him. Gregoire's not allowed to get involved with
passengers. It's a career-threatening situation.'

'Would you really kill to save your job on a particular ship?'

'On any ship, Francis. He'd never get a reference if he'd been
caught with a passenger. The cruising world is tiny, especially when
it comes to these small, high-end liners.'

'OK,' said Francis. 'And what about Eve in all this? If she didn't
die of natural causes, could there be a link?'

'Nothing obvious. They're not even the same nationality.'

'The only thing we know they have in common is that they were
both on that previous cruise to Antarctica at Christmas. Was Gregoire
on that too?'

'I've no idea, I wasn't on it. But yes, probably. Unless he was
on leave, he would have been.'

'Can we find out?'

'Of course.'

'Sebastian also mentioned Daphne and Henry and Colonel Joe. I think Brad and Damian were on it too, if my eavesdropping was accurate.'

'Your eavesdropping?'

'On the coach. On the way down to Tema dock.'

'Nothing gets past you, docs it, mate? OK, let's go find them. Check the fitness centre first?'

Francis laughed.

'They are two of the major users of that place,' said Carmen. 'Apart from me and Colonel Joe, of course.'

But Brad and Damian were not in the fitness centre; nor were they in their cabin down on deck three. Francis and Carmen eventually found them having coffee and playing piquet in the Panorama Lounge. On the linen tablecloth between them was a plate of petits fours.

'D'you mind if we join you for a minute?' asked Carmen.

There was a moment of puzzled surprise and then effusive politeness.

'Please do,' said the older of the pair, putting his cards face down and holding out a hand. 'Brad,' he said. He did indeed, Francis thought, have something George Clooney about him, if only in his obvious awareness of his classic American good looks. 'Have one of these delicious sweet things. Save us from ourselves. That's the problem with these cruises. Endless temptation. Shall we order you some coffee? Or tea?'

'We're fine,' Francis said, looking over at Carmen.

'Hi, I'm Damian.' The younger man was altogether slighter; his voice a register higher.

Carmen introduced Francis. 'You've heard about Lauren?' she said.

'Of course,' said Brad, quietly.

'Awful,' said Damian. 'We didn't even know until the briefing this morning. Apparently, the ship turned round and everything, but we both slept through it.'

'The whole thing?' asked Francis.

'Pretty much,' said Brad. 'I was aware there was some kind of movement in the ship, but it never occurred to me it would be someone overboard. Why didn't they sound the alarm?'

'Didn't want people to panic,' said Francis. 'They've got enough crew to check the sea and man the rescue if they need to.'

'I always sleep like the proverbial log,' said Damian. 'Didn't hear a thing.'

Carmen explained what the captain had asked Francis and her to do. And then the differing accounts of the Don and Lauren relationship. 'So we're just trying to work out the truth. You spent quite a bit of time with them, didn't you?'

Brad looked at Damian and Damian looked at Brad.

'That's all hokum about Don having the money,' Damian said. 'Sebastian's right. He's broke. And Lauren was like a pop heiress.'

'I don't want to sound unduly cynical,' said Francis, 'but what did she see in Don?'

'The thing was,' said Damian, 'they'd been together for a long time. Since Lauren was in her twenties. She worked for him originally. I guess he was more of a big cheese then. And at one point I think he did have a whole load of dough.'

'So why would an heiress need to work?'

'Don had magazines,' said Damian. 'Quite glamorous ones. From what I gathered, she was involved with the art direction. It was like a job she didn't need to have, but enjoyed. You know the kind of thing. Arty status.'

'I see,' said Francis; it was all becoming clearer. 'Did you get a sense of what they argued about?' he asked.

'The usual,' said Damian. 'Money, sex, bad habits.'

'Don told us she wanted to marry him,' said Francis, 'and that that was the problem.'

Damian looked at Brad. 'That might once have been something she wanted. But I'm not sure she was that bothered now.'

'Shirley thought she might have been.'

'You have been thorough,' said Brad. 'Well, I guess there's a certain type of girl who always wants a ring on her finger.'

'Enough already!' said Damian.

Brad laughed and looked at Francis. 'We're getting married in the fall.'

'Congratulations.'

'Our home state's only recently made it legal, so it's kind of exciting for us.'

'Which state is that?'

'Montana. It's been quite a fight.'

'I imagine,' Francis said. 'To go back to Lauren,' he went on, after a moment. 'When you say "sex", d'you mean just between them, or were there others involved?'

Damian looked at Brad; it was as if he were seeking permission to speak.

'Both,' he replied. 'If you want to know about this, my feeling was Don still wanted her, but she didn't reciprocate. Maybe she also had little flings here and there and that wound him up. But then he kind of needed her, not least because she's got the money now. Perhaps he found it hard to accept that. You know, getting older, losing allure, losing control . . .'

'The great relationship analyst, my fiancé,' said Brad.

'I notice these things. Dumb ass here just sails on regardless.'

'She was dancing quite intimately with Gregoire last night,' Francis said. 'And the other evening too.'

'Oh, Gregoire,' said Damian. 'Such a tease, that man.'

'Just a tease? Or do you think something was actually going on between them?'

'There was a flirtation, no doubt about that. But to be honest, I'm not sure Gregoire isn't catered for below stairs.'

'How d'you mean?'

'He's a handsome fellow. And an officer. He's more than likely got some little house mouse tucked away. At least while his contract lasts.'

'House mouse?'

'Watch him with that pretty Latvian receptionist on deck three. There's a definite blush in her cheeks when he ruffles her hair.'

'What d'you think, Carmen? Is that likely?'

'That pretty Latvian receptionist is called Larisa,' Carmen replied. 'I can't say I've ever seen them together like that, in the crew bar or whatever. But then again, these things do go on, not always above the radar . . .'

'Damian has a very overactive imagination,' said Brad.

Before they got up and left the pair to their card game, Francis had one other question for them. They had both, he thought, been on an Antarctic cruise the previous winter. Had it been the Christmas one?'

'No. We did one earlier in December. Just the basic round trip from Ushuaia. None of that Falklands nonsense; we're not interested in that. But it wasn't last winter anyway. We did it the year before. It was spectacular, though. These icy white coasts which dwarf the ship. You should do it sometime.'

'And nobody died?'

'What are you suggesting?' Damian said, with a puzzled look. 'No. Not that we heard about.'

NINE

Francis and Carmen weren't yet ready to go back to the captain and Viktor. At Carmen's suggestion they retreated to Francis's cabin and ordered tea to calm the nerves and get them thinking constructively. Hentie the butler appeared like a squat genie. She hurried off and returned with a white china pot on a tray containing yet more unasked-for treats.

'You could get seriously overweight if you stayed on this ship too long,' said Francis, reaching out for one of the home-made ginger biscuits, which was embedded with tasty chunks of the crystallized root.

'They do, they do,' said Hentie, laughing as she backed out.

'She seems like quite a character,' said Carmen, as the door clicked shut.

'You don't know her?'

'No. Why would I?'

'I thought you might have met in the crew bar or something?'

'Contrary to your fantasies, Francis, there isn't some swinging scene going on below the waterline. We expedition lot tend to hang out together in the passenger areas anyway, since we're allowed to and they're nicer spaces. The rest of it is frankly quite hierarchical. The officers do their own thing in their mess. The Filipinos work so hard they only have time to sleep and Skype their relatives. Ditto the Bangladeshi types you never see, who work in the engine room. And the Chinese in the laundry. As for the butlers and receptionists, I'm only on nodding terms with most of them.'

'And yet, a handsome officer like Gregoire might have a "house mouse"?'

Carmen laughed. 'Where did Damian get that idea? I've never even heard that expression. Maybe he's been having fantasies about Gregoire he can't share with his fiancé.'

Francis laughed and poured himself a cup of tea; then one for Carmen too.

'So where are we?' he asked.

'Getting nowhere fast,' Carmen replied, with a smile.

'Did you ever read Agatha Christie's *Death on the Nile?*'

'I'm sorry to say this, mate. To you of all people, but I've never read a single one of these murder mysteries you like so much.'

'I write. Don't necessarily like. Anyway, in that story, a beautiful heiress is murdered on a ship – albeit a ship that people can get off. There are twenty or so other passengers. And pretty much all of them has a good reason to kill her. Our problem here is the opposite. We've got two dead bodies, but there's no one on board with any obvious motive at all, as far as I can see.'

'Apart from Don.'

'So it has to be him, then? Desperate to get control of Lauren's inheritance, and/or jealous of her flirtation with Gregoire, which he thought was something more.'

'It might well have been something more.'

'It might,' Francis agreed. 'OK, imagine this: some time ago, Don got Lauren to leave him some, if not all, of her money, which he badly needs to prop up his ailing magazine empire or whatever. In return, maybe she gets a say in how things are done. Which would explain why they were arguing about financial decisions. And why he made that emotive little speech about not letting a woman into your business life. But he would never have thought of laying a finger on her; despite their up and down relationship, as everyone keeps telling us, he loved her. But then here, back on this ship with Gregoire again, suspecting or maybe even knowing something has gone on, Don flies into a fit of jealous rage and pushes her over. He doesn't mean to. But they're out on deck, late at night, trying to sort it out. She's drunk. She insults him. Compares him to her other lover. He flips.'

'OK, but the bloke on the lifeboat didn't see anyone push her off.'

'From what the captain said, the bloke on the lifeboat hardly saw anything anyway. Just a body flying down. But do we believe that? The lifeboats are on the top deck. There's nowhere higher than that. Is it possible he saw more?'

'What are you saying?' said Carmen slowly. 'The captain misreported him?'

'Or he misreported himself.'

'You think this guy might have seen . . . what, Don . . .?'

'Pushing her off? Maybe. Or maybe it wasn't Don.'

'Who then?'

'I've no idea,' Francis said. 'But we'll find out shortly.' He looked at his watch. 'Ten to three. The captain said we could talk to him at three thirty. We need to be on the bridge promptly. I don't want him making any more difficulties about this interview.'

'You think he's deliberately making difficulties?'

'He's not making it easy, is he?'

'Fair enough to let the guy get his sleep.'

'Is it? When he's the most important witness. We must also keep asking, what link might there have been between Eve and Lauren?'

'There's nothing obvious.'

'Except the one very obvious thing. Which links so many of the other guests on board too. Daphne and Henry Forbes-Harley, Marion and Sadie . . .'

She met his eye. 'I guess . . .'

Francis was rubbing his thumb against his forefinger.

'Money?'

'Exactly,' he said. 'And plenty of it. Because you don't choose to go on several high-end cruises a year like Eve did if you're not seriously loaded. And I can hardly bear to think how much "Chumba Chumba Cha-Cha" might have made over the years. What else?'

'That they might have in common? They were women?'

'That's of relevance too. But something else. Specifically to do with this ship.'

'To do with this ship? I really don't know.'

'Who were they both good friends with?'

'The big English lady and her hubby?'

'No.'

'Sebastian and Kurt?'

'I don't think Eve even spoke to them. No, you're not thinking in quite the right place. Step down a deck or two. Think perfect profile and gorgeous wavy blond hair.'

'Gregoire.'

'Gregoire, exactly. Both were wealthy ladies we know he was friendly with. But how friendly? Friendly enough to get them to leave a little something for him in their wills? Or more than a little something. And then, once that's been discreetly arranged, a gentle helping hand to go to the place they're all going to go one day in any case.'

Carmen's mouth had dropped open. 'What are you saying? That Gregoire is some sort of swindler-cum-serial-killer?'

'It's a thought, isn't it? And the only one I've had so far that gets anywhere near fitting the circumstances. We had a famous doctor in England a few years back who liked to bump off old ladies in his care. Harold Shipman. You may remember the case.'

'I'm sorry, mate, I don't.'

'He was quite a celebrity in a macabre sort of way. He murdered scores of old people – and he wasn't even taking their money. As far as anyone could work out, his motive seemed to have something to do with the fact that they were a burden on society, so why not help them on their way? If you add money to that mix, you get a double "why not?". And Gregoire is in the ideal position to do this. Make friends with these old dears. Flatter them. Listen to stories of how wonderful their dead husbands were. Make himself out to be, perhaps, a little similar, but oh dear, not so fortunate financially. Bingo. He's hit the jackpot. Especially if they have no living dependents. And that's something else that Eve and Lauren had in common.'

'It's perfectly logical,' Carmen said. 'But wouldn't it be too much of a risk? These ships are small places. Everyone knows everyone else's business. And if this really was what Gregoire was doing, would he attempt two in one cruise? Within a couple of nights of each other?'

'Maybe he was getting greedy. Murderers do – especially when they think they're getting away with it. Or maybe, more likely, Lauren realized what he was up to. If he made an unsubtle attempt to get *her* to leave him something, maybe, being close to him, she realized what had happened to Eve. It's a terrible cliché, but a second murder often has to do with someone finding out about the first one.'

'So what d'you want to do?' asked Carmen. 'Tell Alexei and the captain your suspicions? Go and give Gregoire the third degree?'

'Please, neither of those, not yet. I'm not saying that this is the answer to our puzzle, just that it might be. If it is, it's crucial that Gregoire has no inkling of any suspicion at all. Not even a look from the captain or a raised eyebrow from Alexei. Otherwise we could all be putting ourselves in danger. So let's keep schtoom for the time being, while we see if my theory has any legs.'

'How are you going to do that?'

'I guess it would be worth discreetly finding out about any deaths on previous cruises he's been on.' Francis pulled out his notebook. 'Before this Cape Town to Dakar leg, the *Golden Adventurer* did Ushuaia, Argentina, Cape Town via the Falklands, Tristan da Cuhna and St Helena. And before that a string of round trips from Ushuaia to the Antarctic peninsula and back again, including one special cruise over Christmas and the New Year. Before that, a stately progress down the west coast of South America from Colon, Panama, to Guayaquil, Ecuador; then on to Valparaiso, Chile, and finally round the Cape to Ushuaia. Did anyone pop their clogs on any of those trips?'

'Francis, mate! You're on a mission here.'

He shrugged. 'When we were looking at Eve's body in her cabin the captain said something which made me wonder. Something about, "We're not having much luck, are we?" And then: "So what happened with this one?" As if there had been others. Have there?'

'Not that I ever heard of,' Carmen replied. But watching her face closely, Francis wasn't entirely convinced. Were the expedition staff under instructions not to talk about any guest deaths? It was understandable if so, though frustrating, given that Carmen and he were supposed to be working together. His instinct was not to push it. Just yet.

'So, besides the Christmas one, which of those cruises might Gregoire have worked on?' he asked. 'How often do the staff have leave?'

'More than the crew. But less than us lazy expedition staff, who might just do one cruise – and then be off.'

'OK. If we could find a pattern, we'd be halfway there.'

'I guess so,' said Carmen. Then, after a few moments: 'I wonder . . .'

'What?'

'Blue-sky thinking, but . . . is there any way of discovering whether Gregoire has ever received money from a passenger's will?'

'If you have a name and a date you can check a will online,' Francis said. 'As long as the person is dead and the will is proved, the beneficiaries are listed. But you'd need a name. And an idea of where the will was registered. Then you'd generally have to wait a day or two to see it, so it's not something we could do right this minute.'

'OK,' said Carmen. 'It's kind of the wrong way round, isn't it? For our purposes.'

'Then again, if there was sufficient suspicion by the time we got to Dakar I suppose Gregoire's bank accounts could be accessed by the police. That is, if we can find a police force interested in following any of this up.'

'If Gregoire was really doing this sort of thing, do you imagine for one moment he'd be stashing the cash in his own account anyway? Surely he'd be hiding it somewhere.'

'True,' Francis agreed. 'Oh, well, perhaps I'm barking up completely the wrong tree.'

Carmen smiled. 'Perhaps you are. But it's an interesting idea. Maybe we can catch Gregoire out some other way.'

'Maybe,' Francis said, glancing at his watch. 'And now, if you'll excuse me, I think I ought to go and find Sadie and see what she was so eager to tell me. Shall we meet up on the bridge in half an hour? Keep the captain to his word?'

Francis hurried up to the Whirlpool Bar at the back of deck six. But if Sadie had been waiting for him earlier, she wasn't there now. He ran up the curving metal stairway to the back of deck seven, where assorted guests were still basting quietly in the powerful afternoon sunshine. No joy there either. He was just heading back through the bar area and into the cool interior when he heard a familiar voice.

'I *vas* looking for you,' said Klaus, approaching with a tall glass of some swanky pale beer. '*Vundering* where you'd got to. But perhaps they have hoisted you into the inside track.'

Francis smiled. 'By which you mean . . .?'

'*Vat* I say. The captain is employing your investigative powers to try and solve a double mystery before either a) something else bad happens or b) we dock at the next port and the *Golden Adventurer*'s guests are free to leave the ship. Because if Goldencruise does not stick to the itinerary as described, people will be asking questions. Even more questions than they are asking already.'

Francis smiled at the German doctor's amusing ability to get to the nub of things.

'What questions are they asking?'

'You would like me to be your sidekick? The *Vatson* to your

Holmes. The . . . what was that stupid one in the *Poirot* books called?

'Captain Hastings.'

'Very good. Yes, the Hastings to your Poirot?'

He really was absurd. 'No,' said Francis. 'I was just asking.'

'Of course you were. So, to answer your question, in a nutshell, naturally people are very concerned about the poor young, or maybe not quite so young, lady who went overboard. Everyone has their own theory, which is dependent on how little or how much they know. Some of them think she was thirty-something and unmarried, a penniless companion to an older man, with no influence over him other than her how-to-say sex appeal. Some think she was forty-something and married, altogether more of a problem. Some think she was older than that. Some even think that she was the one with the money.'

'And you?'

'I have my own ideas.' Klaus gave Francis a flat smile and took a hearty gulp of his beer. 'And then,' he added, 'you should also know that these guests are running more than a little scared. Some of them have wild thoughts about a murderer stalking the corridors. I even heard one lady advance the theory that a stowaway was responsible for pushing Lauren over. Though, as I said to her, I'm not quite sure what would be the advantage for a stowaway of killing passengers. Unless he wanted to take over their cabins. In which case, presumably, he would target the singles. Like me and you. But no, I expect we will find more than one trying to leave the cruise at the next port.'

'Passenger?'

'Yes.'

'Leaving at Freetown?'

'If we stop there.'

'We are stopping there. It's on the itinerary.'

'Let us wait and see.' Klaus raised an eyebrow. 'So. Will you join me for a refreshing beer?'

'I would love to, Klaus. But I promised to talk to Sadie.'

'Ah yes, Sadie. She was up here earlier. Drinking coffee. Not quite her usual lively persona, I have to say.'

TEN

B ut Francis never got to Sadie's cabin. As he turned into the central staircase and headed down towards the lower decks he met Carmen coming up.

'There you are!' She seemed breathless, excited. 'Come quickly, mate.'

On the blue-carpeted landing of deck five, she took his arm and pulled him towards the wall.

'Another Operation Rising Star,' she whispered, as a doddery couple proceeded slowly past them towards the Panorama Lounge. God help him, it was Henry and Daphne Forbes-Harley.

'Good after-*no-o-on*,' fluted Henry, with his usual beatific grin.

'You're not serious,' Francis muttered to Carmen. 'Who?'

'Come,' she said urgently.

But Henry had paused in his tracks. 'How are you, Tom?' he asked.

'Very well,' Francis replied, edging away. But Henry had moved closer, placing his hand on his arm.

'I always enjoy a day at sea,' he said. 'Lectures, quizzes, relaxing with a book . . .'

'Me too.'

'We'll see you at cocktail time, *Fran-ciss*,' said Daphne, pulling her husband off. She raised her eyebrows a flicker and gave Francis a flash of that ever-determined smile. 'We're just going to have some tea.'

'Three *tiers*,' said Henry, emphatically.

'I'm sorry?' said Francis.

'They have *three tiers* of cake. And sandwiches. Finger ones, my favourite. Imagine that. When I was a child I was lucky to get a blasted cookie.'

'Come on, Henry, dear.'

'We have it so good these days. Nobody understands.'

'Lovely to see you both,' said Daphne.

'Lovely,' Carmen agreed, taking Francis's arm and leading him firmly down the stairs to deck three. Next to the door to the medical centre was another marked *Staff Only*. Carmen pushed it open and ushered him through.

They were immediately in a different world. Talk about the green baize door. Instead of plush blue carpet on the floor there was worn grey lino. Instead of gold-framed pictures of Antarctic icebergs and colourful indigenous people in remote landscapes there was nothing but scuffed white plastic walls. Wires and pipes ran uncovered along the ceiling. As they were now below the waterline, there were no portholes and no natural light; the place was lit with bare bulbs. Also, at frequent intervals, there were watertight doors, with a lip six inches off the floor. The steps were steep, metal, without railings. They rattled down a couple more decks and along a corridor to find Viktor and Dr Lagip outside a much narrower door than Francis had ever seen upstairs. Leo was also there, but an anxious frown had replaced his usual broad smile.

'Thanks for coming down,' said Viktor. 'He's in there.'

'No longer . . . with us?' asked Francis.

'I'm afraid not,' said the doctor. 'I think he's been gone for a couple of hours.'

Francis turned slowly from Carmen to Viktor. Even as he asked the question he knew the answer. 'Who is it?'

'The lifeboat guy,' Carmen said.

'Whom we were going to talk to right away,' said Francis. 'Damn.' He banged the wall so hard with his fist that it hurt.

'We weren't to know,' said Carmen.

'He must have seen something he wasn't supposed to,' Francis said.

'I would agree,' said Viktor. 'Someone tried, but failed, to persuade him to keep quiet.'

'Until now,' said Francis. 'So what d'you think happened here?' he asked the doctor, nodding towards the cabin.

'Snakebite,' Dr Lagip replied. 'There's no doubt about it. But it's very odd, because where did the snake come from? And where is it now?'

'What kind of snake?'

'Hard to tell. Puff adder maybe. They're very common in this part of the world. I carry the antivenom in my medical kit when we go on excursions. But Leo here agrees, it's highly unlikely one could have got on to the ship on its own.'

'Let alone from the hostile environment of a port,' Leo said. 'There's nowhere for them to hide with all that concrete. And Africans kill snakes as soon as they see them.'

'Unless someone brought it on board deliberately,' Francis said.

'I agree,' said Leo. 'That's the most likely scenario.'

'So what are the symptoms?' Francis asked.

'Swelling of the ankle,' said Dr Lagip. 'Blistering on the leg. It's not a pretty sight. Go in and have a look for yourself, if you like.'

'And this is where you found him?'

'We didn't find him. His cabin mate did when he came off shift. But yes. He was on his bunk, as you'll see.'

Francis pushed open the door into the tiny cabin. There was no porthole down here, and two narrow bunks, with a gap of only a foot and a half between them and the opposite wall. A five-rung aluminium ladder led up to the top one. Both had curtains, which drew to the centre from the sides; they were pale blue, flimsy, didn't look as if they'd keep much light out. There were wooden-fronted storage drawers below each bunk and two square shelves in the corner at the far end. The lower of these had a TV on it, the upper a laptop, a pair of white Converse trainers and a row of bottles and sprays: shampoo, conditioner, antiperspirant, and then, in the corner, a half-empty bottle of Captain Morgan rum.

Francis took in all this with a glance, because his eye was drawn immediately down to the bottom bunk, where the dead man lay sprawled, his eyes wide open, his left leg swollen horribly, a deep and rancid purple-crimson, covered with dark brown blisters the size of potato crisps. The doctor, or someone, had sliced through his trouser leg, but otherwise he was still in his work clothes, a brown boiler suit with the initials GC picked out in yellow thread on the front pocket.

No, Francis thought, whatever this engineer knew about what had happened to Lauren wasn't going to be shared with anyone now. Double damn. Why hadn't he *insisted* on waking him up and interviewing him? Was it even possible that the captain had been deliberately obstructive?

So what had this poor fellow seen? If it had been the murderer actually doing the deed, why hadn't he told anyone in authority?

Because the murderer had spotted him and tried to silence him too? Or had he, more likely, been approached subsequently, once he'd revealed that he'd seen something by raising the alarm? If so, how had the murderer got to him? Below decks? Didn't that argue powerfully for a killer among the officers or crew?

If this guy *had* seen the murder taking place, and it was one of his superiors involved, it had been very brave of him to raise any kind of alarm in the first place. So had he wrestled with his conscience, finally compromising on telling the captain there was someone overboard so that the ship could turn and search, but glossing over exactly how that had come about? He would have known that even reporting a version of what he'd seen would put him in danger, in this closed environment from which there was no escape.

There was little doubt in Francis's mind that what he saw here was the result of a deliberate act. Even supposing a snake had made its way on board, this guy wouldn't have just sat here and died, he would have sought help. So either he'd been sedated before the snake had been let loose or the murderer had somehow restrained him. Which argued again for someone strong, probably male, as this fellow didn't look as if he'd easily be held down. And how long did it take for a snakebite to take effect? Surely it was hours, rather than minutes.

Francis knelt and had a good look at the horrid discoloured leg. He'd had no idea that this is what snakebite did to you. If he'd imagined the symptoms at all, he'd assumed a little local swelling maybe, the poison doing its work in the veins. But looking closely at this vile mess, it wasn't even clear where the fangs had gone in. There was a tiny tear in the skin in the soft flesh below the ankle bone, but as far as Francis could see on closer scrutiny, that was on its own. How, in any case, did you persuade a snake to bite someone? It sounded both an improbable and a dangerous method of killing. Where did you find one? How did you keep it or hide it? It was unlikely the creature came from Elmina, as the coach had parked right below the fort, well away from any bush or jungle. Which meant that if someone really had captured a snake and smuggled it on board they would have done it right at the start of this leg of the cruise, on the trip to the villages in Togo. Before Eve had even died.

Francis's eyes tracked slowly round the room, looking for anything that might give a clue as to what had happened. There was clothing hanging from hooks: two thin black waterproof jackets, two grey lifejackets, two baseball caps, one beige, one dark blue.

There was a map of the world tacked up on one wall, with a thin red line marking the progress of the *Golden Adventurer* through the Panama Canal, down the west coast of South America, around Antarctica (the repeated excursions marked by a x4), then across the South Atlantic via Tristan de Cunha to Cape Town, then on up this wild west coast of Africa: Namibia, Angola, the two Republics of Congo, Gabon, Equatorial Guinea, Cameroon, Nigeria, Ghana, back in a mini-loop to Togo and then on. Beside it was a calendar with days boldly crossed off. On the wall at the back of the top bunk there was a row of tacked-up postcards: Antigua, New York, Bermuda, Cape Town. Behind the bottom bunk were family snaps: a pretty, dark-haired woman who was presumably the victim's partner, in a couple of poses alone, in others with three small children. They ranged from toddler up to about eight or nine years old: two grinning girls and a serious-faced boy.

A narrow door at the end led into a tiny closet containing a shower, sink and toilet. There was barely room to stand in this upright tube; and if you took a shower, there was no way the toilet seat was going to stay dry. Halfway up was a chrome basket containing shower gel and shampoo. A shelf above the sink held toothbrushes and razors. There was a little circular mirror above that.

Francis stepped back into the cabin and looked slowly round again; then he knelt to pull open the wooden drawer below the bottom bunk. There was nothing surprising in here: clothes neatly folded, trousers, shirts, socks and, right at the bottom, a thin brown suit, presumably the gear that Daddy would wear when he finished his stint at sea, got off the ship and went home for a while.

A look in the drawer below the upper bunk revealed a similar picture, although there were two pairs of very clean blue jeans and a younger, more casual feel, perhaps, to the tops. Francis got the sense of a single man rather than a family one. Would talking to the cabin mate reveal anything? Well, he certainly wasn't going to miss his chance this time.

There was a light double knock on the door.

'Francis, mate.' It was Carmen calling. 'Are you done?'

'Hang on,' called Francis. 'Just a sec.' What *was* he looking for? Hanging from a hook, lying on a shelf, bluetacked to the wall, fallen on the floor? He scanned slowly round, taking in all the details. No, he decided, even as he nosed into the corners and pulled open the drawers again, there was really nothing here that was going to give him what even five minutes with the living man would have yielded.

Which begged the question: why had the captain been so insistent that the engineer get his beauty sleep?

'OK,' he said, as he pushed back outside to find Viktor, Carmen and the doctor in the corridor. Leo had gone. 'I've seen all I need to see. Pretty grim, isn't it?'

'It is,' said the doctor.

'I have two questions. Well, two and a half.'

'Go on.'

'One: surely if this man had been bitten by a snake, he would have called you long before he died?'

'Of course. Even the most rapid venoms take half an hour to act. He must either have been sedated, or tied up and gagged. But there's no evidence of restraint.'

'So you think sedation?'

'Must have been.'

'So how would a murderer get a snake to actually bite someone? Wouldn't that be an extremely dangerous procedure?'

'That I don't know the answer to. You could ask Leo, I guess. But yes, even if the victim was drugged, you'd be dealing with someone who's an expert in handling snakes. And your half question?'

'It wasn't obvious to me where the fangs had gone in.'

The doctor smiled, impressed, it seemed. 'I checked that,' she said. 'Tiny incisions. Hardly visible because of the swelling. But they're down by the ankle. You can tell because around them is the worst of the blistering.'

'I could only see one, more like a tear in the skin.'

'There are two. But the second has already sealed over.'

'Quick work,' said Francis.

'Yes, amazing, isn't it? Even though the body is in trauma, it's still trying to heal itself.'

Francis turned to Carmen and Viktor. 'So, are you going to be doing a cabin hunt then?'

'We were just discussing that,' said Carmen.

'Carmen thought, quite sensibly,' said Viktor, 'that the snake, having served its purpose, would probably be in the ocean by now.'

'Don't you think?' said Carmen.

'I suppose so,' said Francis. 'Unless our killer has other plans for it.'

It was a chilling thought: a poisonous reptile in the hands of a clearly determined and unscrupulous murderer. Francis would be checking his cabin very carefully tonight.

'Maybe we should search the cabins,' Viktor said.

'You'd have to announce it,' Carmen said, 'which would cause a panic. Any killer in his right mind would then dispose of the snake immediately. You're just not going to find it in someone's cabin.'

'What do you think, Doctor?' Viktor asked.

'My expertise is only medical. But yes, that sounds like a likely psychology to me.'

'Francis?'

'I suppose the only risk is that if you don't announce a search the murderer might keep the snake.'

'True,' said Viktor. 'But Carmen's right. An announcement would cause mayhem. People are going to be having heart attacks just worrying about it. I'll have to refer the decision to the captain.'

'I can tell you his answer now,' said Carmen.

'I realized while I was in there,' Francis said, ignoring this, 'that I don't even know the poor man's name.'

'George Bernard,' said Viktor.

'You're joking. Is that some kind of made-up name?'

'Not at all,' said Dr Lagip. 'Filipinos generally have English or Spanish given names.'

'George Bernard what? Not Shaw, I'm assuming.'

Neither Viktor nor Carmen got the reference. Dr Lagip tittered.

'Sure?' queried Viktor.

'It's the name of a famous British playwright,' said Francis. 'George Bernard Shaw.'

'Oh, OK,' said Viktor. 'No, his surname is Dimagiba.'

George Bernard Dimagiba. Fair enough. Francis was a long way from his cultural roots, he realized. 'What I'd like to do now,' he said, 'is to talk to the cabin mate, if that can be arranged. Presumably *he's* not asleep.'

'No,' Carmen agreed. 'Not yet, anyway.' She turned, deferentially, to her boss. 'Is that possible, Viktor?'

'Of course it is,' said Viktor, brusquely; he didn't even mention referring this to Alexei or the captain.

They met in the crew bar, which was even further down in the bowels of the ship, on deck one. The little room was as functional as the rest of the below-stairs area, though at least in here there was a ceiling, and the wires to the oblong overhead lights were not exposed.

The bar was closed, but there were indications that it could be a jolly enough place at the right time of day: a collage of postcards on the wall below the optics, a small blackboard offering happy hour cocktails and a big brass bell at one end. Mounted to one side was a large, flat TV screen.

There were metal benches built into each wall. Up against them were four small square tables topped with blue Formica. Black plastic chairs completed the seating. There was nothing as comfortable as a cushion.

George's cabin mate Ray was waiting on one of the benches. As Carmen and Francis came in, he got to his feet, and his lean features were instantly animated with that typical Filipino smile. He too was in the brown boiler suit with the GC logo. The three of them shook hands and introduced themselves.

'Thank you for talking to us,' Francis said, though he knew that Ray would have had little choice in the matter.

Ray nodded. 'That's OK, sir.' He yawned, covering his mouth with the back of his hand.

'Let's sit,' said Francis.

Ray made a move to offer Francis and Carmen the bench but Francis waved him down.

'No, no,' he said, taking a plastic chair. Then: 'This is a shocking state of affairs.'

'Yes, sir.'

'And I understand you were the one to find the body?'

'Yes, sir.'

'So, what happened?' Francis asked. 'You came off shift, returned to your cabin and there was your colleague, lying dead on the lower bunk?'

'Yes, sir.'

'Do you want to add anything to that description?'

Ray met his eyes. His nervousness was tangible. 'How do you mean, sir?' he asked.

'About exactly how you found your cabin mate . . . how you felt . . . if you don't mind.'

'My shift was finished, a bit early, in fact,' Ray said, speaking slowly, almost jerkily, 'so I went back to cabin for some rest. George had shift at four, so when I open door I am not surprised to see him. For one moment I think he is sleeping. But then I look again. And see his ankle, all big, swollen. I run to him. I pull off his shoe and sock. I see . . .' He made a face, expressive of total disgust; Francis didn't need to be reminded of the blistered mess he'd just seen. 'I think immediately – snake. And then I think maybe snake is still in cabin. So I look quickly to find. But our cabin is small and even under bed there is no snake. So now I go up to George and slap his face. Nothing. I slap his face again; his cheeks are flared red, but nothing in his eyes. He is dead like fish. So I take his wrist to check pulse. Nothing. So I phone to doctor.'

'You did all the right things.'

'Thank you, sir.'

'May I ask: what time exactly did your shift normally finish?'

'Four, sir.'

'And today?'

'Three, sir. I was out searching last night when I should have been sleeping. And all my work was anyway finished. So first officer let me go back to cabin early. I was – am – very tired, sir.'

'I imagine. This is First Officer Alexei Ninishivili?'

'Alexei, sir, yes. I do not know his other name.'

'Were you and George friends?' Francis continued, after a moment.

Ray shrugged. 'We like each other. Enough. As cabin mates. George was good guy. You know, sometimes you get cabin mate who is . . . problem. He comes in when you are sleeping and puts TV on. He makes big noise getting up. Maybe he brings back woman.'

'A woman? To that tiny little cabin?'

Ray grinned. 'It happens. Not on this ship, in fact. These guys are OK. Most of them. But yeah, it happens. And others, you know, they leave stuff everywhere. Clothes on your bed, shoes on your shelf, rubbish on floor. But George was not like that.'

'I see,' said Francis. 'Did he say anything to you about the incident last night? The woman overboard?'

'No.' The reply was very quick. Ray looked up, but his eyes didn't meet either of his interrogators, swerving sideways towards the bell at the end of the bar.

'He didn't speak to you about it at all?' Francis asked.

'I didn't see him, sir. Our shifts are not at same time.'

'But last night, you said you were part of the search. Surely you saw him then?'

'I saw him, sir, yes. But I didn't speak to him. We were all too busy looking over sea. And then when search was over I went straight back to cabin to sleep.'

'While George stayed out there?'

'Yes, sir. He finishes at eight, when I start.'

'So there was no crossover, no conversation while you were getting up and he was going to bed?'

'No, sir.' The guy was adamant. Either he was telling the truth, or he had a firm story which he was sticking to. 'We don't see each other. I was away from cabin before he gets in.'

'And you didn't see each other on the stairs? Or anywhere else?' Even as he spoke, Francis realized how little he knew about the operation of the ship. Was there a place other than this bar where the crew might meet: a canteen, a mess, an operations room?

'No, sir.'

Francis paused to let this repeated denial sink in; to let Ray imagine he had convinced them.

'I'm surprised you didn't go looking for him,' Francis went on, in as relaxed a fashion as he could. 'Given that he had such a story to tell. If I had been you, I'd have been dying to know the details of what he'd seen.'

'I only found out that it was George who raised alarm right at end of search, sir. We were just up there looking. Only at end, sir. So then I thought maybe tonight I would get to see him and talk about it. He had single shift, four till eight. I have no shift tonight. Bar is open for a couple of hours. Cabin is bit crowded with two. Maybe we could go for beer.'

Francis played along. 'I see,' he said. 'You were holding back your curiosity, knowing you would see him later.'

'Yes, sir,' said Ray.

'So did you two often go for beers together?'

'Sometimes. If we had break at same time. That is not very often, though, sir.'

Francis tapped his fingers on the blue Formica and looked over at Carmen. She gave him a slight, acknowledging smile; then she nodded, barely perceptibly, to indicate that she was happy with him leading the questions.

'George was a family man, wasn't he?' Francis asked. 'I saw the photos on the wall of your cabin.'

'Yes, sir. He had family. Wife and three children. Back in Philippines.'

'He talked about them?'

'Of course. He was very proud. Paying for them all to go to good schools. One day he was hoping to return and live with them.' Ray looked down at his feet for a moment, then back up again. 'But you understand. I have only been sharing cabin with him on this cruise. Since Cape Town. So we were not so close.'

'And you're a single guy?'

'Yes, sir.'

'With a partner at home?'

Ray was silent. His face revealed little. Perhaps, Francis thought, once again, he had pushed his questioning too far. Ray was under no obligation to talk about his private life. On the other hand, if he were prepared to answer, that might be interesting. In Francis's experience, the most unlikely parts of any particular scenario often turned out to be the most significant.

'I am promised in marriage, sir,' he said eventually.

'I see. Congratulations. When is the wedding?'

'Maybe next year. Maybe the year after. I am saving.'

Francis almost felt ashamed. This was a world he knew nothing about, where men worked year-round on the cramped lower decks to pay for another life back home. Would Ray stop working on the ships when he got married? Or would he, more likely, immediately return to cruising?

On the other hand, there had been no photos of a beloved fiancée in the cabin. Maybe Ray was a more private person, who didn't want a home gallery up on his wall like George Bernard. Or maybe he wasn't telling the truth. That pause before he'd answered the question about a partner had been long. Nor was Francis entirely convinced by Ray's other denials. But he didn't think he was going to admit anything right now. If George Bernard *had* spoken to him, and told him anything compromising, Ray had clearly decided to keep it to himself.

'Carmen,' Francis said, opening his fingers in her direction to offer her the chance to ask her own questions.

'That's fine,' she replied. 'I've nothing to add.'

'Thank you, Ray,' Francis said. 'That was good of you to talk to us. We must let you get back to your work.'

'Thank you, sir.'

The smile had returned. Flash. Was it something they hid behind, these guys? The impression of seamless happiness. Always obliging, always ready to please, with all the irritation that showed on the faces of Westerners buried altogether deeper? Or did they just not allow themselves to have such negative feelings?

As Ray left, Francis caught his eye. It wasn't saying the same as the smile. Francis raised his eyebrows and gave him a slight nod, as if to say, *If you need to talk to me privately, Ray, I am trustworthy. But for the moment, I will accept your story at face value.*

When Ray had turned the corner, Francis smiled at Carmen. 'So,' he asked, 'what did you think?'

'He seemed sincere enough.'

'I'm fairly sure he's hiding something.'

'Really? What?'

'I think he spoke to George. And the reason he doesn't want to tell us that is that George saw something. Something that compromises him.'

'Ray?'

'Yes.'

'Are you saying what I think you're saying?'

'That George saw someone push Lauren over? Maybe. And that that someone was not a passenger, but a person higher up in the crew? Maybe that too.'

Carmen nodded slowly. 'Wow! That's quite an accusation, mate.'

'It's just an instinct. Ray didn't ever really meet my eye. Or yours either, for that matter.'

'I wouldn't read too much into that. It's another culture. You are a total stranger asking very probing questions. This isn't the UK. Or even America or Australia.'

'I appreciate that. I still think he wasn't telling us all he knew.'

'So why "crew"?' Carmen asked. 'Is this Gregoire again?'

'Maybe.'

Carmen smiled. 'You're fixated on the poor man. Bear in mind, if George really did see someone, it might well have been a passenger. Guys like Ray and George would be just as scared of them. You try and implicate a passenger in some crime and there's no knowing what might be unleashed on you. Your employers, the police, attorneys, the terrifying power of the West. A little guy like Ray wouldn't want to risk anything like that.'

'I see that,' said Francis. 'Though how would a passenger get below decks to bump off George?'

'Good point.' Carmen sat quietly for a few moments, clearly thinking things through. 'I suppose it wouldn't be impossible. Or to somehow get to George while he was out of the crew area.'

'With a *snake*?' said Francis. 'If we were playing hard ball,' he went on, 'we could ask the captain to summon Ray to his office and threaten him with his job. That might work.'

'Or it might not,' said Carmen. 'These guys are tough. And below decks it's *omertà*. Silence in the ranks.'

'Yes,' said Francis. And now, he explained, he urgently needed to go and find Sadie. He was worried about her; the way she'd been when she swooped in on them in the restaurant. There had been an unsettling intensity, Carmen agreed. But no, she wasn't expecting to accompany Francis. She would have a little quiet time, digest what they'd learned.

'I guess drinks and dinner will be as usual,' Francis said, 'since the captain is so keen to keep everything on an even keel.' He smiled. 'As it were. So we can talk again then.'

'There's a party this evening,' Carmen said. 'The Neptune Society. For first-time cruisers. I don't think they've cancelled it.' She looked at her watch. 'Six. God, just over an hour. I'll see you there, if not before.'

ELEVEN

'Wait a moment,' came the voice from the other side of the door. There was the click of the electronic lock and then there was Sadie, in one of the white waffle-pattern robes provided free to guests. Her hair was down. Her feet were bare, apart from some deep maroon nail polish on each toe. It didn't look as if she were wearing much underneath the robe.

'Come in,' she said; her smile curved up, distinctly flirtatious.

'Your aunt not here?' Francis asked.

'Got rid of her. By moaning about my boyfriend in Cape Town. Works a treat every time. She's gone off upstairs to play deck quoits or bridge or something. Maybe chat to one of the cranky old bores she's made friends with. Jesus. They're all of a type, aren't they? Republicans with hearing aids who love to boast about what great lives they've got back home, what a great cabin they've got, what a great discount they managed to negotiate, how many million nights they've already spent on these ships. To be honest, it makes me ashamed to call myself American. The only thing approaching a Democrat on this floating hellhole are the two gay guys.'

'From Montana.'

'Is that where they're from?'

'A state which has recently made gay marriage legal.'

'Whoopeedoo. Lucky them. So can I get you anything? I've got champagne, if you'd like a glass.'

'I'm fine.'

'That butler woman, what's her name . . .'

'Mine's called Hentie.'

'Hentie, that's the one, we share a butler, hey, that's a good sign, came in and said to me, "Ma-*dame*, I see you have not opened your welcome champagne yet. Are you OK with that vintage?" "No, I am not freaking OK with this vintage," I screamed. "How dare you? Get me something ten years older at least."' Sadie laughed, tipsily. 'No, I didn't. I decided to open it. She brought me a lovely bucket full of ice. And now I've drunk half the bottle on my own. Are you sure I can't get you a little glass?'

'OK then, just a little one.'

'There's my boy.' Sadie went over to the ice bucket, pulled out the bottle, filled a flute for Francis and topped up her own. 'D'you mind if I get back into bed? You can sit on the end here if you like.'

'It's OK,' said Francis. 'I'll pull up a chair.'

'You can't pull them up, you freak. They're stuck to the floor. Didn't you realize that? Although they try and give the impression this is an uber comfortable drawing room, it's actually a cabin. In a ship. That's way out on the ocean. Which could be invaded by pirates. Or hit a rock and sink, if our rugged Ukranian captain makes a tiny misjudgement sometime.'

'How do you know he's Ukranian?'

'Klaus told us, remember. Anyway, I chatted to him at the Captain's Drinks Party. He was surprisingly friendly for such a heavy-looking guy.' Sadie looked hard at him over the rim of her glass. 'So how's it all going, Francis? What's going on with our Australian friend?'

'She's helping me,' he said.

'With your investigations?' Sadie teased.

'Yes.'

'It may not be obvious to the rest of the passengers what you're up to – but it is to me.'

What did she mean? That she thought he fancied Carmen? The horrid truth was that if he were attracted to anyone on this ship, it was to her, Sadie. Didn't she see that? Perhaps she did, because even as she tried to get at him about Carmen, she was doing her best to play the part of seductress, with her long legs spread out over the counterpane, the thin white robe open loosely at her neck. The folds of the waffle-pattern cloth failed to conceal the creamy swell of her breasts below that. One simple move would render her completely naked in front of him, and they were both aware of that.

He decided to call her bluff. 'So what exactly *am* I up to?' he asked.

She looked at him measuredly. 'Two people have now died on this ship, Francis. For all you told me the other evening about poor Eve I'm not convinced that either was a natural death. We are still in the middle of a cruise, for which a lot of stuffed shirts and their hideous tinselly wives have paid a shitload of dough. So the captain and cruise director are not going to piss off their bosses back in Monaco or London or wherever they hang out, they are going to do their utmost to keep the show on the road. They are not heading at speed to the nearest port, and I don't think they intend to invite the police of Sierra Leone to step on board and solve the mystery. In the meantime, they are pretty keen to work out whether this is just a case of an old lady dying of old age and a drunk falling off the edge of the ship or something more sinister. Like, Francis, a double murder. With all that that entails. So, knowing your pedigree as a writer and solver of mysteries, they have hired you as an ad hoc private investigator. And given Carmen the job of being your sidekick-stroke-minder.'

Francis found himself laughing. 'Not bad,' he said. He had completely misunderstood her about Carmen.

Sadie swung her legs round on to the floor and walked, a little unsteadily, across to the ice bucket. 'More champagne? Go on, it's a very good year.' She scrutinized the label. 'Lanson 1994. What were you doing in 1994, Francis? I was a little girl, with bows in my hair, running around Brooklyn Heights.'

He accepted a top up. He certainly hadn't been a little girl, or boy, in 1994. He had been just out of college, living in a damp basement in Kennington, working behind a bar in Covent Garden every evening while his new wife trained as a lawyer; those all-too-short years before Kate had died had been the happiest of his life.

'Not very good at resisting temptation, are you?' Sadie teased, as she sat down on the bed again. 'Although you did quite well the other evening, I thought. Given that we're on a ship miles from anywhere and you have no attachments at home. Or so you tell me.'

Francis didn't want to upset her, but he thought it was probably the right moment to call time on this interview. He took a fizzy gulp of his champagne and got to his feet.

'I'd better go. I'm sorry, Sadie. I thought from your tone upstairs that you had something important to tell me.'

'Don't rush off. Maybe I do have something important to tell you.'

'Don't mess around, Sadie. If you've got information I need to know, let's have it.' Francis was tempted to tell her about George Bernard Dimagiba, but then again, could he trust her?

'Sit down for a minute,' she said. 'Here, beside me. I'm not going to pounce on you.' She took a breath and composed herself. 'I don't know whether this is of interest, but what I've been wanting to tell you while you've been avoiding me . . .'

'I haven't been avoiding you.'

'Was that I saw that woman that went overboard.'

'Lauren?'

'Yes, her, in a clinch the other evening.'

'In a clinch?'

'Snogging. In a doorway. Up on deck seven.'

'With?' he asked, though he already knew the answer.

'That French hotel director guy, what's his name . . .?'

'Gregoire.'

'Yeah. I'm not sure they realized I'd seen them, because I was over the other side of the deck, but . . .'

'When exactly was this?'

'A couple of evenings ago. The night before we went to see those slave forts. Sunday, I guess.'

'And it was definitely Gregoire?'

'Oh yeah. There's no one else on the ship with hair like that. Unless she'd found a blond stowaway in her wardrobe.' She laughed. 'No, it was Gregoire all right.'

'And she didn't see you?'

'No. She was far too busy with him. Whether they were actually doing more than snogging I don't know. They were very close. I didn't stick around for long. Just glanced over, saw them wriggling up against each other, and kept going.'

'And that's all you've got to tell me?'

'Hey, that's significant, isn't it? Maybe he had something to do with her going overboard.'

Francis shrugged.

'You know something?' she asked.

'There are a number of things we're looking at,' he replied. 'But what you've told me is very interesting. Thank you.'

'Oh, Francis. You've become so dry and distant. You weren't like this last night.'

'A lot's happened since last night.'

She fixed him with a considered, quizzical look.

'Have you and . . . whats-er-name . . . actually . . . got it together?'

'Don't be ridiculous. We're working together. The captain has asked me to look into things, and since Carmen is on the expedition team, and knows how the ship works, she's helping me.'

'Uh-huh.' Sadie didn't sound convinced. She got to her feet, walked over to the ice bucket and plucked out the glistening green bottle. Droplets fell from it as she teetered back to where he sat on the bed.

'One for the road?' she asked, filling Francis's glass before he could stop her. She topped up hers, put the bottle on the bedside table, then sat down next to him.

'So nothing's going on?' she said. 'With her?'

'No.'

'And you don't want anything to go on?'

'No.'

'I'm a little puzzled by you, Francis. Here you are, this attractive guy, who knows he's attractive, with women making it fairly plain to you that they're interested, and you do nothing about it. Are you in fact gay?'

'No.'

'Maybe that's what you like. Just swanning around, soaking up the admiration. But it seems a waste to me, when you could be having a good time.' Her hand came over and rested on his upper thigh. 'A seriously good time,' she added.

When he didn't move away, she started, very slowly, to stroke the bare skin of his legs with her fingers. He could feel his hairs bristle. Inside his shorts, he was aware, damn it, of an all-too visible bulge.

Sadie's hand moved up. 'You see, Francis. You're not such a dry old stick as you like to pretend.'

It was time to go, very definitely time to go. But still he sat there, mesmerized, as, very gently, with two fingers, she stroked him through the thin fabric of his shorts. She knew exactly what she was doing, as she watched him, intently, her lovely dark eyes fixed on his, weakening his best instincts. Then, slowly, theatrically, she ran the tip of her tongue around her lips. Her little seduction act was corny, ridiculous, but it was working; he was breathing heavily, succumbing fast. Now she cupped him with her fingers.

'I don't think that wants to stay in there much longer,' she said,

as her thumb and forefinger reached for the brass oblong catch of
his zip.

He breathed in sharply and got to his feet. 'No,' he said, abruptly.
'I'm sorry. It's not the right time. There's one hell of a lot going
on, Sadie. I need to get on with it. In any case, this isn't wise.'

She let out a bark of laughter. '*Wise!* My God, Francis, you've
got one heck of a lot of self-control. There's not many men who
would walk away from a girl as horny as I am right now.'

She had let her robe fall open, so her flushed nakedness was all
too visible.

He laughed in return. 'I'm sure there aren't. You must forgive
me, Sadie. Maybe we can have a drink or something later. Dinner.'

She was watching him in quiet amazement. 'Are all you English
guys like this? You know what, Francis. I'd love a drink later. Or
dinner. If you can fit me in to your busy schedule. Maybe I can
suck you off under the table while you savour your freakin' black-
currant sorbet.'

He turned and headed for the cabin door. If he didn't go now,
that would be it.

'Don't I get a little thank you for my useful info?' she called.

'Thank you,' he said. But unlike Lot's wife, he didn't turn.

'Remember. We're all in the same boat. Ha ha! Ship. We're not
go-o-o-ing anywhere.'

His hand was on the gleaming brass handle – and he was out of
there.

TWELVE

Francis had found the smart little printed card for the Neptune Society on his bed when he'd returned the previous evening, sunburned and windswept, from his day at Elmina Fort. *The Neptune Society requests the pleasure, etc.* Klaus had joked about it, told Francis the whole event was just a marketing exercise, part of the discreet pyramid of privilege that the cruise line liked to create for its guests. 'The next night it's the Ulysses Society, for those who've cruised before. Makes us feel that little bit special, you see. Clever, eh?' The invite even had an RSVP, to be made to Reception; as if, stuck on board with nothing to do after a long day at sea, you were going to turn down such a get-together. Perhaps people did. Perhaps there were reclusive cruisers. Or those who just wanted to be alone together in their cabin, didn't want to make the acquaintance of all the other ghastly first-timers, not to mention the attendant officers and crew.

All the key figures had turned out for the occasion. Bearlike First Officer Alexei was with a trio of other, more junior officers in full kit. Gregoire was here, as gorgeous as ever in four-stripe epaulettes and crisp white shirt. The expedition staff, meanwhile, were out of their khaki uniforms and into colourful African shirts and long trousers. Carmen looked positively feminine tonight, in a dark blue satin evening dress with a low neckline.

Around them swirled the first-timers. There were faces Francis recognized and others who were – amazingly – completely new to him. Where on earth had they all been hiding? Big Shirley and her goateed husband were there, bonding noisily with one of the younger officers. You had to hand it to her; if she really was dying of cancer this was surely the way to go, laughing and drinking margaritas on a warm evening somewhere off Liberia.

Despite the shock of last night, everyone seemed to be making a stalwart effort to have a good time. Nonetheless, they couldn't help themselves from talking about poor Lauren, their own personal experience taking centre stage, already being worked up into the anecdotes that would doubtless continue when they left the ship at Dakar and returned home. 'When I first woke I wasn't sure *whad* was going on' . . . 'I thought maybe something was *wrung* with the ship' . . . 'No idea about a *person* overboard' . . . 'I'm still so *sharked*' . . .

'How did it go with Sadie?' Carmen asked, pulling Francis to one side.

'OK. She was a bit tipsy actually.'

Carmen laughed. 'I hope she didn't make a pass at you, mate.'

'God, no!' His face revealed nothing, even as he thought: this is how it would begin. Within hours of anything having happened, people would know. Osmotically, right across the ship. For the sake of twenty minutes of sweet abandon, he would be linked to her. His cabin would no longer be a haven, where he could retreat and be himself. She would have right of access. Before he knew it, he would be in a *relationship*. God help him. He was heartily glad he'd made his exit.

'So what did she want to tell you?'

Francis looked round, then leant towards her. 'In confidence, she'd seen Gregoire snogging Lauren. The night before we docked in Takoradi.'

'Hey! That's a bit of info, isn't it? Did you believe her?'

'No reason not to.'

'If that's true,' said Carmen slowly, 'that is really something. Maybe we should risk talking to Gregoire again. Even if it's going to put him on his guard.'

'Not here, I don't think.' Francis looked over towards the handsome hotel director, now holding court at the centre of a circle of attentive ladies.

'Definitely not here.'

She tailed off into silence, because there was a hush in the group chatter. Francis looked over towards the door. The captain had arrived, in full uniform, his navy-blue sleeves ringed with four bands of gold, one thicker than the others. He nodded at the company and accepted a drink from one of the white-jacketed waiters. Then he moved slowly on through the crowd, an awkward smile on his face.

'Excuse me,' said Carmen. 'I'd better rescue him. It's the Neptune Society, so he's got none of his old favourites here.'

Francis turned to find Viktor in front of him; the German nodded and moved them a little way out from the throng.

'How's it going?' he asked. 'Carmen tells me you didn't get anything much out of Ray.'

'No,' Francis replied. He hadn't realized that Carmen was planning to relay this – or any – information to Viktor. Was this sharing wise? Had it gone higher? Not that Francis thought that Viktor, Alexei or the captain were in any way *involved*. But who knew who they might confide in as they tried to work out what to do next? The hotel director? Maybe they would. And then, if it were true that Gregoire had something to do with all this, he would surely: a) cover his tracks, b) make sure any compromising info was kept well away from Francis and Carmen. Christ, might they themselves be in danger?

It was not a certainty that Eve had been murdered. Nor that Lauren hadn't thrown herself off the ship. But George Bernard Dimagiba hadn't stepped on a snake accidentally and then sat there stoically till he died. And his cabin mate was very scared of *something*.

'So what do you think?' Viktor was asking, leaning forward, speaking in a voice that was barely audible against the surrounding chatter. 'That Ray knows nothing?'

Maybe Carmen hadn't told Viktor that much after all. Francis would err on the side of caution.

'I don't know,' he replied. 'Ray's line was that he'd been working too hard to talk to George.'

'That could be true. They do work incredibly long hours, these guys. Even harder than me, sometimes.'

'Surely not,' Francis teased. 'So, next stop, Freetown,' he continued, moving the subject briskly along before Viktor could quiz him any more. 'Aren't you worried that our murderer might try and abscond?'

Viktor took the bait. 'We can hardly change the itinerary,' he replied, 'just for that chance. In any case, the ship is too large to dock at Freetown, so we anchor offshore and make all the transfers by Zodiac. Then there's no danger of any random crew member getting off. And I doubt that any killer from the passenger list would want to reveal himself by leaving us. Unless he really thought his game was up.'

'I hope we're not interrupting.' Hearing a woman's voice, Francis looked round to see Bruce and Candy, the Chicago couple. Candy was dressed as if she were just off to a sixties high school prom, in a blue and white sailor-suit dress, her thin blonde hair swept back under a matching blue hairband. Seventy going on sixteen. Bruce was wearing a sports jacket so loud it looked as if it might start singing all by itself.

'Not at all,' said Viktor, switching on his expedition leader smile. 'You two enjoying the party?'

'We are. Very much. The Neptune Society.' Candy tittered. 'All us raw first-timers. But *you've* been on a cruise before,' she added to Viktor. How stupid was she?

'Of course. The crew and staff who are with you here tonight have mostly been doing this for a while.'

'And you, Francis?' asked Candy.

'No, I'm a bona fide member of the Neptune Society.'

'Boner Friday?' queried Candy, turning to her husband.

'*Genuine*,' Francis clarified. 'I'm a genuine member of the society. Never having done anything like this before.'

'It's Latin,' Viktor explained. 'Just the sort of high-end language we expect from our resident lecturers.' He laughed and Candy joined in, albeit with a puzzled look on her face. Did she even know what Latin was? Francis wondered. Not something to do with those ever-encroaching Latinos, surely?

'You enjoying it, Francis?' asked Bruce.

'I am, very much.' Francis turned in Viktor's direction. 'Although I've been lucky, I think, to start with a ship like this.'

'You have, young man,' Bruce said. 'We think this is the best cruise line we've tried, and we've tried quite a few. The mix of high-end luxury and real adventure is what we like.'

Viktor was beaming. 'That's what we aim to provide.'

'I mean that trip to see those pygmies in Cameroon,' said Candy. 'As I said to Bruce—'

'Many times . . .' Bruce interjected.

Candy rolled her eyes in protest, but still barely paused in her flow: 'How else are you going to gain an experience like that? Pygmies. Right out in the jungle.' She turned to Francis. 'We'll have to show you our photos. If you were travelling independently you'd have had to be here for weeks to see that. Making the contacts—'

'Gaining the trust,' Bruce chipped in. 'That's what I think you're shortcutting for us here, Viktor. Remote people like that don't open up to just anybody. But someone on the team's done the legwork, meaning that a bunch of old has-beens like us—'

'Not has-beens, honey. Retired folk.'

'Retired . . . beans, then.' Bruce chuckled throatily at his own non-joke. 'I think maybe that's what we should all be called. Retired . . . beans, ha ha ha! But anyways, my point is, how else are we going to get in to see stuff like that? We're not. It's remarkable. I have to say, I think what you're doing here is *remarkable*, Viktor.'

'Thank you,' said Viktor.

Candy had clearly heard this speech before. She had already moved on, was fixing the expedition leader with a serious look.

'So tell me, Viktor,' she asked. 'You got any more gen on this young lady that went overboard? Was she just drunk, like everyone's saying?'

Viktor's hands were folded together in front of him in a gesture of prayer. 'You were at the briefing this morning?'

'We were. And Bruce was up on deck last night as well. Doing his bit.'

'There's really nothing to add at this moment,' Viktor said. 'As far as we can see, the whole thing was just a tragic accident. She had, as you said, drunk a deal too much.'

'But I had another look at those railings up on deck seven,' Bruce said. 'After the briefing. It's all pretty well secured. I don't see how you'd just fall over.'

'Bruce was a police officer,' said Candy. 'For thirty years.'

'Is that so?' said Viktor.

'With the Chicago force,' Candy continued. 'He rose to the level of commander.'

'Can you level with us,' said Bruce, ignoring this. 'In confidence. D'you think there's anything more sinister going on here?'

'What are you saying?'

'Suicide?' He paused. 'Homicide?'

Viktor was shaking his head. 'I understand your concerns. And obviously, with your experience. But,' he chuckled, manfully, 'with all due respect, this isn't Chicago. I don't think either of those outcomes is particularly likely.'

'Particularly likely?' Bruce repeated the words a little scornfully. 'But possible. Do you think it's at all *possible*? That's the question you should be asking yourselves.'

'The other question a number of us have been asking,' said Candy, 'is why you didn't search the sea for longer this morning? It was barely light when we turned round and steamed on. There were no planes or helicopters. No air-sea rescue.'

'The decision of how long we search for is entirely the captain's,' said Viktor. 'You would have to take that up with him.' He turned from wife to husband. 'But I'm sure you understand, Bruce. This isn't the coast of Florida. This is Africa. We were off Cote d'Ivoire last night. One of the remotest, poorest places in the world. There is no air-sea rescue to summon.'

Bruce had turned a perceptibly darker shade of red. He looked like a lobster in the pan with the heat turned up. A muscle twitched in his cheek. He was doing his level best, Francis saw, to stay polite and in control.

'Of course I understand, Viktor, that this isn't Florida. We wouldn't have come here if it was. We signed up for an adventure – and it looks like we might have got one. I also understand that you don't want to stop the cruise, that you want us all, if possible, to go on having a good time. Goldencruise don't want to be refunding a hundred plus passengers twenty thousand bucks each, of course they don't. But there's an atmosphere on this ship now. People have imaginations. Some of them are wondering whether this lady fell over the edge all by herself – or whether, to be frank, she had some help. And I'd be a liar if I didn't tell you, I'm one of them.'

'I'll be honest with you, Bruce,' Viktor replied. 'Anything is possible here. But we've spoken to this woman's partner and looked into all the circumstances, and a terrible accident really does seem like the most likely option.'

Francis was glad that the expedition leader hadn't brought him into the discussion, though obviously revealing to this ex-cop that he had been asked to act as a quasi-detective in a case of three mysterious deaths would not have been helpful. Fortunately, at that moment, there was a distraction, as the party's decibel level dropped to acknowledge a glamorous young arrival.

Sadie was in a low-cut, backless black velvet dress with slits up the thighs, which were themselves jacked up alluringly on a pair of four-inch black diamante heels. It was amazing, Francis thought, that she was upright at all, let alone striding so confidently across the room. Next to her, her aunt, in a long shirt of orange, blue and black stripes over black trousers, looked positively dowdy, even with her sparkling diamond earrings. Sadie accepted a flute of champagne from one of the waiters and made straight for the captain.

Viktor had taken advantage of this diversion by excusing himself, slipping away through the crowd to do his bit with another group of first-timers. With the object of his indignation removed, the puff seemed to have gone out of Bruce. He shook his head, more mystified it seemed than angry.

'I don't have anything against him personally,' he told Francis. 'But they haven't handled it well. Just for appearances, I would have stuck around searching till well after dawn.'

'It was pretty hopeless, though, don't you think? They weren't going to find her.'

'You know, Francis, it doesn't cost them anything – much – to circle in the sea for a few hours. And then they can throw up their hands and say, "Job done". As for his point about air-sea rescue . . . like anything else that's a question of money. I don't believe there isn't a helicopter somewhere in West Africa. Some of those dictators have at least one, don't they?'

He had regained his humour. But Francis was relieved when another couple joined them.

'These martinis don't miss, do they?' said the male, who was decked out in a colourful Mandela shirt. His accent was sing-song, old-fashioned Aussie, coming from a sun-beaten face whose etched wrinkles spoke of years of politically incorrect laughter. His tiny wife looked similarly baked by the elements; a gleaming grin sat perkily in the face of a cheerful lizard. Her frock was an almost fluorescent orange, with a big frill of orange feathers along the hemline.

'I haven't tried one yet,' Bruce replied.

'Ah, mate, you should. Put you in a much better mood. I need to be, what with all these people falling off the blinking boat.'

'We were just talking about that,' said Bruce. 'Now whadda you think? They could have stopped a little longer to search for her?'

'Yeah. I was just saying that earlier to Noelene here. They could at least have hung around till the sun came up. Quite apart from anything else, it's not very reassuring for the rest of us old battlers.'

Looking up, Francis saw that Viktor was gesturing to him. Discreetly, with the fingers of one hand. He was standing next to the captain, who had now moved away from Sadie. Francis made an excuse to the American/Aussie foursome and crossed the room.

The captain stepped out of earshot of the crowd and Viktor followed.

'Viktor tells me that cabin mate of dead engineer told you he hadn't spoken to George about MOB incident,' the captain said.

'Yes,' Francis replied, cursing Carmen's indiscretion.

'And you didn't believe him.'

Well, if she wanted to share everything with the bosses before she and he had even digested it together, he might as well join in. 'I don't want to get him into trouble,' he said, 'but no, I'm not sure. I got the feeling that maybe George Bernard might have said—'

'We will have to get him to explain himself,' the captain interrupted. 'Can you and Carmen join me on the bridge in' – he glanced at his watch – 'fifteen minutes?'

'Of course.'

'You too, please, Viktor. I will get Alexei to summon him now.'

He turned and headed towards the doors to the lobby. As if remembering at the last minute his obligations as the trustworthy figurehead of the ship, he turned, smiled a fixed oblong smile, and bowed his head a fraction as the hubbub hushed.

'Thank you all very much for coming to Neptune party,' he said. 'We greatly value our first-time guests. I hope you have pleasant evening. And when you cruise again, remember what good time you had with *Golden Adventurer*.'

There was a ripple of laughter at this, though the captain had not, Francis thought, been joking; this was a sincere nugget of pre-rehearsed marketing, to be repeated, presumably, up until the point of a full-on norovirus outbreak or pirate attack.

He was gone.

'What's he going to do to him?' Francis asked.

'Ray?' Viktor replied. 'Waterboard him probably. No, I expect just being in the captain's presence will be enough. Ray knows that the captain has the power to put him off at the next port if he's not happy. And make sure he never works for Goldencruise again.'

Carmen had joined them. 'Are we going to an interrogation?'

'I think we are,' said Francis. He didn't meet her eye, unhappy as he was that she'd passed on his speculations without consulting him. Then, glancing involuntarily over towards Sadie, he saw she was looking at them. Her gaze stayed on him for a moment, then, without meeting his eye, flicked away, as she returned to an enthusiastic talk with Leo. Her gloved hand was resting on his arm.

THIRTEEN

The poor man looked terrified, like the proverbial rabbit caught in the headlights. The captain had put him alone at one end of the L-shaped padded crimson bench that ran along two walls of his little office. He himself was on a big swivel chair, his back to his desk. Viktor, Carmen, Francis and Dr Lagip were squashed up on the other arm of the L. First Officer Alexei, oddly, was not present.

Ray had repeated how he'd found the body of his colleague when he'd come off shift and was expecting to be alone in their shared cabin. Dr Lagip confirmed that Ray had called her immediately on the ship's phone and she had found him sitting there, holding George's hand, clearly in shock.

'Did you know he was dead?' asked the captain.

'I thought he was, yes, sir.'

'So why hold his hand?'

'Don't know, sir. I thought, maybe, I was wrong, sir. His hand was warm. It was like he was still alive.'

'You two were friends, yes?'

'Yes, sir.'

'Not more than that?'

Ray's eyes flickered as he took the captain's meaning. 'No, sir. He was married man. And I – no, sir. I am promised in marriage.'

The captain looked over at Francis and raised his thick black eyebrows. 'These things happen on board ship. Even with married men.' He turned back to Ray. 'So you were part of search, the night before?'

'Yes, sir.'

'And you knew George was one who'd seen this woman go over?'

'Yes, sir. We all knew that, sir. Not straight away, but soon after.'

'And yet, you tell us, that during course of search, and in hours afterwards, you didn't speak to him about what had happened?'

'No, sir.'

'We stopped to search for three hours. Both you and George were up on deck seven.'

'Yes, sir. But George was at other end of ship, sir. He was bow, I was stern. You can ask first officer.'

'I will do,' the captain said. 'And then what happened? When search was stopped?'

'I went back to cabin to sleep, sir. George stayed on shift. He was on midnight to eight hundred hours. I was on eight to sixteen hundred hours, sir.'

'Which means you would have crossed over at eight hundred hours?'

'No, sir. I was already gone before George returned to cabin. It is always like that in morning, sir.'

The captain's expression was one of disbelief. 'That may well have been normal arrangement. I understand that. But. You ask us to believe that on morning when your friend had seen passenger going overboard, you did not stay for few minutes to find out what he saw?'

'I cannot be late for first officer shift, sir. You know him, sir. First officer is angry if we are late.'

'This is true.' The captain turned to the others. 'Alexei is no softie. I think you'd agree, Viktor.'

'Yes, Captain. Alexei is no softie.'

'And this morning,' Ray continued, 'when whole ship is in panic, I must be early for shift, I think. So even though I am eager to speak to George about what happened, I do not speak to him. I go to shift. And then work till fifteen hundred hours, when first officer lets me go off. I return to cabin an hour early, hoping, yes, to speak to him before he goes on shift. And that is when I find him, sir, on bunk. I think at first he has passed out, but then I notice swollen leg—'

'Yes, yes,' said the captain, impatiently. 'You've told us that.' He looked hard at Ray. 'You realize that if this turns out not to be true you will be automatically fired.'

'Yes, sir.'

'You will leave at next port.'

'Yes, sir.'

'Freetown.'

'Yes, sir.'

'Without wages.'

Was that legal? Francis wondered. Ray didn't question it.

'Yes, sir.'

'You will never be hired by *Golden Adventurer* company again.'

'Yes, sir.'

'And if I have anything to do with it, you will never be hired by any other cruise line again. For any job.'

'Yes, sir.'

'Back to Manila.'

'Yes, sir.'

'For good.'

'Yes, sir.'

'No more money for family.'

'No, sir.'

'So that's it then. You are telling us all that George said nothing to you about what he'd seen?'

Ray was looking down at the floor. Now he looked up and round the little group, entreaty in his eyes. Francis did his best to look as sympathetic as possible. 'Please, sir,' Ray replied. 'I told you. I didn't speak to him. Of course I wanted to know. We all did. But then I think: today I finish at sixteen hundred hours. So either I speak to George then, or later, because he comes off shift at twenty hundred and this evening I have not shift. So maybe we can go to bar for an hour and I can hear story then.'

'OK,' said the captain. 'So what did you hear from others? While you were all up there looking out for MOB?'

'That it was woman, sir. Who had fallen from top deck.'

'And that George had seen her?'

'Yes, sir.'

'And that was all?' said the captain. 'Nothing about who woman was, or what exactly George had seen?'

'Yes, sir. I mean no, sir. Nothing. Except . . .'

'Except?'

There was a pause.

'Except what?' the captain repeated.

'Some people say she drink too much, sir.'

'Who said that?'

'Some of the bar staff.'

'Who?'

'It doesn't matter, sir.'

'I'm asking you: who?'

There was another long pause, during which Ray was visibly struggling with mixed loyalties.

'Alfredo,' he replied, eventually.

'Our pianist?'

'Yes, sir.'

'Not bar staff.'

'No, sir.'

'What exactly did he say?'

'He said that on two nights she was crashing around dance floor, sir. Like elephant. With husband. And also—'

'And also?' asked the captain, his eyes like a predator who has his claws on the throat of his prey.

'And also . . . with others . . . sometimes.'

'Did he mention any particular others?'

'You better ask him that, sir.'

'Or I can save time and ask you. Which others did he mention?'

'Another passenger maybe,' said Ray, feebly.

'And someone else? A member of staff? Tell us, please, Ray.'

'I did not say this, sir.'

'Just give us name, please, Ray.'

'Mr Gregoire, sir.'

'What were they saying?'

'That he had been dancing with her, sir.'

'Nothing more?'

'No, sir.'

'Not that he was seen later, in dark corner of upper deck, kissing her?'

Ray looked genuinely shocked. He was either an extremely good actor, or this was a surprise. It was to Francis too. He hadn't realized that Carmen had relayed Sadie's information to the captain as well. He tried to meet her eye, but she wasn't looking his way.

'No, sir,' Ray said. 'Nobody said that. They were just saying that she had been drunk, and had been falling over when she was dancing.'

'OK, Ray. I understand.' The captain looked him slowly up and down. 'Is there anything else you want to say?'

'No, sir.'

The captain turned to the other four on the bench.

'Is there anything any of you would like to ask Ray?'

Francis waited, but there was no response from the others. 'If I might,' he asked, after a few moments.

'Please . . .' said the captain.

'We do understand, Ray,' he said, 'how difficult this is for you. This death has been a horrible shock. You are the one who has to live below deck, and if you tell us some secret that only you know your loyalties may well be compromised. But you have to trust us. We will not pass on anything you tell us. That's a promise, isn't it, Captain?'

The captain nodded.

'On that basis, Ray, may I just simply ask: do you have any idea, any idea at all, who killed your cabin mate?'

There was silence.

'No, sir,' the engineer replied.

'He hadn't argued with any other crew member that you knew about?'

'No, sir.'

'This is between us, Ray,' said Viktor. 'It won't be reported back. You won't be in trouble with anyone if you tell us anything.'

'Even if it seems unimportant,' added Francis.

'There was nothing, sir. George was much-liked fellow, sir. Family man, sir.'

'OK,' said the captain, looking round after another long pause. 'Is that all?'

There was a general murmur and no more questions.

'You can go now,' said the captain.

Ray was on his feet.

'Have they taken body from cabin?' the captain added.

'Yes, sir.'

'So you can get some sleep?'

'Yes, sir.'

'I should go and do that. When does your next shift start?'

'Four hundred hours, sir.'

'OK, you get some quiet time in, then.'

Ray scuttled off, with barely a nod to the other four. Francis was annoyed that he hadn't managed to catch his eye again, to reassure him that he was in a separate category of trustworthiness to the rest of the investigation panel.

'So,' said the captain, once he'd gone. 'Do we believe him?'

'I wasn't sure before,' said Carmen. 'But I think he was telling the truth this time. You put enough pressure on him.'

'I could have been harder,' the captain replied. He didn't specify how. 'But I agree. So we draw blank.'

'Not entirely,' said Viktor. 'There's still Gregoire.'

'It is no secret Lauren was dancing with Gregoire,' said the captain. 'Did she kiss him too? Or more than that? Who knows? We only have word of one passenger for that.'

Francis looked over at Carmen again, who shrugged. Apologetically? Hardly.

'Sadie,' said Francis. If his information was going to be out there, it might as well *be* out there. 'But why would she make something like that up?'

'Women do these things,' the captain said. 'Maybe she was jealous.'

'With all due respect,' said Francis, 'I don't think Sadie has any designs on Gregoire.'

'At least that is one man she is not interested in,' said the captain, with a chuckle. Even though Francis had not succumbed to her charms, he felt slightly offended on her behalf.

'Don't you think that it's a piece of information we should take seriously?' he said. 'I thought members of staff having relations with passengers was strictly against the rules.'

'It is,' said the captain.

'Career threatening, even? Doesn't that provide Gregoire with a motive?'

'If it was true, it might do,' said the captain. 'How shall I put this? Gregoire has been my hotel director for three years. Each year we do close to twenty separate cruise segments on this ship. Gregoire is on eighteen of them, and me also. So I know him well. He is vain, yes. Ambitious, also. He comes from nowhere, he would like to be something, wouldn't we all? As for this supposed flirtation . . . OK, so he is good at his job. He dances with many passengers. Younger and older. Makes them feel special. "Oh Gregoire, so good to see you again." So they rebook. He is asset to us. But. Actually kissing passenger. Or more than that. I doubt it. Why? Gregoire is not one to break rules – there is too much at stake for him. Also, he is well-catered for in that area, believe me.'

'On the ship. Or off the ship?' asked Francis.

'Both, probably.' The captain laughed. 'Don't get me wrong. I don't go in for such liaisons myself, it would not be professional. I would be compromised. But if hotel director wishes to sleep with receptionist, or butler, or masseuse from beauty salon, who am I to care? If they are still doing job properly, that is fine. If it interferes with job, I will put one of them off at next port.'

'I see,' said Francis. He turned to Carmen. 'Did you know this?'

She nodded; a little bashfully, it had to be said.

'So you presumably all know who he is involved with?' he asked.

He looked round the room and realized from their faces that they did.

'You may look no further than your own cabin,' said the captain.

'My cabin?' Francis asked, feeling stupid. Then: 'What? *Hentie?*'

The captain nodded. Carmen and Viktor smiled. Francis looked down at the hard grey surface of the floor. He was furious, he realized suddenly, that while they had been freely passing his other information around, this unlikely fact had been kept from him.

'I think,' he said measuredly, 'that if you want me to help you with all this, it would be useful if you disclosed this sort of thing. Otherwise – to be frank – I feel as if . . . I'm just wasting my time.'

'What do you want?' said the captain, tersely. 'A list of every bunk-up on lower deck? That might take a while.'

FOURTEEN

F rancis retreated to his cabin. The bed had been turned down, there was a chocolate on each of the two pillows, and between these another flannel animal, though this one looked more like a lizard. He pinched it at the neck and hopped it slowly across on to the right pillow, so that it was apparently eating the chocolate. Maybe Hentie would find that amusing. Then he walked through into the living-room area and sat down on the couch by the porthole.

He stared out through the thick double layer of glass at the ocean. It stretched away, an undulating blue-black, to the distant flat line of the horizon. The sun had recently set and the clouds parading high across the darkening sky were a brilliant pink, like so many puffs of backlit candyfloss. Even as he watched, their glow faded to a lifeless grey. He turned away and drew his curtain; on the dark night falling on the endless empty ocean.

Was he sulking? No. Francis wasn't a sulker. But he was reassessing. His contribution. That was for sure. I mean, how on earth could they expect him to make any sort of serious effort to get to the bottom of all this if they were going to hold things back from him? Gregoire being involved with Lauren had been part of his thinking, if not his central theory. Why hadn't Carmen said something to him, when he'd told her that Sadie had seen them snogging? Why hadn't she just said, 'Er, unlikely, I think, given that Gregoire is hooked up with your butler Hentie?' He had been relying on Carmen as a sounding board and she had disappointed him. First, by passing information that he'd intended to be confidential straight on to Viktor and the captain. And then, this.

So how did this new information fit in with his theory about Gregoire the serial killer? Not well. Unless Sadie really was lying. But why would she? The captain's suggestion that she was jealous was surely ridiculous. Wasn't it?

Well, first things first.

Francis got to his feet and walked over to the desk, picked up the phone receiver and jabbed nine.

'Good evening,' came that clipped, flat, guttural accent. 'Butler service.'

'Hentie, hi, it's Francis in 312.'

'Good evening, sir. And how are you this evening?'

'Fine thanks. I just wondered . . . could I have a pot of tea in my cabin?'

'Of course, sir. Would you like anything with that? Cake, biscuits, canapes or something off the room service menu?'

'Just the tea, thanks.'

'I'll be right along, sir.'

Sir, sir, sir. Keep me at arm's length, why don't you? They had to, he supposed.

He did want the tea, but he also wanted another look at Gregoire's supposed girlfriend. Francis wouldn't have picked her, stocky, muscly and workaday-looking as she was, for such an exotic bloom as Gregoire. Indeed, he was starting to wonder if he could trust any of them now. Was this story really true? It had certainly been odd, Francis thought, the way the captain had been so protective of his hotel director. Almost as odd as the way, earlier, he'd insisted that George Dimagiba needed his beauty sleep. For a moment, Francis found himself countenancing a scenario where the captain himself was involved in these mysterious deaths. *In charge?* The murdering sea captain. He wouldn't have been the first.

Why had they let him stay in Eve's cabin in the first place? Francis wondered. At the time he had thought it a little odd that the captain hadn't just asked him to leave. And why had he called him back after the MOB? *The captain is keen to have you present at our discussion!* What if he were just a pawn in a bigger game? If they had got him involved as part of a cover-up? 'We even asked the resident crime writer to look into it. You can't accuse us of not trying.'

Oh, you vain and foolish man! Of course they didn't give a hoot about your so-called detective skills. The story of Mold-on-Wold means nothing to them. They were just using you.

But they had all been disappointed just now, hadn't they? All hoping that Ray was going to crack under pressure, reveal that, yes, George had told him that he'd seen something terrible. Gregoire tipping Lauren overboard. Admit it, Francis, that's what you'd been hoping for. And then everything would have fitted neatly: either

Gregoire *had* been involved with Lauren, or he'd told her something incriminating, or both.

Francis had been planning to talk to Gregoire again. With Carmen. Put him under a bit more pressure. But did he want to do that now? Did he want to be involved any more at all? He really didn't need to be. Quite apart from anything else, why should he put his own personal safety at risk?

There was a knock at the door.

He got up and went to it, stupidly nervous suddenly. 'Who is it?' he called.

'Hentie.'

'Thanks, Hentie,' he said, opening it. 'Just checking. That was quick.'

'Ah, they're mostly all having dinner at the moment, sir. Are you sure you don't want me to get you a little something to eat?'

'Maybe in a bit. You can put that down there.'

She bent to lower the tray she was carrying on to the narrow table. She had a nicer figure than he'd thought under that brown uniform.

'There you go, sir.'

'You working all night?' he asked.

'Just till eleven, sir. Then I get my head down.'

Francis nodded. Get her head down where? he thought mischievously. But could he ask her about Gregoire? Here, now, directly. *'By the way, are you in a relationship with the hotel director, M. Le Guard?'* No. It wasn't worth the risk. If she was, she would pass it straight on. Le Guard's suspicions would be aroused.

Instead he said, 'I expect you need that. It's a long day for you.'

'You get used to it, sir.'

'Please don't call me "sir". Call me Francis.'

She looked embarrassed. 'As you wish.'

'You enjoy your work?' he asked. He felt very stilted, suddenly. Like some old man trying to be chatty, though in fact he was probably no more than fifteen years older than her. If that.

'After a fashion, yes, s . . .' The 'sir' faded into a hiss. It was not replaced by a 'Francis'. 'The money's pretty good. For me, from South Africa. The main thing is – it's easy to save.'

'I imagine it is.' He picked up the white china lid of the teapot and gave his tea a stir with the spoon. 'Got to give it a little whirl around,' he explained, 'otherwise it doesn't taste of anything.'

'You English with your tea,' she said with an indulgent smile.

'So what are you saving for?' he asked.

Her eyes lit up. 'I have a couple of dreams.'

'Such as?'

'What I would love to do, one day, is have a game farm.'

'Like a safari place?'

'Ah, yes, safaris would be part of it. If we had enough hectares. Nice, high-end accommodation. Luxury tents maybe too, for our more adventurous visitors.'

'In South Africa?'

She shook her head. 'Namibia. For me, there is more space. Less people. Less trouble.'

'The crime rate in South Africa isn't good, is it?'

'Very bad just now. Actually I had an aunt who was killed on her farm last year by thieves who turned up one afternoon in a *bakkie*.' From his time in Swaziland Francis knew what a *bakkie* was: a little van with an open back. 'They took one old-fashioned TV,' Hentie continued, 'and a laptop. For that they tied her up and shot her in the head. That's how bad it is now.'

'Your people are Afrikaans?'

'We are, sir.'

'So it's your country too.'

'Yes, sir. It is.' *It ees.*

'Nowhere else to go?'

She smiled at that. 'No,' she said. 'It's a shame. I'm not saying apartheid was right, it wasn't. When I was a teenager I used to argue with my dad about that. It was right to free Mandela, to give the blacks their share of power. But the politicians mishandled the transition. Gave people guns who should never have had guns. "Kits constables", they called them. Boys from the townships who were trained up to be police in eight weeks. Eight weeks! And then given a flippin' AK47! And now they wonder why we have the worst crime rate in the world.'

'So you have another reason to want to get away. To the safety of the ship.' Francis smiled. 'Or maybe not. Given the things that have happened in the last couple of days . . .'

'Yes, sir.' Hentie's eyes flicked hurriedly away from his. 'I'd better be getting back,' she said.

'Really? I was enjoying our chat.'

'I can't neglect my other guests, sir.'

'I was interested in your take on it all.'

'Thank you, sir. I'm glad to help. If you need anything else from the menu, please call the restaurant.'

Just like that, she was gone. If Francis had hoped for a discussion about the MOB, or even their joint witness of the sad demise of Eve, he hadn't got one. What else did Hentie know? Everything, presumably. Everyone below deck surely knew about George Bernard Dimagiba. So what had he glimpsed there in her eyes in that moment before she'd run away? More than just knowledge. Fear. It wasn't that she didn't want to talk about all this with a passenger. She was genuinely scared. *Of what her boyfriend might do to her if she told? Of what he might want her to do next?*

Francis leant forward and poured himself a cup of tea. He had told Hentie he didn't want biscuits, but there was another little plate next to the pot with a selection of four or five. He picked up a sugar-dusted shortbread and chewed it anxiously.

Was Hentie really Gregoire's girlfriend? Or was that just another tall story for the dimwit amateur detective that the senior crew had decided to have fun with?

He urgently needed to clarify his thoughts. He got up and went over to the narrow desk by the mirror. He picked up a pen and one of the pieces of printed writing paper that sat in a pile there, headed GOLDEN ADVENTURER. And below that: *From the suite of Mr Francis Meadowes* in an elaborate curling font.

On one side he wrote: *Victims.*

Eve – octogenarian widow. Obviously wealthy, in that she spoke about going on several cruises a year. But not otherwise at all ostentatious about her money. Manner of death not clear. Surely those dodgy prawns wouldn't have killed her? But Dr Lagip suspicious. Although about what wasn't entirely clear. Suffocation? Poisoning? Has she heard back from the Takoradi lab yet? If she has, she's not shared it with me. Eve was also in the Antarctic last Christmas with several others on this cruise. Henry and Daphne, Sebastian and Kurt, Don and Lauren, Col Joe. Suspicious? Or just one of those real-life coincidences?

Lauren – glam (forty-something?) partner of apparently broke
Don. Fell overboard after drinking too much. Or was pushed?
By Don? Or someone else? After discovering something she
shouldn't? Maybe about Eve's death. Or because she had been
involved in a career-threatening fling with Gregoire? Don
certainly thought she had been – just his paranoia? Or was it
suicide? Don didn't think that possible. They were also both in
the Antarctic on the Christmas cruise.

George Bernard Dimagiba – forty-something crew member.
Victim of snakebite, doctor thinks. Surely she's right about that?
The evidence is horribly clear. Herpetologist Leo backs her up.
But how did the snake get on the ship? And when? Did whoever
brought it on intend to use it? On George? Or perhaps one of
the earlier victims? And where is this reptile now? In the sea?
Or hidden in someone's cabin, waiting for a reprise? As for
George, he witnessed Lauren's fall. But what – or rather who
else – did he see that night?

On a second piece of paper Francis wrote: *Suspects.*

Gregoire – was friendly with Eve, would have had access to her
cabin. Was also close to Lauren. How close? Is it possible that
he was murdering passengers after getting them to change their
will? Too far-fetched, as Carmen thinks? Or could it be that that's
what Lauren found out? Was he grooming her as his next victim?
Did she really snog him? If so, did Hentie know? Is Hentie really
his girlfriend? Or did the Carmen/Viktor/Captain team just make
that up, another piece of misinformation for their joke detective?
Whatever: the captain was surprisingly supportive of him.

Don – driven to the edge by his beloved partner's infidelities?
Or just fed up with her and wanted money all for himself? Or
both? Might he have brought her on the cruise specifically to
bump her off, having found out about this extraordinary loophole
in international law on a previous cruise? But how would he have
got access to the lower deck to kill GBD? And where and how
would he have got hold of the snake (unless that was Plan B for
Lauren)? In any case he's been sedated in his cabin since Lauren's

death. Hasn't he? Final point: if he is a suspect for Lauren, that assumes that Eve died a natural death. Doesn't it?

Who else? If Hentie really is an item with Gregoire, is it possible they're working together? Would that explain that sudden flash of fear in her eyes and rapid exit just now? She has a financial motive, in wanting the game farm. But would she have idly disclosed that ambition to me if she and G really were murdering passengers and stealing their money? On the other hand – the butler did it!

He jotted down other possibilities:

Klaus? Something distinctly creepy about him and he always knows too much. Certainly about Africa – so would know all about snakes. That bulky excursion bag of his is certainly big enough to hide one. Could he have popped one in while we were out in Togo? But really a murderer? Why?
And: he was not on the Christmas Antarctic cruise.

Shirley? A terminally ill woman might not care about what she does, if she had a cast-iron motive to kill. But what on earth would be her motive for these two very different women? One of whom is from a different continent to her. Also this is her first cruise ever.

Brad and Damian? Happy with each other, well-off, soon to be married, zero motive. However: a bit odd that they claimed they slept through MOB drama. Believable? Also: how/why did Damian know about Gregoire's 'house mouse' below decks?

Sebastian and Kurt? Ditto re. MOB. Kurt a bit spooky.

Sadie? Confused perhaps, dangerously horny, but surely no killer. First-time cruiser.

Colonel Joe?
The captain and/or his sidekick, po-faced Alexei?
Henry and Daphne?

This last scrawled question brought a laugh. *The Alzheimer's Murderer?* Francis could see it now, in the *Mail* Online. 'Concealed beneath a brilliantly maintained act of pretending not to know who anyone was, Henry Forbes-Harley not only knew exactly who they were, but he was actively killing them off . . .'

Absurd. In any case, all these passengers had far too much money to have any need of murdering anyone for money. If Daphne and Henry were anything, they were Gregoire or whoever's next victims.

As he scrawled the words *More than one murderer?* there was another knock at the door. Francis hurriedly turned over his piece of paper and walked nervously up the little corridor. Had Hentie rushed off to tell Gregoire? Could this be him now? With a poisonous reptile clutched in his fists?

'Who is it?' he called.

'Carmen.'

He opened the door. She was standing in the corridor, in her blue party dress and high heels. Her grin was infectious.

'Aren't you coming up for dinner?'

'I didn't think I'd bother. Might have something from room service tonight. Stuff to think about . . .'

'Oh, come on, mate. You can't hide yourself away in here.' Her eyes danced with amusement. 'Are you cross with me, is that it?'

'No.'

'Are you sure?'

'Seriously, Carmen, I thought we were working together. I didn't realize that you were concealing things from me.'

She pushed past him into the cabin, filling his nostrils with the waft of some musky, almost sickly scent.

'You mean,' her voice dropped to a whisper, 'Gregoire and Hentie?'

He nodded.

'Hand on heart, I didn't know about that. Until we went up to the office. The captain told me. Viktor knew, but I didn't.'

Did he believe this?

'You also told the captain what Sadie told me about Gregoire and Lauren.'

'Was I supposed not to? We're all working on this together, aren't we?'

'Yes, but I thought we'd agreed we didn't want Gregoire to be suspicious. The captain seems very supportive of him. Who's to say he hasn't already repeated this back to him?'

'Sooner or later he's going to know. Anyway, it looks like Sadie might have made it all up.'

'I'm not sure about that. Why would she?'

'Come on, mate, don't stay in here sulking. Come up and have some food. We can sit together and do some hard thinking. Thrash this all out.'

'It somehow doesn't feel right. To eat an elaborate dinner with all these dead bodies on the ship.'

'And what's more right about hiding away in your cabin? You need to be in the dining room. Getting a sense of what people are feeling. Saying.'

'Have they all forgotten poor Lauren already?' Francis said. 'Dressed up in their finery and moved on.'

'Not at all. "Poor Lauren" is very much the main topic of conversation on this ship. But you need to hear it.'

'Do I?'

'Come on, you saddo,' she replied. 'Chuck on a jacket and let's go upstairs.'

Was it only last night, he thought, as he followed her out of the door and along the narrow, claustrophobic corridor, that it had been he who was persuading Sadie to go and join the diners?

FIFTEEN

I n the Panorama Lounge after dinner Alfredo the pianist sat behind his instrument, his head tilting back and forth in time to the music, his fingers dancing expertly up and down the keyboard, extracting the maximum feeling from every note he played. 'Love Story', 'Lady in Red', 'The Way You Look Tonight', 'What a Wonderful World' – the tunes were as predictable as they were schmaltzy. Every now and then a passenger would get to his or her feet, dodder over the blue carpet and lean down towards the Filipino's ear with a suggestion for a tune, then drop a bank note into the outsized brandy glass that sat on the gleaming ebony lid of his Bechstein.

The bar was more crowded than Francis had yet seen it. Rather than be got down by the shocking events of last night, the guests seemed to have decided to live it up. Bolstered by five courses, a sorbet and petits fours, the unease that Francis had detected at the Neptune party had been replaced by a much more boisterous mood, one of backslapping and loud laughter.

But he wasn't paying much attention to this rowdy conviviality, because he had at last got Carmen alone. The 'hard thinking' she had promised him had not been possible at the mixed table of eight they had ended up sitting at for dinner. Francis had spent half his meal listening to the life story of a construction magnate from Bolton, UK; the other half in conversation with Martha, a waxy-faced American who had been confined to her cabin for three days with the norovirus. 'Not that I had it so bad,' she said, 'but Sean did. Oh, boy! My travelling companion,' she added, nodding across the table to a handsome fellow who looked as if he'd been dipped in a vat of teak wood stain. She'd suffered less, she reckoned, because she took probiotics, as well as something called Digest Gold, which was really amazing for upset stomachs – Francis should get some. But the 'confining thing' was serious. She and Sean had had this letter from the captain, saying that if they were found outside their cabin – *at all*, while they were still ill – they would be put off at the next port. 'It was like, really, heavy, but then' – Martha cackled with laughter – 'it had this typo right in the middle which made it ridiculous.' But it had made them wonder. 'I mean, how many other passengers are similarly imprisoned?'

'So,' Carmen asked him now. 'Did you pick up anything useful over dinner?'

'Some remedies for upset stomachs and an insight into the building industry in the north of England, but no, not much more than that.'

She laughed. 'You're a patient listener.'

'So people tell me.'

'They didn't talk about the MOB?' Despite the background din, she mouthed the acronym.

'The woman on my left did. Eventually. But she was convinced Lauren had fallen off.'

'That's mostly what they think. An awful tragedy, but no more than that.'

'The old boy on my right didn't even mention it.' Francis gestured round the room. 'Less than twenty-four hours later, life seems to be carrying on much as normal.'

'Or else people have just decided to make the most of things.'

There was a pause while they sipped their drinks and looked round at the partying passengers. Then Francis leaned forward. 'So you really didn't know about Gregoire and Hentie before that meeting?' he asked.

'No,' Carmen insisted. 'I'm not holding stuff back from you, mate, if that's what you're worrying about.'

'Or from the captain, as far as I can see.'

'What are you talking about? Gregoire's supposed snog with Lauren again.'

'Call me old fashioned, but if someone tells me something in confidence, I would keep it to myself.'

'In this situation?' Carmen cut in. 'Where we're trying to find out who killed a man? Possibly even a man and two women. Don't you trust the captain?'

'I'm not sure trust comes into it particularly. I don't think that he's involved, put it that way.'

'*Involved.*' She laughed. 'The captain! That's even crazier than your idea about Gregoire the serial killer.'

'Is it? So why is he so protective of him then?'

'Of Gregoire? He's worked with him for ages, and he rates him. You often find that people in authority can't countenance the idea of their favoured subordinates doing any wrong at all. Even trivial stuff.'

'You could be right,' Francis said. He sat in silence for a bit. 'I suppose that's it,' he concluded.

'Of course it is. What are you suggesting? That Gregoire and the captain are bumping off the passengers together and sharing the money?'

Francis laughed. 'Before you came to find me, I was sitting in my cabin with a piece of paper trying to work out how any of these deaths could possibly be related. And I can't say I was getting anywhere much. The only even half-likely suspects I have are Gregoire and Don. And Don has been in his cabin in a sedated state since Lauren went overboard.'

'So what about Gregoire being involved with Hentie?' Carmen asked. 'Does that make him more – or less – of a suspect?'

'It makes it less likely that he was involved with Lauren,' Francis replied. 'Doesn't it?'

'Which would make your friend Sadie a liar. With who knows what motives.'

'It would. But if Gregoire is the killer, then Hentie would make an excellent accomplice. She can go anywhere, upstairs or downstairs. She has the perfect reason to be in any of her passengers' rooms at any time. Mine included.'

'Eve was on her corridor,' said Carmen.

'She was.'

'Her motive presumably being the same as Gregoire's. Money.'

'I had a chat with her when she brought me a cup of tea earlier. Her ambition is to own a game farm in Namibia. I don't imagine they come cheap.'

'Depends what currency you're buying in. The US dollar gets you thirteen South African rand these days. That's why you get plenty of South Africans doing these jobs. Because they can earn a relative fortune . . .'

She tailed off. There was a hush in the bar. Sebastian was up by the piano, striking quite a pose in a knee-length cream *kurta pyjama*, decorated with a filigree of orange-gold, a purple scarf slung over one shoulder. Sebastian the glam serial killer, thought Francis for a moment; he certainly looked the part. Now he was asking everyone to be quiet please while his friend Alfredo sang 'Nessun Dorma'.

'We are listening here to a man who reached the finals of "The Philippines Have Got Talent".'

This announcement was greeted by loud laughter. Alfredo gracefully bowed his head, as if this patronizing derision were a compliment. Sebastian's face remained composed and serious, as he held out a straight arm towards Alfredo.

The chords rang out; and then, from this little smiling man, came a deep, rolling tenor that took everyone by surprise. By the time he'd reached the final lines, the Panorama Lounge was quiet. Women – and men – were dabbing at their eyes. On a banquette to the left, big Shirley was sobbing loudly, hubby Gerald rubbing her shoulders with his scrawny right hand.

> *All'alba vincerò!*
> *Vincerò! Vincerò!*

The last note, the sustained high A made famous by Pavarotti, faded into the pin-drop silence. Someone clapped. The bar broke into noisy applause.

'The Filipinos *have* got talent!' came an Australian shout.

Sebastian was weeping too. Next to him, Kurt was stony-faced.

'May I?'

Francis looked up to see a familiar face. Klaus was in maximum twinkly mode tonight, dressed up in his navy blazer and a striped blue and crimson tie that looked as if it might belong to some English sports club or public school, rather than anything more European. He was clutching a large whisky.

'Please,' said Francis politely. He gestured at the empty seat next to his companion. 'You know Carmen, I'm sure.'

'Yes.' Klaus nodded. 'I have been on some little Zodiac expedition captained by you. And of course I heard your very interesting lecture on the pygmies of Cameroon.'

'Thank you,' said Carmen. 'I hope you enjoyed it.'

'I was particularly interested in their language having a totally different root from the Bantu peoples around them.'

'Ubangian. Yes.'

'This is one of the lesser known stories of this fascinating continent. How the Bantu superseded the indigenous peoples. Of course, further south it was the Khoi and the San who were wiped out. There's not much left of them now either, except perhaps in the genes of the so-called Coloured people of the Cape.'

'You know your history,' Carmen said.

'Just a little,' Klaus replied smugly. Now he turned to Francis. 'So, have you solved any of the mysteries yet? Found any murderous stowaways tucked away?'

'No stowaways, that's for sure,' Francis replied. Carmen was looking puzzled; but it was hardly Francis's fault, was it, that Klaus had such an unashamedly intrusive nature. 'How about you?' he added. 'Have you got anything more to tell us?'

'I think the drink has calmed the nerves of the guests a little,' the German replied. 'Although some of this laughter is a bit on the hysterical side. But nobody is going to be taking a lonely walk up on deck seven tonight, I don't think. We may laugh and joke here in company, but we will be straight back to the cabin and locking the door. How is your stomach, by the way?'

'Fine, thanks,' said Francis.

'Keep using the disinfectant gel. I would. Nobody is saying anything, but the norovirus is spreading. I see some familiar faces are not here tonight.'

'Really? I thought it seemed rather crowded.'

'It is. For the bar. Many of the diners have come through for a how-to-say nightcap. But there were fewer at dinner. I notice these things.'

'You certainly do,' said Francis, rolling his eyes discreetly at Carmen.

She half rose. 'Another drink?' she asked. 'I'm getting one.'

The invitation had been to Francis, but Klaus was no slouch in saving himself a trip to the bar. 'If you are offering,' he said, 'I *vill* have another *visky*. It's a Scottish malt. Frederick knows which one.'

'Frederick's the barman?'

'Of course. An old friend of mine. Though whether that's his real name I have no idea.' This last remark was made, it seemed, without irony.

'OK then, why not,' Francis said, smiling up at Carmen. 'I'll have another of these fine brandies. But just a small one, please.'

Once Carmen had gone, Klaus turned towards Francis with a conspiratorial smile. 'So this attractive blonde lady is your Hastings, I think?'

'Not quite Hastings,' he replied. 'A bit too bright for that.'

'Perhaps you are her Hastings then,' said Klaus, with a chuckle. 'At any rate I notice your heads pushed together. What have you concluded?'

Francis gave him a blank smile. 'Not very much at all. Though obviously if we had, it would have to stay confidential.'

Klaus was not to be so easily put off. 'And have your collective thoughts been affected by this latest incident?'

Francis tried to look as if he had no idea what Klaus was talking about.

'I'm sorry,' he said. 'I'm not with you.'

'It is lucky you are a writer,' said Klaus, 'and not an actor, because I don't think you would have got far in that profession. We both know what we are talking about. The shocking murder of this crew fellow who saw poor Lauren go overboard.'

Who had told Klaus about this? Hadn't the captain insisted that George's death be kept entirely under wraps? In addition to being on chummy terms with barmen, how deep below deck did Klaus's information network go?

'You're very well informed,' Francis replied. There was little point in denial. Strange thought – maybe Klaus would be able to help?

'Clearly this man saw something,' said Klaus. 'And by something, I mean someone, as mere things don't go round doing random killings by themselves, do they? Do you have any idea who might have helped our glamorous lady friend over the railings?'

'No.'

'But you've spoken to his cabin mate?'

'You seem to know as much as me, Klaus.'

'And he told you he never got the chance to talk to his friend. So he wouldn't know either. Do you really believe that?'

'He seemed pretty adamant.'

'Of course he would. If what his friend told him was that it was one of his bosses he saw, he's probably running scared for his life.

There's no getting off this ship. Until the day after tomorrow, at least.'

'No,' Francis agreed. 'Is that what you think? That it's one of his bosses?'

'I don't know. This is one of the reasons I thought I would come over and have a chat with you. But one thing is worth considering: that a guest is less likely to know how to get around in that strange industrial area beyond the *Crew Only* doors.'

'You sound as if you've been down there yourself, Klaus.'

'Bear in mind that I admit to being an inquisitive man. Also that I have been on several cruises and occasionally – how should I put this? – when the weather is bad and the place is deserted, my curiosity overcomes me. Never, when my wife is with me, would I dream of stepping outside the hallowed luxury areas. But yes, sometimes when I am alone, I have explored. Though not far, because as you know, when we are at sea, those watertight doors are often locked and it really is a maze down there. Every corridor looks the same. One time I got seriously lost and thought I would never get back. Finally I found myself in the laundry, deep in the bottom of the hull, staffed by three Chinese I never saw before or again, even on those party nights at the end of the cruise when they bring out what they tell us is the whole crew to be paraded before us. One of these anonymous oriental gentlemen kindly showed me back to civilization.'

'Do any of the other passengers have any clue about this latest death?' Francis asked.

'I have no idea. But then I have not had this conversation with any of them. To be honest, I doubt it. Even with the shock of this poor female who went overboard, most of them are just thinking about their next meal. Or their next excursion. Or what they can next complain about. The noise of trolleys in the corridors early in the morning. Some fixtures and fittings that are not as smart as they would like them to be. The food, which is not exactly what they are used to in New York or Los Angeles. The wind on the deck, even; I once heard one lady grumbling about that.' He chuckled. 'So you don't have any suspects lined up?' he added.

'I'll be honest with you, Klaus. I'm baffled.'

'One of the more amusing aspects of this case, I think, is that there are plenty of our fellow guests who would love to murder their cabin companions. That young Sadie, for example, would happily finish off her aunt, given half a chance. Daphne, for all her gracious smiles, is always encouraging that demented husband of hers on to more and more exhausting excursions. Sometimes I look at the stern face of Kurt and wonder about his feelings for his talented younger boyfriend. And as for Gerald and his enormous wife, well, this hen-pecked individual is probably too cowed—'

He broke off, as Carmen was approaching with a small round tray containing the drinks. 'But here is Hastings,' he added. 'With our *sniv-ters*.' He raised an eyebrow. 'To be continued, as they say.'

SIXTEEN

Day at Sea. Wednesday 26 April.

There was another full day at sea, as the *Golden Adventurer* made its way on from Cote d'Ivoire and along the long, straight green coastline of Liberia. Was it just that there was nothing appropriately touristic for the passengers in the ports of Abidjan, San Pedro, Harper, Buchanan, Monrovia and their environs? Or perhaps there was a security issue? Maybe the police of these two countries had refused to play ball? Whatever, the next stop on the itinerary was Freetown, Sierra Leone, and that wouldn't be reached until early tomorrow morning. For today the view was strictly waves, wake, horizon and the occasional wildlife: the gulls that flew in from the wider ocean to escort the ship; the flying fish that you could spot leaping from wave to wave, gleaming darts of silver; and every now and then, if you were lucky, something bigger – a shark, a school of dolphins.

Francis had woken early and taken a pre-breakfast walk up and around the top deck. Today was his lecture and he wanted to get his head in the right place. At seven fifteen a.m. the sun was already hot, though the breeze off the sea made it refreshingly cooler, especially in the long shadows behind the various big structures up there. What were they – funnels, satellite receiving stations, secret cabins? Glancing through the darkened windows of the fitness centre, he spotted a couple of familiar silhouettes pounding around on the machines: Brad and Damian keeping themselves in enviable shape. Out on the wide deck itself a procession of walkers in shorts or tracksuit bottoms and trainers were making their way round the edge of the ship in a loose oval. Two of these were the Australians he had met at the Neptune party, he realized, as they got closer.

'G'day, Francis!' shouted the bronzed male.

'Er, good morning,' he replied.

'And *moy* name is?'

'Uh,' Francis began, embarrassed. Had this guy even introduced himself last night?

'Derek. Why on earth should you remember that?' He cackled. 'This is Noelene, my wife. Gorgeous up here at this time, isn't it? You should join us.'

'Maybe I will.'

'I mean right now, mate. Get your joggers on and get up here. Lose a couple of pounds before breakfast.'

Francis laughed. 'Maybe tomorrow.'

'"Maybe tomorrow." You hear that, Noelene? Maybe tomorrow. This guy's a joker.'

Francis escaped down the steps to the open tables at the back of deck six. John-since-1972 was standing waiting by the bar in his gleaming cream jacket and black bow tie.

'Good morning, Mr Meadowes, sir. May I get you some tea or coffee this morning? An omelette-with-everything perhaps?'

You had to admire these guys. Not only were they relentlessly cheerful, they also remembered the names of all the passengers and exactly what they had ordered before, as if there really was nothing they would rather be doing than bringing you the breakfast you had forgotten you liked. Handy for the Alzheimer's crowd, Francis thought irreverently, to have John-since-1972 on hand.

He chose a table right by the end rail. Below, you could see down to the stern of deck four, where the six Zodiacs were stored – big black inflatables with powerful outboard motors. A couple of guys in brown boiler suits were working on the two visible ones just below him, checking over the mechanics, getting everything ready for disembarkation tomorrow.

His omelette-with-everything arrived. 'Everything' was tiny squares of chopped ham, cooked slices of tomato and peppers, chewy strands of half-melted cheese. Francis had just started on this now familiar tasty dish when he was aware of a shadow next to him. He looked up to see Mike, the bearded Aussie marine biologist.

'Shall I join you?'

'Please,' Francis gestured, his mouth full.

Mike sat opposite, then started to munch his way through his muesli.

'You've not cruised before, have you?'

'No,' Francis replied.

'How are you finding it all?'

'Eventful.' He wondered how much the expedition staff had been told; about everything that had gone on below deck, quite apart from his role as ad hoc private investigator. If even Klaus knew about George Bernard, surely Mike did too.

'Certainly has been,' Mike replied, raising an eyebrow. 'You looking forward to Freetown tomorrow?'

'I've no idea what to expect. But it'll be good to get off the ship for a bit.'

'It does all feel a bit stir crazy, doesn't it? Everyone's a bit on edge since the incident on Monday night.'

'Hardly surprising,' said Francis. 'Have you been on a cruise where anything like that has happened before?'

'Never an MOB, no. There was a death in Antarctica, and another one on the Kimberley cruise I did last April, but that's only to be expected with this demographic.' Mike gave the confident chuckle of a fit young man. 'Not that MOBs are actually that unusual. There's several a year worldwide. Just a couple of months ago there was some Chinese woman who went overboard during a Mediterranean cruise; there were even suspicions that the husband might have helped her.' He raised an eyebrow. 'It's not always passengers either. There was a young female crew member who went missing from a Norwegian ship in Alaska last summer. Then there was that woman from your country who vanished mysteriously off the coast of Mexico a few years ago. Rebecca somebody. It made big news at the time because she was only twenty-five and perfectly fit and cheerful and all that. There was no obvious reason why she might have done herself in.

'For passengers,' he continued, 'sometimes it's just some drunk falling over the rails, but often it's weirder. There was some old bloke who threw himself off a ship in Tasmania last year after a nice dinner with his wife and some friends. Left a note saying he thought getting old was shit. Then there was an engaged couple who went over somewhere near Brisbane after a row. She went first, he tried to save her, neither of them survived.'

'So what happened with this one, d'you think?' Francis asked.

'Who knows? That was some crazy lady. Always getting drunk and rowing with that husband of hers.'

'I don't think they were married.'

'Boyfriend, whatever. Man friend, old geezer friend. Their behaviour became quite a feature of the Antarctica cruise at Christmas. We used to laugh about it. Though I guess it's not so funny now.'

'No,' Francis agreed. 'I was shocked. And also at the speed with which the ship turned round.'

'They only go back because they're required to by maritime law. But nobody really expects to find someone who's gone overboard in the middle of the night on an ocean like this. It's just too vast. And anyway, if she was drunk, she'd not have lasted that long. There's plenty of sharks out there, too.' Mike made a horrid little munching gesture with his right hand. 'The truth is, it's more of a formality. As well as a reassurance to the other passengers.'

'Is that so?' Francis topped up his coffee from the steel jug. 'And when there's just an ordinary death,' he continued innocently, 'as in Antarctica, is that something you expedition staff get to know about straight away?'

'They tell us, yeah. Not always immediately. But the news kind of gets around.'

'Or if you know the passenger personally, I guess you'd be aware.'

'There is that.'

'You didn't know either of these people? In Antarctica . . . or Kimberley?'

'Not, not really,' Mike replied. 'The guy in Antarctica was an American. Big fat tycoon type, didn't look terribly healthy. Cruising on his own. I have to say it was hardly a surprise he karked it.'

'Cruising on his own?'

'I think he was. Yes, come to think of it he had a few golden girls after him, so definitely.'

'Golden girls?'

'Widows. Gold-diggers. There's always a couple.'

'You don't remember his name?'

Mike frowned. 'Krug, something. Krugminder – something like that. Viktor might remember. He was leading the expeditions on that cruise.'

'And Kimberley?'

'That was on a different ship. But yeah,' he grinned, 'we all knew about her. Famous lady. There were obituaries in all the Australian papers. She was the widow of one of Australia's richest men, Dougie Wyldestone, d'you ever hear of him?'

'Can't say I have.'

'He was one of those guys who was in on the discovery of minerals in Western Australia at the start of the last century. He got in there quick and grabbed the relevant leases. Anyway, she was much younger than him. Like in her twenties when he was in his eighties. She was his housekeeper before she became his wife. So everyone was fascinated by her. Thai. You can imagine the rumours.'

'About her death?'

'No, about why she'd married him. You know, the old story, bit like our friends on this ship.' Mike made a face which indicated that the friends he meant were Don and Lauren. 'This one managed to get most of the loot when the old feller died, though there was a fight with his children from his first marriage, I believe. She lived for years in this massive mansion in Perth and had a string of younger boyfriends. Tennis pros, gym instructors, that kind of thing. I don't think she ever married again.'

'And what was her name?'

'Ah, didn't I say? Marikit . . .'

'Marikit Wyldestone . . .?'

'Yeah. Even though she might have got her money in a dodgy way, she was always very generous with it. So she was much-loved by the ordinary Aussies.'

'Interesting stuff. And you say that cruise was on a different ship?'

'Kimberley, yeah, that's a regular one for the *Golden Mermaid*. Sister Goldencruise vessel, which then goes on up to Indonesia and Japan and places like that.'

Mike had got to his feet and indicated he was off to get some more food.

'So tell me what happens in Freetown?' Francis asked, when he returned with a plate piled high with cooked breakfast.

'Ah, it's a good day out,' Mike replied. 'Sierra Leone is amazing. The port at Aberdeen – that's the district of Freetown where we land – is too small for us to dock, so we have to anchor offshore and do a Zodiac transfer. Which is great fun, the guests love that, scrambling up on to the rocky beach. We didn't do it the last two years, because of the Ebola epidemic, so it's going to be interesting to see how the place is now.'

'So when were you there before?'

'April 2014, literally just before the epidemic broke. God knows, we might have been taking a terrible risk, trailing round Freetown, but nobody knew anything about it then . . .'

'And none of the guests contracted the disease?'

'Not that I ever heard about. Then last year they were technically in the clear, but the WHO didn't give the thumbs-up till mid-March, after we'd sailed from Cape Town, so Goldencruise didn't put it on the itinerary. But no, all back to normal now, I hope.'

'So then, after the beach . . .?'

'Yeah, we bus them up to the amputee hospital, which was always a bit of a wake-up call for them. To see the mess the civil war left behind, even years later. You tend to find them all getting their cheque books out after that.'

'Not that you're being cynical.'

'Not at all. But it's a funny thing about Americans, don't you think? Not that they're naive – well, maybe they are. But it's like' – he slipped into a hick accent – '"Ah gee, I didn't realize there would be so many guys with no legs and arms, please, let me chuck some money at you." It all works well, because of course what the hospital wants *is* for money to be chucked at it. The whole place is run by an American anyway. That's why they take them up there – it's not too alien. She's some incredible missionary woman who came here on holiday or on a fact-finding trip or something and then saw all these limbless guys without any help and decided to stay. Amazing really. I love people like that, who see something terrible and decide they can't turn away. On a human level, it's impressive.'

'Sounds like it is.'

'And then for a bit of light relief after that we take them up to the chimp sanctuary. That's good fun. The chimps are cute. Pose for photos and yawn and scratch their crimson arses and stuff like that. They really do look almost human, loping around with their long arms. You can certainly get your head around evolution when you see them in action. Then it's back down to the beach for cocktails and the amputee-leper football match.'

'I saw that on the itinerary.'

'Only in Africa! One team is like the amputees from the civil war and the other team is the lepers. I shouldn't laugh, but you gotta see these guys. They really go for it. Zooming around the sand on crutches. Kicking with one leg.' Mike shook his head. 'It's pretty awesome stuff. And the beach is beautiful. A great big curve of sand and palm trees. You know, if they got their act together they could have some serious tourism in Sierra Leone.'

'So it's all totally safe now, is it?'

'So they tell us. Still, you won't catch me snogging the local guide, that's for sure.' He laughed. 'Then we bring the guests back here in the Zodiacs at sunset and take them off to Banana Island.'

'The same night?'

'Hell, no. They need their five-course dinner, don't they? After a full-on day like that. No, the ship goes up the coast and anchors by the island overnight, and we offload first thing in the morning.'

'And what happens on Banana Island?'

'Bugger all. There's a scruffy little village to look at and a walk through the jungle for the more adventurous guests. You might see a couple of monkeys in the wild, if you're lucky . . .'

He tailed off; his boss had joined them.

'Morning guys,' said Viktor. 'All set for another long day at sea? I need to talk to you, Mike, when you've finished breakfast. There's been a bit of a change of plan.'

'So what's happening?' Francis asked.

'There'll be a passenger briefing later,' Viktor said, coolly. 'You'll find out then.'

Secrets, secrets, secrets. As Francis paced round the ship after breakfast, gearing himself up for his lecture at ten thirty, he felt there were too many. Two deaths that none of the passengers were yet aware of, and now . . . what? It was, he supposed, fair enough that Viktor should keep his operational info confidential. But still, a little galling. Especially since Francis knew so much more than all the other guests.

Around him they were all getting on happily with their 'at sea' days. Whatever Viktor had up his sleeve for tomorrow, today the programme was running as planned. Lectures by himself and Mike (replacing the one cancelled yesterday); a game of competitive quoits on deck seven; even a teatime birding quiz with Leo in the Panorama Lounge. For those who couldn't be bothered with such worthy pursuits, there was of course the Whirlpool Bar, which opened pretty much as soon as breakfast had been cleared away. Two deeply tanned ladies were already waist deep in the central spa pool, pink cocktails in hand at ten in the morning. Twelve feet away, on the other side, a flabby gent with a threadbare carpet of white hair down his back was reading from a Kindle while sipping a pint of lager. God forbid that his bony fingers should lose their grip on his device!

At ten thirty Francis stood waiting by the lectern in the theatre as the guests trooped in and took their places. Bruce and Candy had made it; Derek the Aussie and his wife Noelene; Brad and Damian; even, he noticed, Shirley and Gerald, in an audience that numbered close to thirty. With the sparkling blue ocean outside, his subject felt very drab and English as he took them through his usual well-rehearsed account of the crime genre, from the Newgate Calendar and Godwin's *Caleb Williams*, through Poe, Conan Doyle, Chesterton, Christie, Sayers, Allingham, James, right up to the gorier narratives of today. Some of his jokes got chuckles; the less obvious ones seemed to miss the mark. They had just started on questions at the end when he was interrupted by an announcement over the tannoy. For a moment, hearing Viktor's voice, Francis thought they had decided to move the briefing forward. But no: Mike had spotted a school of tuna and the ship had slowed down and diverted for people to see it.

The theatre emptied in under a minute, with barely an apology. Francis followed his audience out to find an excited crowd gathered at the back of the sun deck, cameras in hand; though you needed, he thought, a telephoto lens as powerful as Damian's foot-long proboscis to catch the tiny surface splashes a couple of hundred yards off the port side of the ship. Sadie was out here too, in a turquoise sarong, with a pair of binoculars, chatting to Leo. Her laugh was rather stagey, head thrown back, and Francis wondered for a moment whether she had noticed him. She hadn't been to his lecture; he kept his distance.

If Francis was mildly cheesed off that a school of fish had proved more compelling than questions about his talk, he was also glad to have got his obligations out of the way. He had a quick coffee in the Whirlpool Bar, then headed back round the ship, feeling increasingly like a hamster with nowhere to hide. There was, he supposed, safety in numbers. Even the most determined killer was hardly going to have a go at him when most of the guests were out and about, enjoying the fresh air.

Daphne and Henry, in matching maroon tracksuits, were making their way at a dodder round deck seven. Daphne was right behind her hubby, pushing him on with encouraging little shouts.

'Attaboy, Henry! You know you can do it.'

The old man's colour was high; crimson shading into purple.

Francis chuckled at Klaus's thought that she was trying to finish him off. Or did exercise alleviate Alzheimer's? Who knew – perhaps she just wanted him to be fit.

Francis returned to his cabin, wondering if Carmen might have left a message for him. He had felt rather sidelined yesterday, despite her pre-dinner apologies and the chat they'd had afterwards. Now he felt more so. Viktor had made it clear that he wasn't sharing the 'change of plan' with the likes of him. So what was it? Was there new information? Were they finally going to tell the passengers about Eve and George? Ah, well, he would have to find out later, with all the others.

Meanwhile, he wasn't giving up on his own ideas, whatever Carmen thought of them. Now Mike had confirmed that there had been deaths on other cruises, what did that mean? There was no harm in having a closer look, was there? Following up the names and details of those who had died. It was the sort of Internet challenge he enjoyed, especially as he was operating from a remote satellite connection somewhere off West Africa.

Francis had thought he would be in for a bit of a search, but a helpful – if improbable – site called cruiseshipdeaths.com provided everything he needed. There they all were, from Sir David Frost, seventy-four, on board the Queen Elizabeth en route from Southampton to Rome in August 2013 (he too had been lecturing), to Baby Doe, aged one day, abandoned by her twenty-year-old mother on board the *Carnival Dream* in the Caribbean in October 2011.

Mike had been almost right. It was a Mr Krugbender, an American, who had died last Christmas on the *Golden Adventurer*'s twelve-day round trip from Ushuaia, Argentina, through the Falkland Islands and on down to Antarctica. He had been travelling on his own and there was nothing suspicious about his death. But Mike had understated things. There were no less than two other deaths registered for the *Golden Adventurer* in the past year: a Mrs Drew-Huggins, seventy-nine, on the Ecuador to Chile leg in October; and Major Ralph Walden Fisher, eighty-six, on the ship's Tromsø to Longyearbyen passage in July. And yes, here she was, on the twelve-day April cruise from Broome to Darwin on the Interluxe Goldencruise *Golden Mermaid*: Marikit Wyldestone, aged just seventy-three. He skipped through a couple of obits of her, which confirmed what Mike had told him. An undeniably merry widow, known for both her charity work and her lovers; by the looks of it, the former sometimes provided the latter. The general tenor of the write-ups of her death was one of surprise. No one had thought lively Marikit would pass on so suddenly and so soon.

Then Francis dived a little deeper, amazed, as so often, at what you could find online these days. Getting hold of a copy of a will would once have meant a personal visit to the Supreme Court of New South Wales in Sydney and similar trips to find probate records in Ohio and Illinois. Now you could order one online, pay a small fee and have it delivered to your inbox in days; or, for a bit more cash, overnight.

Serious researches in hand, Francis took his laptop up to the breezy sunshine of deck six. The Whirlpool Bar was busy. The early-morning boozers had moved on to pre-lunch aperitifs and been joined by others. Loud laughter rang from the groups around the tables. There were shrieks and splashes from the central spa pool.

Francis took a seat in the last available space, a table for two right in the corner by the steps down to the back of deck four. He ordered a beer and clicked through to Facebook. Out here in bright sunshine in the middle of the ocean, the whole thing seemed surreal. Who *were* these people, his so-called 'friends'? A sprinkling were real friends, or at least real acquaintances, as in people he liked and occasionally saw. But there were many others who had joined his list by a strange kind of osmosis. People he had known at college, years ago, for example. The act of clicking 'confirm friend' hadn't even led to a catch-up message, quite often, let alone a catch-up meeting. There they were, these forgotten people, in his news feed, with their strange lives and alien opinions; and odder still, the reactions and opinions of *their* 'friends'.

Francis enjoyed eavesdropping. He was always up for listening in to a conversation on a bus or train, or increasingly, these days, of a one-sided nature, on a mobile. But Facebook licensed snooping on other people on a grand scale, with lives and motives and delusions laid horribly bare. This one was finding her teenaged daughter impossible to live with, that one was going through a messy divorce (friends who had once cooed over the endearing things that hubby had got up to were now invited to unfriend him – pdq). This one had just taken up yoga and was finding her new class hostile, that one was floored by depression. This one was standing to become a local councillor, that one had moved to New Zealand and become a climate change activist. This one fulminated batily from the right, that one pontificated self-righteously from the left. Francis rarely commented. Instead, he lurked. Lurked and learned.

He clicked open his newsfeed. There were the usual posts. 'Friends' opining about news items and public figures; grumbling about neighbours, bosses, partners, parents, children; boasting about parties they'd been to, restaurants and bars they'd visited, famous people they'd seen or even met, holidays they were on, flowers they'd planted, books they'd written; asking for help with this charity run or that worthy appeal. After each post came the stack of thumbs-up 'likes' and the trail of inane comments. 'Wow!' 'Amazing!' 'Sounds lovely', 'Clever you', 'Big hugs' etc.

Oh, what a lot these indiscreet individuals told you about themselves, even as they imagined they were in some online version of a chat in a pub or at a private dinner party. And what was this latest post? Input from his very newest 'friend'.

Sadie Solomon
2 hours ago

This cruise I'm on just gets weirder and weirder. The night before last, as I wrote yesterday, we had an MOB (man overboard). Or rather a WOB (woman overboard). A fellow American, no less, not that much older than me, albeit with a much older partner (not like my lovely Louis Pienaar – hey Lou, I miss you!).

Anyway, the ship turned round for a bit, failed to find her, then we turned promptly back and steamed on, up this empty West Coast of Africa. Apparently we are somewhere off Liberia at the moment, though how would you know with nothing but mile upon mile of ocean to look at? We are not stopping at Monrovia, presumably because it's too poor and genuinely 'African' for my high-end fellow 'guests' – as they call us passengers – to be allowed to see.

As you can imagine, since the MOB, as we so casually call it, the ship has been a hotbed of gossip. Basically: did she fall – or was she pushed? I have some thoughts about that, based on something I happened to see a few nights ago. I tried telling the captain about this, but he didn't seem interested. Then there's this English crime writer guy on the ship who fancies himself as a bit of a private dick. I told him too, but he doesn't seem that bothered either. So now I'm feeling a bit stymied. It's not as if there's any police on board this ship. So my question to you guys is: should I just let this lie or what?

We are stopping in Freetown, Sierra Leone, tomorrow, for a day's excursion. So I guess I could report to the police there. But whose business is it really that I saw the female victim, the night before she died, snogging one of the senior crew members?

Nothing like sharing! Had Sadie forgotten that she and he had become Facebook friends? The post had already garnered fifty-four 'likes' and twenty-nine comments, including five 'Wow!'s. Sadie's friends, scattered around the globe, were adamant that she should do something. Three thought she should contact the police as soon as they docked in Sierra Leone. You have to, Sade. I can't believe the cruise line aren't taking this seriously. One had even posted the FBI's contact details for her. I'll do it, hon, if it's too hard to call from there and no one else will.

More important than that, from Francis's point of view: she was sticking to her story. Would she really post a fib based on jealousy – or whatever – online like that?

SEVENTEEN

At three o'clock, as most of the guests were snoozing after lunch, Viktor came on the tannoy to tell them that there would be an important passenger announcement at five p.m. in the Panorama Lounge. When the time came, Francis followed the other guests upstairs to find the expedition leader at a lectern, pulling nervously at those bushy, greying sideburns of his.

'I'm very sorry to report, folks,' he told the hushed guests, 'that there has unfortunately had to be a change to the itinerary for tomorrow. We will not be stopping in Sierra Leone.'

A public health warning had just yesterday been issued about a suspected new case of Ebola, he went on, as a gasp was heard in canon across the room. It was in a rural district, but there was no way that Goldencruise could now take the risk of docking at Freetown.

'Though "dock",' Viktor continued, 'is probably not the right word, as we usually anchor offshore and make landfall in the Zodiacs. I really am so sorry that we cannot do that tomorrow, because Sierra Leone is one of my favourite destinations. It's very poor, yes. In fact, it ranks number 177 out of 187 in the UN human development index. But the spirit of the people is wonderful. Especially considering all they've been through in recent years.'

'But we're not going,' heckled a passenger, 'so why harp on about it?'

The accent was Australian. Francis looked over to see Derek, with his lizard wife sitting loyally beside him, tonight in a frock of electric turquoise. Noelene's mouth was a downward curve, highlighted crimson.

'I'm sorry,' Viktor replied. 'This is really not a situation we could have foreseen. As I said at the very start, when we set off from Cape Town, and again to those guests who joined us at Tema, Africa is always unexpected. That is part of the adventure we are on.'

'Not much of an adventure if we're stuck on this ship for another two days,' Derek interrupted.

'Once again, sir, I can only apologize. But these really are circumstances beyond our control.'

The scheduled visit to Banana Island was also cancelled, Viktor continued, as that was just to the south of the Freetown peninsular and geographically part of Sierra Leone. The good news was, however, that the *Golden Adventurer* would be able to press on with the rest of the itinerary and stop, in just under twelve hours, ahead of schedule, at the Bijagos Archipelago in Guinea-Bissau.

'Bijagos is a most beautiful and unspoilt area, and we will still be able to visit the traditional village that we have been to before, which I can promise you is more remote than anything you have yet seen, apart, perhaps, from the pygmies in the rainforests of Cameroon. Last year it was mentioned as the highlight of many of our guests' trips. And because of the cancellation of Freetown, we can spend a little longer out there, and have plenty of time too for our birding trip in The Gambia. For those of you twitchers on board, and even the non-twitchers, the birding is spectacular on the Gambie River. Isn't that right, Leo?'

'It certainly is!' cried the Nigerian, flashing a wide white smile, and holding up a balled fist.

'So how do you know that there isn't any Ebola in this Bijagos place?' came an American voice. It was Candy, with Bruce beside her.

Viktor replied with tact and patience, pointing out that the Bijagos Archipelago was three hundred kilometres north of Freetown and in any case well out to sea, and that there had been no incidence of Ebola at all, ever, on the mainland of Guinea-Bissau. But Candy was not happy. Nor Bruce. The strange mood of disbelief and frustration spread. On the one hand, the guests didn't want to have the trips they had been looking forward to removed from the itinerary; on the other, they didn't – absolutely did *not* – want to be exposed to anything even potentially dangerous. It was one thing to have a look at these exotic, impoverished societies close up; to take photos of the bizarre costumes and well-toned bodies; to enjoy the trees and flowers and birdlife and animals, the sumptuous empty coastline; and then to go home and boast about how adventurous you had been. It was another thing to risk being made ill.

Had it been wise, Francis wondered, watching the protest as it got exponentially noisier, to keep this briefing until the formal cocktail hour? Many of the guests had been boozing all day. But that of course was one thing that Viktor could never say: 'You were drinking margaritas in the spa pool this morning, wine at lunch, beers and more spirits in the sun all afternoon, and now you're back on the cocktails. If I may respectfully suggest, sir, madam, you are arseholed.'

Francis wasn't really in the mood for dinner. There was part of him that wanted to retreat to his cabin, order a club sandwich, watch a film and please Hentie by finally opening his personal bottle of vintage champagne. But that needling curiosity of his won out. Even though he had pretty much given up on the idea of trying to help the ship's authorities with their Operation Rising Star, he couldn't resist hearing what the guests had to say. Were they all angry, or had the meeting just heard the most vocal? And how many of those were, under this surface discontent, suspicious? Did they believe Viktor? Had Klaus been telling tales? Apart from the MOB, how much else did they *know*?

So he followed the shuffling couples out past the ever-smiling cocktail waiters and down to the restaurant at the back of deck four. There was a strong swell tonight, so progress was slow, as people used the gleaming brass rail to help them down the stairs, trying not to topple into each other, though inevitably this was happening too. Were they that much further out to sea, Francis wondered, or was there a storm coming?

At the entrance to the restaurant, he waited alone in the queue that backed up from the maître'd's welcome desk. Gregoire was standing to one side, looking box fresh in his white jacket, his four gold stripes gleaming on his shoulder. His smiles to the guests looked particularly insincere tonight, or was that just Francis's imagining?

'Nice to see you again, Tom.' It was Henry Forbes-Harley, his childlike grin wreathing his face. As Daphne stepped forwards Francis held up a hand. There was really no need for her to correct the poor old fellow yet again.

'And you, Henry,' he replied.

'So what d'you make of all of this then? Sudden resurgence of E-*bo*-la.' He pronounced the 'bo' with mocking emphasis. 'Sounds unlikely to me.'

'I'm sure it's kosha,' Francis replied.

'Who's issuing the warning? The World Health Organization? I'm sure they'd have told us if it was. You want to know my opinion? I think it's got something to do with this woman that fell off the ship. *If* she fell off. Who's to say?' He leaned in close to Francis. 'A lot of people get fed up with their wives after a number of years.'

'Henry!' Daphne cut in. 'We need to take our seats.'

Henry rolled his eyes. 'And where best to get shot of the old bitch than on a cruise ship?' he went on, lowering his voice as he leant close to Francis. 'The cruise line doesn't give a damn what happens. As long as they get their money. They make you sign a piece of paper that shields them from class action lawsuits. Did you know that? Most of these idiots don't even read the small print.'

'Henry! Please, come *along*.'

Henry winked at Francis and wagged a finger. 'More to talk about, Tom. See you later in the bar?'

Poor Henry. He had clearly been as sharp as a razor once upon a time. But no way would Daphne allow him up to the bar after dinner. It was five courses and then beddy-byes for him. He watched the old man and his wife being taken by Gregoire to join a table full of other septua-, octo- and possibly nonagenarians.

'Mr Meadowes, sir,' said James the head waiter. 'Are you dining alone or would you like company tonight?'

'Company, thank you.'

'Follow me.'

James led off across the crowded room. Over the far side, by a wall of curtained portholes, there was one place left at a table for seven; it was between Carmen and Sadie. Also at the table were Aunt Marion, Klaus, Leo and Colonel Joe.

'Good evening, all,' he said.

Taking his seat, he smiled at Carmen, then turned to Sadie. Things might be awkward if he didn't deal with her immediately. After all, the last time he had seen her, those elegantly varnished fingers of hers had been curled around his cock.

'Hey,' she said quietly.

'Nice to see you, Sadie.'

'I'm glad it is. Sorry about last night. I was a bit tipsy.'

Was it only last night? It felt like a week ago. Sadie, at any rate, seemed to have recovered her equilibrium. She was drinking, but not with the desperation, the abandon she'd displayed then. She seemed altogether calmer, more dignified.

'We're both grown-ups,' he said.

'Let's hope so.' She leant towards him and raised an eyebrow. 'D'you believe this Ebola bollocks?'

'You clearly don't.'

'The WHO declared the country free of the disease over a year ago. Why should there suddenly be a resurgence now?'

'Don't you think it's possible . . .?'

'Possible, yes. But this is nothing to do with that. Goldencruise just don't want even the slightest risk of meddling authority. Who knows what might happen during eight hours in port?'

'But Freetown isn't a port,' Francis said, 'from what I understand. They don't even dock.'

'If people are landing, customs officials still have to come on board. You only need one passenger – or crew member – to step out of line and say something and they could have a load of Sierra Leonean police pitching up. Trundling round the ship looking for evidence. Not letting the captain sail on. Can you imagine that?'

She had no clue, Francis realized, that he'd seen her Facebook post. As long as he didn't post anything new himself in the next couple of days, it was unlikely that she would remember they were now 'friends'. Maybe she would post again. Paradoxically, he was more likely to learn what she was really thinking that way than by asking direct questions sitting right next to her.

'So what do you reckon, Francis, to this Ebola story?' It was Colonel Joe, his pudgy features crimson with excitement. He leaned forward over the table and took a hearty gulp of his Merlot.

'I know *vat* I think,' said Klaus, turning to Sadie with a courtly twinkle.

But the colonel's question had clearly been rhetorical. Wiping his lips with the back of his hand, he ploughed on. It was clear to him, he said, that the captain didn't want any contact with the land for operational reasons. 'This so-called new case all seems a bit convenient to me. Why didn't we hear about it before? If I'd used a trick like that when I was in the military, to justify the cancelling of an operation, no one would have taken me seriously. These people think that because they've got a boatload of civvies they can get away with it. But I'm telling you, it's hogwash. Hogwash,' he said again, as if the repetition made it truer.

Cue Carmen. She had been leaning forward waiting her turn. Starting a sentence of protest and getting cut off several times. Repeated 'buts' now ended with a 'Colonel, *please*'.

She had to defend the captain, she continued. With all due respect, this warning was for real. She had seen the printouts in the doctor's office. Goldencruise was reluctantly doing what it had to do.

Even as the conversation grew freer, the ship started to pitch. The waiters were doing a sterling job, balancing expertly on the rocking floor as they hurried back and forth with sorbets and main courses and puddings and cheese. A surreal sense of urgency had taken over. Could they get the five courses over and done with before it became impossible to serve any longer?

It seemed that they could, though there was, right at the end of the meal, one mighty lurch that sent plates sliding across tablecloths, while several glasses toppled and spilt their contents. Excited shrieks followed; the immediate mayhem was providing a distraction from the deeper unease.

Meanwhile, as Francis watched and listened to the general round-the-table badinage, it dawned on him that Sadie's romantic interest had moved on to Leo. Whenever the Nigerian spoke, her eyes shone. If he was making a serious point, she hung, patiently, on his words; if he made a joke, she tittered loudly, a tinkling American counter-point to his rumbling African laughter. How far things had gone, Francis couldn't help but wonder. Whatever, he himself had clearly been left behind. The neediness that she had displayed towards him last night had vanished. God help him, but this easy poise made her attractive again, to the point where he was almost regretting his rapid exit from her room.

When dinner was over, there was a general move towards the bar. The rough sea had encouraged the idea of a drink. Klaus was recommending brandy as a stomach settler. If Leo was up for a *digestif*, Sadie certainly was. As she followed the herpetologist up the circular stairwell, head tilted in to his, she was all but holding his hand. Aunt Marion stepped behind, in yellow suede shoes, a redundant chaperone.

Francis decided to leave them all to it. Up on deck six he pushed open the solid metal door to the Whirlpool Bar with some difficulty. It slammed behind him, almost catching his fingers.

Outside it was wild. The water in the central spa pool sloshed from side to side, splashing out on to the deck as it had when the ship had turned for the MOB. Francis paced carefully over to the rails at the back, held them tight against the wind, gusts so strong in his face it felt as if they could have thrown him toppling back on to the deck. The ship's wake had vanished among the mighty blue-black waves. You could only glimpse the horizon here and there. High above, dancing through racing clouds, the moon was waning, but still all-but full. Its strong light picked out the foaming white crests like the T-shirts of dancers at a disco.

Up on deck seven it was crazier. A propellor attached to a weather vane was turning so fast it seemed it should surely spin off. The orange covers of the lifeboats, though tightly tied, flapped madly. Francis clutched the rails and stared out. This was near where Lauren had stood. And yes, if you had wanted to end it, it would have been easy enough. To climb over. Hang for a moment in a final decision before letting go and plummeting down the long smooth side, past the three rows of lighted portholes and the black hull beneath. Perhaps that was all it had been. Suicide. Lauren should have waited for this weather.

He jumped. There was a hand on his shoulder. He spun round. It was Ray, right in his face. He tensed himself. *Is this the killer?* He looked for a blade; sprung-loaded, he was ready to disarm him.

But: 'Sir! Sir!' the crewman was yelling. 'I must talk to you.'

Ray pulled Francis over to the shelter of an oval funnel in the centre of the deck.

'Yes. What?' Francis shouted back. He kept his distance, watching the crewman closely, in case this was a trick.

Ray leant in, till his mouth was right by Francis's ear. 'My friend *did* tell me something,' he shouted. 'George. George Dim-a-gi-ba.'

'Yes, what? What did George tell you?'

Francis's words were swept away by the wind.

'You must not tell captain.'

'OK.'

'Or first officer.'

'OK.'

'Or any – of – *them*. Please, sir. This just for you. I am scared.'

Francis looked in the man's face and saw that he was. He took his hands, held them firmly between his. Partly to reassure him, partly, still, yes, for safety. 'OK. You can trust me,' he yelled in his ear.

'They will kill me. If they know what I know.'

'Know – what?'

'George did see – someone,' Ray shouted back. 'From up on lifeboat, sir. With drunk lady.'

'Who was it?'

'He didn't know, sir.'

'A crew member – or a passenger?'

'No one he knew from crew, sir. This man not in boiler suit uniform, sir. Nor staff uniform. He was in long trousers, sir. And shirt with flowers, George said.'

'Shirt with flowers . . .'

'Yes, sir. And not old, sir. Young and strong. With yellow hair. He tipped her.'

'Tipped her?'

'Over railings. Like that.'

Ray gestured with both hands, an evocative circular movement.

'OK,' said Francis, nodding slowly. 'Anything else?'

'No, sir. That was all he said.'

'He definitely said "yellow hair"?'

'Yes, sir. Sorry for this, sir. I had to say to someone. But not to captain. Captain is angry if I say.'

'Why?'

'He would not like this story, sir. Better she went suicide. Easier for him. And the rest of them. And the big company. Who employ us. You understand.'

'I understand.'

'Please, sir, don't say I tell you.'

'No. Of course not.'

He was gone. Like a dark wraith, streaking through the shadows towards the *Crew Only* door at the far end. Francis saw a flash of electric light, as the door opened and closed, then he was alone in the blue-white moonlight.

EIGHTEEN

Bijagos Archipelago, Guinea-Bissau. Thursday 27 April.

The ship pitched and tossed through the night. Francis pitched and tossed with it, wondering about young strong passengers with flowery shirts and 'yellow hair'. If it were true that that's what George had seen, and not some kind of mad Chinese whispers, this threw his previous theorizing right up in the air. Because what *passenger* – apart from Klaus – would have managed to get downstairs to bump off George? And Klaus was strong enough, sure, but young, certainly not; nor was he blond (unless he had come prepared with a wig).

So who?

Well, Don was a regular wearer of flowery shirts, but he was neither young nor blond. Francis had seen him once in the gym, but did this mean he was strong enough to tip poor Lauren over the edge in the firm way indicated? So how close had George been? Could he have been mistaken about the hair colour? Why mention it, if so?

Who else? Brad and Damian were relatively young, and certainly strong, but neither were blond, and what in any case could possibly be their motive? They had never, to his knowledge, spoken to Eve, and were no more than drinking buddies with Lauren. The Australian with the lizard wife was another one who favoured flowery shirts, but his hair was white. Nor by any stretch of the imagination could you say he was young or strong. There were other guests Francis could eliminate. Henry Forbes-Harley was way too old – and white-haired too. Colonel Joe was bald. Neither would be seen dead in a flowery shirt.

Gregoire was young, strong, and yes, undeniably, blond. Francis had never seen him in a flowery shirt, but that was not to say he didn't wear one off-duty. Ditto Viktor. But neither of them were passengers. Was it possible that George, who operated way below stairs, could have mistaken them for guests? Or not known they were staff? Mike also fitted the description, but could Francis see that nice, easy, straightforward young man as a murderer? In one of his books, he might well have been, because he was so above suspicion. But in life as it really was? No. Surely not. And if so, why? Why, why, why?

Eventually he fell asleep, waking some time later with the persistent sting of a full bladder. The moonlight was still shining through the half-drawn curtains, but the sea seemed to have calmed a little. Just a gentle rocking motion now. He swung his legs out of bed, pulled back the curtains, and looked out. The waves were half, a third of the size of earlier. The white crests fewer. The storm had passed; or else they had steamed through it.

He eventually found the light switch for the little bathroom. He peed carefully into the rocking bowl, watching his tired features in the mirror. A restful cruise, with plenty of time to think and write. Pah!

He woke his sleeping laptop and clicked on to an Internet session to check his emails. As yet, nothing from the Supreme Court of New South Wales. Nor any of the American probate repositories. Well, what had he expected? An immediate response?

He returned to the smooth, starched sheets. Hentie's little flannel rabbit was beside him on the pillow. He held it tight, like a child, to calm his racing mind.

When he woke again the light from outside was pink on the curtains. It was the rumble of the anchor going down that had disturbed him. He got out of bed and looked out, to see the huge red disc of the sun perched an inch above the horizon, surrounded by a flaming trail of crimson and yellow clouds. It was almost six forty-five a.m. He checked his email again, but there was nothing new except junk.

At seven thirty the parasols were already up on the Whirlpool Bar deck and John-since-1972 was standing ready to serve breakfast in his cream blazer. Two others had beaten Francis to it. Mike, who smiled and waved; and – well, well – Don, who didn't. The old man was wearing his trademark dark blue baseball cap, and under that . . . a beautiful flowery shirt. This one had yellow blooms and twining green leaves on a background as blue as the sky.

Beyond, the sea was sunlit and totally calm. On the starboard side of the ship, towards the horizon, there was land. Long, low-lying islands, bleached to a pale green in this shimmeringly bright sunlight. The jungle vegetation petered out into rocky points strung with the tiny silhouettes of palm trees.

Francis went inside to fetch his starter: white melon, yellow banana, purple passion fruit, orange paw-paw. He ordered coffee and an omelette-with-everything.

He sliced his fruit into little cubes and forked these up one by one into his mouth. Over the deck Don was tackling what looked like a full English breakfast: sausages, eggs, bacon, the works. Was there an equivalent in the good ol' US of A? The full American? Without looking too obviously in his direction, Francis watched the old man's mouth working, that baggy jaw chewing carefully, eyes down. What was that face? A man who had murdered his rich, neurotic partner and had – so far – got away with it? Or a man who was stoically consumed with grief for the bright, beautiful younger woman he had loved from the first time he had seen her?

It was brave of him to come out and sit in a public place where he was bound, if he stayed, to be offered sympathy, if not asked questions. On the other hand, perhaps he'd had enough of being cooped up in his cabin. Perhaps he'd decided he would join today's excursion and to hell with it. For a collector of remote places, Bijagos was surely up there. An archipelago in a country that few outside West Africa had ever heard of. Guinea-Bissau.

'Morning Francis!' It was Mike, holding a mug of tea. 'Looking foward to Bijagos?' He gestured towards the distant land mass.

'I am.'

'It'll be good to get our feet back on dry land. That was quite a storm last night.'

'It all seemed over very quickly.'

'We powered through it. As our captain likes to. It was heading south anyway. Lucky we didn't try and stop at Freetown, as it happened. With waves like that we'd probably not even have made landfall.'

'And today. When do we disembark?'

'That'll depend on the tide. We'll be sending out a recce soon to have a look at the state of the channels. We need a high tide to get all the way up there. Should be OK with this full moon. Means it's springing. But you never know until you have a look.

The mud may have shifted since last year. Anything's possible out here.'

Mike sat down and leaned forward. 'I see you've got company,' he said quietly.

Francis made a warning face. 'I expect there'll be plenty of others out soon.'

'I meant . . .'

'I know what you meant,' said Francis. 'Tra la la la,' he sang. 'Tell me more about Bijagos.'

Mike took his point. 'You'll love it,' he said. 'It's an awesome place.'

'What's an awesome place?' It was Carmen, with a heaped bowl of muesli.

'Bijagos, of course,' said Mike.

'Awesome is actually the word, mate,' she said, sitting down. 'I think of everywhere on this cruise, it was my favourite destination last year.'

'Mine, too,' said Mike. 'Apart, maybe, from the pygmies.'

'Maybe I'm too close to them,' Carmen said. 'You know, there's unspoilt Africa and unspoilt Africa. For whatever reason, there's no sense of envy out here in Bijagos. The villagers are genuinely pleased to see us. To welcome us as strangers. In lots of places in the undeveloped world you take out a digital camera and people give you a scowl.'

'They've had too many visitors,' said Mike. 'The novelty's worn off.'

'Perhaps they just want a bit of what we've got,' said Francis, 'if we're going to come and gawp at them, like they're animals in a zoo.'

'Totally get that,' said Mike.

'But here,' Carmen said, 'as you'll see later, they're lining up to have their picture taken. Children mostly, but adults too. And when they see themselves on your little screen they're thrilled. Leaping up and down with excitement. But it's not as if they want us to give them the cameras. Or even send them the pictures. Though I happen to know that Leo has brought a special present this year.'

'I've seen it,' said Mike. 'Brilliant.'

'In addition to the usual pens and notepads,' Carmen explained to Francis, 'they're getting a collection of laminated portraits, from photos that Leo took last year.'

'Nice touch,' said Francis. Across the deck, Don had finished his breakfast. Francis watched him stop to say something to John-since-1972. Then he turned and made his way along the outside gangway, his left hand gripping the rail as he walked.

'The old man's gone,' said Mike. 'D'you think he'll dare to show his face again?'

'Why shouldn't he?' said Carmen.

'Isn't he, like, the chief suspect?'

'Mike!' said Carmen. 'Lauren was his partner of many years. He's shocked and grieving.'

'Shocked that he's suddenly come into so much money,' laughed Mike. 'Hasn't he? Everyone knows the story now. "Chumba Chumba Cha-Cha." How many squillions has that made over the years? I'm surprised the captain hasn't stuck him in the ship's jail.'

'Mike, this is very loose talk,' said Carmen. 'Nobody knows what happened to Lauren.'

The young man shrugged and got to his feet. 'They can have a pretty good guess,' he said. 'Anyway, I've got a recce to be getting on with.' He headed over to the steps down to the back of the deck below, where the Zodiacs were kept. 'Laters!' he called cheerily.

Francis waited for him to be out of earshot. 'So Mike has no idea about Eve?' he said.

'Luckily not. Nor about George. Christ knows what he'd be saying if he did. There's a good reason for not briefing all the expedition staff about everything.'

For a moment Francis wondered if he should tell Carmen about Ray, George and the young, blond passenger with the flowery shirt. At one level, it would be good to share. But he didn't trust her not to immediately pass on whatever he said to Viktor, Alexei and the captain. And that would in no way be fair to poor Ray, who for whatever misguided reason had trusted him, and him alone, with his precious and dangerous secret.

'Did you manage to sleep OK?' she asked.

'Yes, pretty well, thanks.'

'You're not one to get seasick?'

'No. I'm lucky like that.'

'Me neither. I'm not sure I could do this job if I did. Some of the passengers suffer dreadfully.'

This desultory exchange petered off into silence. There was no doubt that a certain caginess had descended between them.

'So how long is the expedition today?' Francis asked.

'Because of the tides we can only stop for two or three hours. Which is a shame. But that's all part of the experience. It's intense.'

'And then it's on to the Gambia. And the remarkable birdwatching.'

'Yes. Leo will be in his element.'

'And finally Dakar. Where the FBI and the Bahamian police will be waiting. What are you and the captain planning to tell them?'

Carmen laughed out loud; then looked at him levelly, the lines around her eyes crinkling with amusement.

'Are you still upset with me?'

'No. Not particularly. I just got the strong feeling, I suppose, that you'd got what you wanted from me.'

'What exactly did I do wrong, mate? I told Viktor that we'd got nothing out of Ray. He knew we were interviewing him. He was bound to ask, and I was bound to answer.'

'Did you have to share our reservations with him?'

'About Ray? Why not?'

'And with the captain too?'

'I don't understand you, Francis. We're all in this together.'

'I thought you'd agreed with me that it was possible that Viktor or the captain were maybe part of the puzzle.'

'Ah, come off it! Viktor may be many things: a philanderer, a man who thinks he is cleverer and more interesting than he is, the possessor of a dodgy ponytail, but he's not a murderer. Nor is the captain.'

'Or his surly sidekick?'

'Come off it. The security officer as the murderer, that would be novel. No, he's just a useless stooge. Anyway, how do I know that you're sharing every last observation or speculation you have with me?'

'You don't,' said Francis, with a somewhat forced laugh.

'Good morning. I hope I am not interrupting some important pow-wow?'

It was Klaus. For once Francis was glad to see the German. He was carrying a plate of salami and cheese and a cup of black coffee.

'Good German breakfast,' Francis observed.

Carmen had got to her feet. 'I'll see you later, Francis. On the boats.'

'Ah, yes,' said Klaus. 'I am looking forward greatly to our little excursion. I have been feeling a bit – how-to-say – boxed up on this ship. Wondering if I was ever going to put foot on dry land again.'

He followed Carmen's sashaying backside with his eyes. 'Such a pity,' he said, turning back towards Francis with that familiar provocative glint in his eye.

'I'm sorry, I'm not with you. What's a pity?'

'That Hastings bats – as you say with your *vunderful* English cricketing metaphor – for the other side.'

Francis eyeballed him. 'You mean . . .'

'She's of the Sapphic persuasion. Her island is Lesbos. I had wondered for a while, because even though I am fully aware I am past the age when I might attract the gentler sex with my physique, rather than my brain, I was not getting any vibrations from her at all, if you follow me. And even your flashing-eyed Jewish admirer was giving me the occasional frisson.'

'Sadie?'

'Of course.'

'No longer my admirer. Perhaps you hadn't noticed, Klaus, but she's moved on.'

'Has she? I don't think so.' He chuckled. 'She's playing the long game with you, my friend. Pretending to be enamoured of the Nigerian bird expert to excite a little envy in the English gentleman.'

'Don't be ridiculous.'

'I am older than you. I am out of the game. I can see these things. He is too much of a how-to-say geek for her.'

'So what makes you think Carmen . . .?'

'As I say, I had my suspicions. And then, last night, I went for a breath of fresh air in that magnificent storm and I saw them.'

'Them?'

'Hastings and her girlfriend. There was no mistaking it, I'm afraid. Pressed up against a funnel at the back of deck seven. I don't imagine they thought anyone else would be out there that late in that weather.'

'Doing what?'

'What lovers do. If I were less politically correct, I might have said that it would have been enjoyable to have been wedged between them.'

Klaus twinkled roguishly, but Francis wasn't going to humour him. Even as he asked his next question, he knew the answer. 'And who is this girlfriend?'

'That pretty doctor. I don't imagine her culture is particularly forgiving of her inclinations either. That may be one reason she likes to travel.'

NINETEEN

Early afternoon. The sun was glinting brilliantly on the water as the guests made their way down the steps from the Whirlpool Bar and on to the Zodiac area at the back of deck four. Some were in shorts, some in loose trousers, some in skirts. On their heads they wore everything from bog-standard baseball caps to Daphne's magnificent floppy straw hat, which made her look as if she were going to a wedding in New England rather than a remote village on an island off Guinea-Bissau. They all had the tubelike grey lifejackets slung round their necks and tied tight around their waists. Most were also wearing or holding the little black Adventurer backpacks, which had a pocket on each side for a standard aluminium water bottle.

Francis was excited. He had returned from breakfast and his chat with Klaus to find an email waiting for him from the probate authorities in Illinois with a copy of the will he'd asked for attached. Once he'd read that, a busy morning had followed, as he'd chased around the Internet to pursue the hare that had now been unleashed. So well had things gone that he'd been tempted to skip the Bijagos outing and get his case completely watertight before taking his findings to a higher authority.

But a couple of hours wasn't going to make that much difference, was it? Everyone on the expedition team had told him how amazing the archipelago was. They were landing on a remote island and then returning to ship, so no one was going anywhere. More important, in the informal atmosphere of the excursion he might get a chance to double-check his suspicions with the reality.

As they passed down the steps and along the deck the passengers' identification cards were slid by another po-faced Asian crew member into a reader attached to a laptop. For a moment their grinning, solemn or perplexed mugshots filled the screen, then they were allowed through. For trips like this, *Golden Adventurer* counted them out and they counted them back. Just to make sure they didn't leave anyone stranded in the jungle. As long as they were still alive, they were still valued customers.

The expedition team were waiting in the Zodiacs, which were grouped in a loose circle around the embarkation steps, which ended a couple of feet above the heaving surface of the sea. Mike, Carmen, Leo, Viktor and the others, each standing at the back of an inflatable, hand on the throttle of a powerful outboard motor. As each of these bobbing craft filled up and moved off, another came in to the steps where two wiry crew members in brown boiler suits were ready to help the next lot of guests on board.

There were about twelve to a boat. Francis found himself stepping down into Carmen's Zodiac, just behind the redoubtable Daphne, who was as ever urging on her husband.

'That's it, Henry. Attaboy!'

Henry, meanwhile, had fixed Francis with that familiar look; of someone who has spotted, after a long while, an old and favourite friend.

'Now *you*,' he said, waving an enthusiastic finger. 'Didn't we meet you on the Antarctica cruise? At Christmas? Tom, wasn't it?'

'It's Francis, honey,' said Daphne. 'Fran-*ciss*. He joined us on *this* cruise. Not the Antarctic. He wasn't *on* the Antarctic cruise.'

'Wasn't he?' Henry seemed taken aback. 'We've met before,' he said, 'I'm sure of that.'

'On *this* cruise, sweetheart. You met Francis on this cruise.'

'Did I?'

The old man seemed cheered now. You had to hand it to Daphne. She was dutiful, devoted even with her constant corrections, though that understandable edge of impatience wasn't far behind.

Others were bundling on. Sebastian in an embroidered African smock, long bell-bottomed maroon trousers and pale blue reef shoes; his stocky boyfriend neat in starched khaki beside him.

'Good morning!' the designer called in Daphne and Francis's direction. 'What a relief to be getting off the bloody vessel for a bit. I am *so excited* about this village.' Kurt followed silently in his wake, his features impassive as ever. As he plonked his substantial backside on the fat plastic tube that made up the boat's side, the whole craft rocked visibly.

Next up were Brad and Damian, in identical white singlets and blue shorts, which showed off their muscled physiques to fine effect.

'Afternoon boys!' called Sebastian.

'Good afternoon, Sebastian,' Brad returned, a little coolly.

Shirley and Gerald were next.

'D'you mind sitting this side?' Carmen asked Shirley tactfully. The craft sank several inches in the water, but she and Kurt were now balancing it beautifully.

The last pair down the steps were Bruce and Candy. They took their places opposite Shirley and Gerald.

'Hiya, folks!' said Bruce, who clearly wasn't going to be fazed by any hostility from the critical Brits.

There was only Leo's Zodiac to fill and then they were off. It was no surprise to Francis that Sadie had somehow engineered to be in that boat, up by the tiller in knee-length cut-off jeans and a flowery bikini top, surely not the ideal costume for a visit to a remote island village. And whatever Klaus thought, the devoted looks she was giving the driver of her little craft spoke volumes.

The flotilla of seven boats raced across the gentle swell towards the low green line of the islands. Nobody spoke. It was enough just to feel the rushing sunlit air on your face and look out over the sea, shimmering silver-gold under the sun. The mother ship receded to a tiny silhouette, the island shore grew more distinct. Soon they were entering a channel between banks of mangroves: low, dusty green trees with their dense tangle of leafless brown stems just above the waterline. The boats slowed, the engines reverted to a purr, above which could now be heard the cries of circling birds. Damian's paparazzo lens was out again. He half-stood, knees bent as he clicked away furiously at his visual prey.

After twenty minutes or so they came round a corner to a muddy little beach below a tall tree with a thick trunk spreading out to branches which made for a shady canopy. In the sunlit foreground, a couple of long wooden canoes lay stranded, face down, on scattered stones.

There was a welcoming committee of small boys, some squatting on the hulls of the boats, others standing on the beach. Most wore long trousers and T-shirts, a few had shorts, one pair a brilliant yellow. Some of the tinier ones had nothing but tight pants, above which belly buttons protruded on skinny frames. There were a couple of adults there too, to greet the expedition team. Francis wondered if they had mobile phones out here, or perhaps the whole visit had been set up this morning on Mike and Viktor's recce.

The guests disembarked, clambering over the sides of each

inflatable and on to the stony mud along a portable landing stage made up of three or four low black plastic boxes.

Carmen's boat was fifth, and by that stage, the first groups of visitors had walked up past the big tree and on along a narrow path into the forest.

Viktor and Mike stood in the shade, arms held out, pointing. 'Welcome to Bijagos,' Viktor was saying. 'The village is two hundred yards up this track. Please be careful to stick to the paths and as always in Africa, keep an eye out for snakes. Our last boat out to the ship leaves in three hours, at five o'clock sharp, so make sure you're back on the beach by then, as there is no arguing with the tide, and we wouldn't want to leave you alone on the island. I have heard that the cooking isn't at all bad, but not as delicious as that of Gregoire's amazing team.'

Dry brown leaves crunched beneath the well-shod feet of the guests as they filed inland, eyes down. In a bright clearing, butterflies swooped above tall yellow grass in the sunlit air. Just ahead, one of the boys was waiting for Francis's group. He was naked bar a pair of grubby crimson briefs. He grinned broadly as he rolled a rusty steel hoop in front of him, turning every thirty yards or so to make sure his selected charges were keeping up with him.

'I love these little characters,' said Bruce to Francis. 'Give him half a chance and he'd be running the country.'

As they got closer to the village, they could hear the heavy rhythmic beat of drums. More boys with hoops appeared from left and right. One wore a crimson T-shirt on which was written: *Junior Arctic Aviator – Snow Zone*. Another had a portrait of Barack Obama on his chest, with the very faded strapline *Yes, we can!*.

Suddenly they were there: in a wide clearing stood a series of mud brick rondavels, with conical roofs of low-hung, untrimmed thatch. At the centre of the hard-packed dry earth of the village floor was an enormous tree of who knew what antiquity. Branches as big as trunks spread up from its base, which had a diameter of twenty feet at least. This behemoth cast a wide circle of shade, dark at the centre, dappled with pools of sunlight towards the edge. A long line of teenaged girls was dancing round it in a loose circle, toyi-toying in that effortlessly rhythmic African way. They were wearing Western tops: T shirts or low-cut sleeveless. Their skirts made an African contrast: straw, in two tiers, dyed black, orange and purple, with shell necklaces hung loose around their shimmying waists. Some had bare feet, some colourful flip-flops. A number of the bigger girls also had anklets around their right legs; giant seed pods strung together. What did this signify? That they were already married, taken, promised?

When all the guests had made it up to the village, there was a shout from Viktor. A presentation was now going to be made, he announced, to the – good God! – king, an even older man than the Togoan chief, with rheumy eyes and a sprinkle of white stubble. He was sitting on a low chair to one side of the clearing, extravagantly attired. On his head a patterned oval *kofi* was topped by a khaki felt cowboy hat, with feathers stuck into the leather headband, on which you could just still read the engraved legend *Vegas*. Below, he wore a baggy blue shirt, hung around with scarves and cloths of various bright colours. Next to him, on a mat on the ground, his queen was even more burdened down with fabric, swathed in what looked like a red and white tablecloth, with a patterned yellow and green blanket over her shoulder. Her eyes darted suspiciously from a smoother, younger face. On the top of her head, above a tightly-wound orange scarf, sat an upturned gourd. As in Togo, the king had a taller, younger, beefier henchman to one side, similarly wrapped in cloths and scarves. He wore a battered old pair of crimson Doc Martens and carried a stout stick.

Viktor made a short speech, thanking the king and queen for allowing the *Golden Adventurer*'s guests to visit. The presentation was then made: one box containing colourful cloths (surely coals to Newcastle?), the second the inevitable pens and pads of paper. And this is what we bring you: not a digital camera or video, those magical white man's machines we are all slung around with, but something simple for the children's lessons. Which we must all approve of, of course, education surely being the thing. To lift you out of your colourful poverty and let you approach the elevated world we have called First. Did they even have a generator here? Francis wondered. Or would a gift digi soon run down and be left as a treasured but useless possession?

A wild burst of drumming announced the resumption of the dancing. And now there were new characters, gleaming, muscled young men decked out in theatrical costumes. One wore a dome of reddish-brown straw on his head, from which protruded shiny – and real, it looked like – black horns. More straw circled his neck, with a couple of red and white scarves thrown in for good measure. Wrapped tightly round his bare arms were strips of patterned cloth and a trio of straw pom poms.

Another had a big wooden shark's fin strapped to his back. A cowhide apron was tied to his jiggling bottom over khaki shorts. Below were knee bandannas and elaborate straw anklets.

Others appeared, in equally glorious assortments of straw, cloth, necklaces and other add-ons. One had a wooden model of a naked girl in a red bikini attached to his head. Another wore a full – and horned – cow's head, with a mouth that served as a lookout for his eyes within. Another's face was invisible behind a headdress of fluorescent green, which matched his skirt, but not his crimson Fly Emirates top.

'And so,' said a familiar voice in Francis's ear, '*ze* whiteys stand around, wishing they had this much fun in their lives. But of course they do not. Not legitimately, anyway. The nearest they will get to it is some embarrassing dance at their daughter's wedding.'

It was Klaus, in khaki, with a fluorescent green money belt at his waist, his large excursion bag slung over his shoulder, a compact digi in his right hand.

'You know,' he went on, 'this is an interesting society here. Matriarchal. The women have real power in Guinea-Bissau. They propose marriage to their men by giving them some soup made of fish eyes, and then later if they want to divorce them, they can. These dancing boys here are all about to go off for initiation, which will take them seven years. By the time they get back, the wives they already have will be living with someone else, so they will take another one, and have a second family. If only it were so easy in the West.'

Francis laughed. 'How on earth d'you know all this, Klaus?'

The German tapped his nose. 'I do my research. No point in travelling if you don't understand what you're looking at. Not in my bible anyway.'

'I suppose not.'

'Pretty frightening looking, some of these costumes, don't you think?'

'They are.'

'But little do they realize that it is not they who are the

frightening ones in this case. They are playing at killing. It is we who have the murderer among us.'

'You think?'

'I do.'

Francis looked at him, at that smug but oddly nervous smile playing under the bushy white moustache; at the clear blue-grey eyes that radiated the confidence of a well-off professional but simultaneously craved your attention. Klaus prided himself on being dry and worldly, and after his long career as a surgeon, he had every reason to present himself in that way, but there was still a small boy in there who was trying to please.

'You know who it is?' Francis asked.

'I have my suspicions.'

'Which you want to share with me?'

'Perhaps later. When we are back on the ship. Not here, I don't think. Let sleeping hounds lie. If they are cornered, they might otherwise get savage. Don't you think?' He smiled. 'And you?'

'If and when I have solved this puzzle completely, I promise you will be the first to know.'

'Can I believe that? Maybe you have already solved it.'

'Maybe I have,' Francis replied, looking levelly at him.

'This I like,' said Klaus. 'The famous evasive English sense of humour.'

The drumming around them had reached a crescendo. At the centre of the clearing the shark-man was throwing himself to the ground in a frenzy. One of the guys in straw had mock-stabbed him with his all-too-real spear, and now he was 'dying'. Dust rose up in clouds, sunlit red-brown as it cleared the shadow. The surrounding circle of young women was hunched over, arms out before them, intense in their concentration as they moved their hips.

Around them the guests took it all in in different ways. Many were following the action with their videos and cameras, trying to capture something of this extraordinary spectacle to take home to their families and friends and computers. Damian was diving around with his big lens like a man possessed. Sadie stood beside Leo, talking, laughing, clearly enjoying the scene without feeling the need to record it. Shirley, likewise, was living in the moment, doing her own crazy toyi-toyi with Gerald. Terminal illness, Francis thought, did nothing if not make you unselfconscious.

Just beyond him, Francis noticed a familiar figure leaving the edge of the clearing, pacing away through the huts, looking round nervously from time to time.

'Excuse me,' he said, backing away. Klaus took no offence. He smiled and hoisted up his camera, before heading back into the fray. Francis walked nonchalantly away, past older women and men standing watching from between the thatched huts, wrinkled, bent, with just a tooth or two between them. He picked up speed as he went deeper into the village, catching glimpses through darkened doorways on each side of the different households inside: some cluttered, some as tidy and swept clean as a London show flat. Here and there, thin trails of smoke rose from ashy fires.

He paced on, pretending to be taking photographs as he kept his object in clear view. Scrawny-looking hens clucked around, pecking madly at the dry ground; in front of one little homestead a skinny dog looked up at him with red-rimmed eyes and yelped.

Francis reached the far side of the village, where he lurked by a rondavel, watching and waiting. After five minutes or so, he continued through the undergrowth, under the canopy of tall trees, looking ahead to make sure nobody had spotted him coming, and behind to make sure that no one was following. The drumming was more distant out here, but still loud enough to cover the noise of his footsteps. He took care not to step on any dry branches or leaves that might give away his approach with a crackle or a rustle. At the same time, he kept a careful eye out for snakes. It was all very well to tread quietly, but he didn't want to step on a sleeping puff adder.

After a hundred yards or so he came upon them, sooner than he'd thought he would. The two women were right in front of him, across a small clearing, pressed up against another mighty tree, oblivious in their intimacy. He suddenly felt nervous, wondering what had led him to confirm his suspicions, his burning curiosity, dammit, now, here, of all places. In a very short time, if he didn't duck down or retreat, this was going to upgrade to a confrontation, which could easily be postponed till later, back on the ship, when he would have supporters around him. Maybe, on second thoughts, he would do better to leave his showdown until then . . .

He was about to back away when Carmen turned and saw him.

'What the fuck!' she cried.

The little doctor looked up too, then pulled away from her girlfriend. She looked terrified.

'I'm very sorry to interrupt,' Francis said. 'But I need to talk to you.'

'What are you playing at?' said Carmen, 'following us out here like some peeping Tom?'

'I'm sorry. But I think you know why—'

'Do we?'

The charm had gone; an unsmiling she-wolf was revealed.

'Yes,' said Francis; there was no going back now. 'You've been very clever, covering your tracks, but I'm afraid I can't pretend I don't know any longer who murdered Eve. And then Lauren. And then the poor man who had the misfortune of seeing you with Lauren.'

Carmen laughed, but it was a hollow rattle of a laugh. 'You are – seriously – joking me. Where on earth do you get this mad idea from?'

'I get this mad idea from the fact that Ray, whom we interviewed, was told by his cabin mate George that he'd seen someone with Lauren on the night she went overboard. And not just with her, throwing her over the edge. This person was young, strong, and blond. But no one he knew from staff or crew.'

'So?' said Carmen.

'It was not Gregoire, as I'd originally thought. In any case, George would have known all the officers and cruise staff, uniformed as they are. But being very far below stairs he wasn't perhaps aware of the distinction between a passenger and a member of the expedition staff who slept on the same corridor as the passengers.'

'I'm sorry,' said Carmen, 'I have no idea what you're talking about.'

'Had Ray told me,' Francis continued, 'that George had seen Lauren pushed over by a little old lady with grey hair I would have had my work cut out. But there are no other young strong blonds on the ship. Apart from Mike – and I ruled him out some time ago. This also explained another problem I had, that a passenger couldn't have done away with George, deep down on deck one, where no passengers, except possibly the adventurous German, Klaus, ever go.'

'I don't know where you think you're going with this, mate,' said

Carmen. 'But I had absolutely nothing to do with George's death. For Christ's sake, I was with you when he was murdered.'

'Of course you were. Setting yourself up with a foolproof alibi. The murder was the work of your accomplice, also your girlfriend, the medical expert who knows all about poisons and carries the snake antivenoms with her on all expeditions. Wasn't it, Alyssa?'

The doctor's dark eyes darted sideways at her companion. She wasn't a great actress. 'This is ridiculous,' she said. 'What makes you think . . .? This makes no sense at all.'

'I'm afraid it makes perfect sense. That the doctor, who has access to all the drugs she could want or need, could find a way of sedating George, before injecting him with snake venom, through the single hole that I observed in his ankle.'

Alyssa was doing her best to look outraged. 'As I told you,' she stuttered, 'there were two incisions—'

'Don't bother,' Francis cut in. 'I know an injection mark when I see one. More to the point, you were also responsible for kicking the whole sequence off by murdering Eve, whose only crime was to be rich and old and trusting. You told me yourself how much you liked her, Alyssa. What good friends you were. And she told me the same thing. How the staff were like family to her. You had been close for more than one cruise, hadn't you? She was in the Antarctic at Christmas, and also in Greenland last summer. The caring doctor was on both those trips, looking after her elderly guests, making friends, lining up the next victim, one of the ones who would return.'

'Francis, really,' said Carmen, and now, with a brittle laugh, the charm had returned. 'When we were working together, trying to solve this mystery for the captain, I thought you were pretty sharp. But now, mate, I'm sorry, you seem to have lost it. Yes, Alyssa and I are lovers, and I'm sure you understand why it's easiest if we keep that relationship a secret. There's always gossip on a ship – and although we are supposed to be living in the twenty-first century, a lot of the attitudes onboard are pretty unreconstructed. If all the crew knew we were a couple, it would impact on the way they treat us. I'm sorry to say that, but it's true.'

'I understand that,' said Francis. 'That's one of the reasons I wanted to speak to you alone.'

'But that's where it stops. Really. This idea that either of us is involved in all this is ridiculous. So please, go back to the village, see a bit more of the dancing. Then, when we return to the ship this evening we can review all the evidence and see where we've got to. Not that any of this is your problem any more, because as you may or may not know, the FBI are joining us in Dakar.'

'Yeah, right,' said Francis. 'Bringing with them a crack detective squad from the Bahamas and a couple of DCIs on secondment from the London Met. Pull the other one.'

'It's true,' Carmen replied, but she wasn't convincing.

'This is why I decided to seize the moment and talk to you now,' Francis continued. 'Away from the ship. Because we can still be discreet. It may very well be that this is a puzzle that gets left to other authorities. Or, more likely, glossed over and forgotten, as has happened who knows how many times on cruise ships before. The bodies will be repatriated, as per international medical protocol, and life will go on.'

'Will it?' said Carmen; for a moment she looked relieved, as if she wanted to believe him; and in that relief Francis knew for sure that she was guilty.

'But if that is to happen,' Francis continued, 'I need to understand your motivation. Both of you. Because as far as I can see, your actions were never particularly selfish. In fact, it strikes me that they were imaginatively, even daringly unselfish.'

'How do you mean?' asked Dr Lagip, leaning forward towards him. Her hands were shaking, but there was hunger in her eyes.

'Alyssa,' said Carmen, but her warning note had barely impinged.

'Shall we sit?' said Francis.

It said something, he thought, that the two of them immediately did as he suggested, and in a moment they were all three cross-legged on the dry brown leaves, the dappled shade all around them. He took them through the reasoning that had led to his conclusion. How, as Carmen knew, he had initially thought that it was Gregoire who was Eve's murderer; that he was some kind of Harold Shipman figure, getting wealthy passengers to alter their wills, then quietly bumping them off.

'It was only later,' he went on, 'that I realized I had the right story, but the wrong protagonists. It was you, Alyssa, who was grooming these old and vulnerable people. It was all quite an art, because among the many wealthy guests on each cruise, you had to pick singles, obviously, and also, ideally, those who had no immediate relatives who might kick up a fuss or contest the altered provision of the will. Eve totally fitted the bill. Her husband Alfred was dead. Because she had cared for her mother for all those years, she had never had children. So who had she planned to leave her fortune to? The donkey sanctuary down the road. Poor, mangy, mistreated animals, yes, doubtless, but compared to many of the human horrors you've seen around the world, laughable, not even on the scale. And the sanctuary wasn't likely to question things when the bequest was changed.'

Francis could tell from Alyssa's face that his words were hitting home but she wasn't as yet ready to crack. Neither of them were.

'I have no idea what you are talking about,' she said primly.

'I was initially confused, of course,' Francis went on, 'just as the captain was, just as you meant him to be. Because you had been very clever, drawing attention to any suspicions around the first murder, just to put him and the rest of us off the scent. Of course the lab at Takoradi – of all places – wasn't going to find anything untoward in the autopsy. You knew that. That's why you insisted on it. And once you'd put your foot down about that – and so publicly, and in such a principled way – it was going to be clear to everyone that you also had nothing to do with the other deaths that had taken place on previous cruises. Poor Mr Krugbender in the Antarctic at Christmas. Old Mrs Drew-Huggins on the Ecuador to Chile leg in October. Major Fisher in Longyearbyen last summer.'

'How on earth . . .?' said Dr Lagip with a gasp.

'There's a useful website that has all these deaths registered. Marikit Wyldestone is also there, though that was on a different ship, as you know, Alyssa. But four deaths on the *Golden Adventurer* in just under a year, no wonder the captain was concerned. More significantly, so was Security Officer Alexei. So you decided to call their bluff. Which you did brilliantly.'

'You are one hell of a funny guy, mate,' Carmen said, with a laugh. 'Deaths occur all the time on these ships. The morgue has room for three bodies, d'you want to know why? Sometimes it's not just three a year, but three a cruise.'

'Alyssa has already told me there isn't a morgue,' Francis said.

Carmen looked over at her partner, and then shrugged. 'Whatever. It doesn't affect the numbers. So let me try and get my head around this mad little theory of yours,' she continued. 'Alyssa was "calling the captain's bluff". So she sent out a corpse she had been responsible for murdering *herself* for post-mortem. Is that what you're saying?'

'You know that's what I'm saying.'

'But in that case what exactly did she do to poor Eve? The old lady was lying there intact in bed. She wasn't shot, stabbed, strangled or even, as far as I'm aware, suffocated. There aren't many poisons that escape the analysis of a modern autopsy. There were no marks of an injection there, as I recall. So what did she use? Something by mouth? Some rare African plant that European forensics has yet to be aware of?'

'Good question,' said Francis. 'And one that kept me guessing for a while. I'd actually worked out the method before I realized it was you who'd used it. I thought Gregoire was responsible. But it all ties in. Because you had to come up with something completely undetectable. You needed Eve to have "died of old age".

'Now as the ship's doctor you had all the means at your disposal to quietly do away with someone. A lethal dose of an anaesthaetic like pentobarbitol, perhaps, or an overdose of diamorphine. But painless and easy as both of those would have been, for respectively the patient and you, they would have been picked up, as you say, by a post-mortem. And though that might have worked in the past, when only you were certifying the deaths, that was no good this time, was it?'

'OK, so how did I achieve my perfect murder?' The doctor asked this wryly, joining Carmen in the idea that Francis's whole thesis was a huge joke. But beneath that brave facade, Francis could hear the controlled breathlessness of her delivery. She was desperate to know how much Francis had worked out, and if so what evidence he had.

'When we were standing in Eve's cabin,' Francis went on, 'looking at her body laid out on the bed, there was one odd detail that puzzled me. The champagne bucket on the side, which is not standard issue. Your butler only brings you one if you ask for it. But Eve didn't drink. More than that, she had once been an alcoholic. There's no way she would have wanted any alcohol in her room – so why the bucket?

'It wasn't on the floor, which is probably where it would have been earlier. You'd had time to clear up. You just hadn't seen fit to remove this anomaly. So what, I asked myself, might a champagne bucket have been used for? As I thought about it, and also about other possibilities any murderer might have had at their disposal, it suddenly dawned on me where I'd seen such a container before. Gregoire had used one to pour out the dry ice during the Togoan dance show. Now these solid blocks of carbon dioxide are harmless, of course, in a well-ventilated room. They're used all the time on stage, in the theatre, at rock concerts and so on. And on the night, for this performance, the gas just produced a little coughing among our elderly guests. However. In a sealed room, such as a cabin, with no windows open or able to be open, and the doors airtight also, you would have been able to build up enough carbon dioxide to suffocate poor Eve. And this would have no after effects other than a high level of carbon dioxide in the blood. Which might lead to bloodshot eyes, but is not in itself suspicious.'

'You can't poison someone with carbon dioxide,' said Alyssa. 'You're thinking of carbon monoxide.'

'Good try. But I'm aware of the distinction. Also that carbon dioxide can be a killer too.'

'Let's humour him for a minute, darling,' Carmen said. 'So Alyssa poisoned Eve, just as she had done away with others, you say, on previous cruises. But how on earth did she persuade her to change her will? And what possible proof can you have that she did, given that she's only been dead for four days? Have you been in touch with her solicitors in Malmesbury?'

'In Malmesbury,' repeated Francis. 'Interesting that you knew where Eve lived.'

'Everyone knew she lived in Malmesbury. She was always talking about it.'

'But not to you,' said Francis. 'Because it wasn't you who was Eve's friend, was it? In fact, she barely knew you. Because that was another part of your strategy. Work separately. Your plan would have been altogether too obvious if anyone had realized you were operating together. Or if anyone had picked up on your relationship. Even I hadn't understood that until this morning, when I was told about it by somebody who'd seen you together last night during the storm.'

'Who?' Alyssa cried. Then, as if to cover that half-admission up, she asked, 'What do you mean, "during the storm"?'

'What I say,' said Francis. 'During the storm. You were observed on deck seven together.'

'But it was wild up there,' said Alyssa. 'Who could have wanted to go—?'

'Well, you two, I think, since you knew it was wild up there. I promised not to reveal my source. But when I saw you today, leaving the celebration, Alyssa first, and then, a discreet ten minutes later, you, Carmen, I knew I had to tie everything up by confirming what I'd been told. And here you are. Very much together. I don't think there's any denying that now.'

'We may be dykes,' said Carmen bluntly, 'but we're not murderers. Give us a break.'

'To go back to your earlier question,' Francis said. 'How did I know what was in Eve's will? I didn't. Even if I had known the name of the Malmesbury solicitor, this wasn't information I could get at from here. Until a will is proved, it remains confidential – even the most expert hacker would find it hard to access. However, the completed wills of Mr Krugbender and Marikit Wyldestone were easy to find online. Ditto that of Major Fisher, though even with the fast-track service I haven't had any luck yet with Mrs Drew-Huggins. Not that that matters. Because in among the beneficiaries of these three very different people, from very different parts of the world, was a common one: the Rising Star Trust.'

There was a gasp from Alyssa. Carmen's features didn't move.

'And what or who,' Francis went on, 'was behind this interestingly named charitable foundation? Ten years ago, I would have had to travel to Grand Cayman, where the trust is incorporated, to find out. Now that information is also online. Among the four trustees I discovered this morning is one Dr A. Lagip.'

Alyssa was shaking her head, slowly, from side to side; why, wasn't clear, as it was too late for denial now.

'So what does this Rising Star Trust do?' Francis continued. 'Is it for the personal benefit of Dr A. Lagip, Dr E. Ongongo, Paula Cordoba and Rachel White? Apparently not. Because the credentials of Dr E. Ongongo, for example, are impeccable. He turns out to be an extraordinary character, well-known in central Africa for distributing funds to NGOs and other charitable causes. He has worked not just with Rising Star, but with Bill Gates, Bono, Bob Geldof and Madonna, among others. Paula Cordoba, it appears, has a similar role in Central and South America. And it turns out that one of her Facebook friends is Carmen Contreras, Australian anthropologist, lecturer and expedition leader on cruise ships.

Carmen's face was a picture. A picture, it had to be said, of one whose back was now against the wall.

'How on earth did you discover that?' she breathed.

'All too easy,' said Francis. 'Facebook is hardly a heavily encrypted department of the US military. Completing the team,' he continued, 'is another of Carmen's Facebook pals. Rachel White. Who is, despite her name, a native Australian who works, she tells us on her much-liked page, on projects with Aboriginals in the Northern Territory of Australia, mainly to do with getting them off alcohol and into productive work. Indeed, it appears that she is directly responsible for two model settlements in the Tanami desert, one of which produced Australia's first Paralympic one-legged long jump champion, Bambam Badjalang.'

There was no mistaking the rapid look that passed between Alyssa and Carmen. Francis had them bang to rights.

'So Rising Star is, it seems,' he continued, 'a thoroughly noble enterprise, funding a string of carefully researched charitable projects across the globe. Is that why it's called Rising Star, Alyssa? Because it is leading the way in the fight against international social injustice? Or is there a darker reason? That Operation Rising Star is the code for a dead body on a ship. Or is it both? That here we have a remarkable charity, apparently dedicated to doing good, but funded by the unfortunate victims of a cruise ship doctor who is also a murderer. Is that about the size of it, Alyssa? The ends justify the means?'

Both the doctor and her girlfriend said nothing. From the village came the sound of renewed drumbeats, mixed now with a wonderful wailing African chant.

'Sounds like the ceremony is reaching its climax, doesn't it?' Francis said. 'We'd better get a move on.'

'So how does Lauren fit into your little theory?' Carmen asked. Her brave face had crumbled totally now.

'That was another ongoing puzzle for me, as you knew. Who would want to kill that poor boozy little rich girl Lauren, and why?

It didn't seem as if it was your strategy to pick on more than one victim per cruise. Eve had gone off nicely. So it could only be that Lauren had somehow worked out what you were up to. And why would she have done that? Had one of you been trying to recruit her to the trust, perhaps to persuade her to set up a legacy? She had a big heart, Lauren, and a history of helping charities. You, Carmen, had become quite matey with her and Don, both in the Antarctic and on this cruise. I saw you dine with them – one night I even saw you dancing with her. So had you been unable to resist telling her about the trust, and then been caught out when she realized exactly how the trust worked? She was, by Don's account, a canny operator. She liked to scrutinize every charity she helped. So had she double-checked Rising Star and worked out, as I did, that Mr Krugbender, who had died on the Christmas Antarctic cruise, was a benefactor? Had she added to that Marakit Wyldestone, from the Kimberley cruise she had also been on? I doubt she would have found Major Fisher, because she and Don never went to Longyearbyen, nor were they with Mrs Drew-Huggins in Ecuador. To be honest, I was surprised that you let all these people be named.'

Alyssa shrugged and looked over at Carmen. 'We had to,' she admitted after a moment. 'It was what they wanted.'

Inside Francis let out a private whoop. 'You never imagined,' he said, 'that anyone would cross-reference them with a list of cruise ship deaths?'

'Of course I didn't,' the doctor replied. 'Who looks at lists of benefactors? Anyway, not all of them wanted recognition. Major Fisher, for example – how did you find out about him?'

'It's all there,' said Francis. 'If you know where to look. Ralph Walden Fisher is hardly a common name. And he did leave a lot of money.'

'I know he did,' Carmen said.

'His fortune was inherited,' Alyssa added, 'from a cousin, and he always felt a bit guilty about it. It came to him late, so he'd lived an ordinary life in the real world; he'd travelled extensively, so knew what suffering could be, and how money could help alleviate it. He was a sweet guy.'

'Until he was murdered,' said Francis briskly. 'So if Lauren had found at least some of these things out, had she challenged you, Carmen? And had you realized that, although you had never been involved in the killing side of things before, now was the time, it had to be done? For the very best reasons: to protect your lover and her wonderful idea. For what really was the ending of the life of one unhappy alcoholic compared to the salvation of large numbers of Aboriginal, African and South American children? Weren't their young lives worth more than hers? Not to mention all those other rich old people who were sooner or later going to die anyway? And what a nice way to go, Alyssa. On a cruise. Falling asleep after a pleasant dinner with friends, with a view of the sea. What could you fault about that? Or about taking the money that was only going to go to greedy relatives or pointless First World charities and spending it where it would really count. A donkey sanctuary! I mean, I ask you.'

'How did you know about the donkey sanctuary?' asked Carmen. 'That stuff's not online, surely.'

'Eve told me.'

Suddenly, the doctor was crying. Great sobs shook her tiny frame.

'Alyssa,' Carmen said, holding her. 'Stop it, darling. Please. Get a grip.'

'No!' she cried, and the strangled noise that emerged from her was like a dog's yelp. 'You're right, Francis. You have worked it all out. It was so stupid to call the trust Rising Star. We were going to call it Better World, but then, I don't know . . .'

'Better World seemed so naff,' Carmen cut in. 'Sounds like a health club. And I'm a sucker for black humour.'

Alyssa was laughing through her tears, her eyes affectionately on her lover. She wiped her cheeks with the handkerchief that Carmen passed her.

'It didn't start like that,' she said. 'I never planned to hurt anyone, let alone kill them. I trained as a doctor, for goodness' sake! But I got into it in stages. It began when I persuaded this one guest, a beautiful old Canadian lady who came on a trip around the South Sea Islands, to support a charity that I know about back home in the Philippines. It's an amazing operation. They take foundlings and orphans and look after them, then place them with stable families. There are so many children that are helped by that. You see them coming into the charity, sad and lonely and frightened, and then a year later, screaming around happily in their new homes. How can you deny them that? So I was so thrilled when Julia agreed to give us some money. She had been British, originally, but she was evacuated to Canada in the war. And then her father had died, and her mother had been on a ship that had been torpedoed crossing the Atlantic, so she had lost them both and grown up in care. She had been luckier later in life and ended up married to a rich and successful businessman, but she'd never forgotten the difficulties of her childhood, so she was more than happy to help. She left us pretty much everything. She must have known she was dying, because she only lasted a couple of months after we docked. We got the money quite promptly and it made such a huge difference.

'And then, on the next but one cruise, from Auckland to Dunedin round the coast of New Zealand, I was talking about her amazing contribution to another guest, an American lady, and she suddenly decided she wanted to give us the bulk of her fortune too. I was very excited, obviously; but then, when she got home, one of her children persuaded her out of it. I was so disappointed about that, because she had been very sincere when she'd been chatting to me, and it was a lot of money we'd been promised. So then, one night, discussing it all with Carmen . . .'

'I talked her into it,' said Carmen. 'Why not just make sure of things while the benefactors are still at sea? Jesus, they're way past their sell-by date.'

'They're all alone in the world,' the doctor continued. 'They hate going home. That's what they always say: "It's so much fun on the cruise, but then I have to go home to an empty house." So why not save them from that? I have the drugs. A hundred milligrams of Propofol finishes them off, in an entirely painless way. I certify their deaths, so there's no need for an autopsy.

'But you're right. Captain Andrushenko had started asking questions. More to the point, Alexei was seriously suspicious of me. So yes, I thought I would, as you put it, call their bluff.' She turned to Carmen. 'Shall I go on?'

'You might as well.'

The doctor looked almost relieved. 'I had the idea about the dry ice on the trip from Argentina to Cape Town. One of the guests passed out at one of the evening shows that Gregoire and Viktor organize and had to be revived. That little faint only lasted a minute, but it gave me an idea. In a sealed room, as you said so correctly, you suffocate, if the levels are high enough. And yes, the only sign is a slightly raised concentration of carbon dioxide in the blood. A lab wouldn't question that, especially if I'd already correctly noted appropriate symptoms, such as the bloodshot eyes. It was me insisting on the autopsy. What more could I do to reassure the captain that I had nothing to do with these onboard deaths? Especially if it wasn't what he wanted. My stand was proof that I was not what the first officer thought I was.'

'Thank you,' said Francis. 'That's very brave of you to tell me that. I totally understand how you could have done it. And now the Rising Star Trust supports charities right across the world.'

'It does.'

'You weren't to know that Lauren would work out what you were up to, or that poor George would be up late checking the lifeboats.'

'No,' said the doctor, her voice trembling. 'I could never . . . George . . . I mean, I didn't think in a million years . . . It was two a.m.'

'Alyssa,' said Carmen. 'Come on. We weren't to know.'

'But still. He had children . . .'

'And they're alive.'

'Orphaned,' she said with a sob.

'May I ask,' said Francis, after a few moments, 'if *your* parents are alive?'

Alyssa met his eyes. 'No. They died when I was little. In a car accident in Manila. And so, yes, I was myself in a home for two years. Before I was moved to my new family.' She had taken a handkerchief from Carmen, and was wiping her face, trembling as she did so. 'I was lucky,' she went on. 'They were not just kind, but also wealthy. So I was sent at a young age to the best schools. I would never have become a doctor if I had not had the support of my new family.'

'And your new parents are still alive?'

'Yes. They are very proud of me. Of course, they have no idea about the Rising Star Trust.'

'For what it's worth,' said Francis, after a few moments, 'I was adopted too. My time in care was mercifully short, and I have no memory of it, but I'm always aware that things might have been very different for me. I'm on your side, put it that way.'

There was silence. Way over in the village, the wailing and chanting had tailed off, but the pounding of the drums was continuing. Francis glanced at his watch. It was a quarter to four. They had just over an hour before they had to leave the island.

It was Carmen who broke the silence. 'I'm impressed, mate,' she said. 'It makes me wonder how much of this you'd worked out when we were going around together interviewing people. And whether your petulant little protests about me passing on information to Viktor and the captain were just a smokescreen.'

'No, I was sincere about that. It was bloody annoying.'

'Maybe it was. But we have a problem now. Because we can't really let you go back to the ship, can we?'

She reached down to her waistband and drew out a hunting knife. It was a good six inches long. As she held it up, it glinted dangerously in a beam of sunlight that shafted down from the thick foliage above.

'Expedition blade,' she said. 'Don't think I'd be afraid to use it.'

Francis didn't move. 'Don't be silly,' he said. 'We're all grownups here. I'm not a policeman.'

'It's hard to explain how it feels,' Carmen said, 'when you've killed someone. Especially when you are not a naturally violent person. You wake up each morning and it takes you half a minute to remember. That that's what you've become. A murderer. There's no escape from that. And no escape from the fact that people are trying to find you out. Clever people like you, Francis. That one stupid slip could give you away.'

She was pacing back and forth, holding her knife up in front of her, dramatizing her position of power. Francis glanced rapidly across the clearing and wondered whether he could outpace them through the woods, a seven-hundred-yard dash back to safety in the village. He doubted it. He could shout, of course, but that would hardly be heard against all that wailing and drumming.

'I shan't forget,' Carmen went on, 'that scream Lauren let out when I tipped her over the railings. Never. Even though she was an unhappy woman, she didn't want to die.' She shook her head, slowly. 'I caught her totally by surprise, so it took her a second to realize . . . It was horrid, that noise as she went down. And yes, poor George. I don't think either of us anticipated the . . . collateral damage.'

Francis was thinking fast; somehow, he needed to talk this maniac round. Softly, softly, he told himself, don't show your fear.

'Why d'you think I followed you into the woods?' he asked.

'I don't know. Because you were curious. Because you wanted to confirm that what Klaus had told you was true?'

'Who said it was Klaus?'

Carmen laughed. 'Don't worry. I saw him. Silly old fool. I hardly thought that he would tell anyone – let alone you.'

'OK,' said Francis. 'You're right about that. But I also came because I wanted to sort this out before we went back to the ship. I wanted to tell you that in the circumstances I didn't necessarily want to turn you in.'

'Necessarily?' Carmen repeated. 'That sounds very convincing. And convenient. Given what we've just told you.'

Francis shifted his weight. Some forest insect had bitten him on the bottom. Involuntarily, he reached down to scratch the itch.

Carmen tensed. 'I wouldn't try running for it, mate,' she said. 'I'm pretty fast, and pretty fit.'

'I know you are. And I guess that if you wanted to finish me off, here, now, the two of you, you probably could. But there's no point. Unless I choose to tell the captain what I know, I don't see why you would ever be caught. The results from the lab are going to confirm that Eve died of old age. However much Don protests to the contrary, poor Lauren will be seen as a suicidal drunk; there's no actual body to investigate. No one except myself and Ray know that George saw something. The snakebite was a surprising thing to happen on board ship, but not impossible – and you are, Alyssa, as you said, the ship's doctor. This would not be the first time you've certified a murder as a death. Even if there are any outside enquiries, which I very much doubt, there'll be no case at all.'

'Why d'you think I'd believe for one moment that you won't say anything?' said Carmen. 'Even if your natural sense of justice doesn't force you to turn us in, if you don't, you're incriminating yourself. Accessory to murder, isn't it? And what about Ray?'

'Ray is a very frightened man. It may cost you a little, but we can square him. And why should the rest ever come out? I've heard your story, and I understand what good work the Rising Star Trust is doing. Why would I want to put a stop to that? For the sake of revealing that a few old people died a couple of years earlier than they might have done?'

Carmen looked doubtful. 'And a middle-aged heiress, and an innocent Filipino father of two,' she said.

'I have factored those two into my thinking. And I have one condition for my silence. That you stop now. Not Rising Star. Certainly not that. But your unorthodox fundraising activities. I really couldn't be party to any further murders, however innocent you present them as being.'

'It's a bit late to be making conditions, don't you think?' Carmen replied. 'Anyway, that's rather a big ask, when we could sort things out right now. So that we can continue as planned. In any case, I don't believe you. Sorry.'

'You told me you didn't like killing,' said Francis. 'You had to kill Lauren. And Alyssa had to deal with George. I understand that. But me. Would you really want my death on your conscience too? And how in any case would you cover it up? It would be the straw that broke the camel's back. If I don't return to the ship, they're not going to steam on this time, are they? A fourth death will mean they have to act. And who knows who saw you both leaving the village? Besides me. As you said, Alyssa, the first officer already suspects you.'

'Very convincing, mate,' Carmen said. 'And thank you for your offer – and for pointing out that we could pay Ray off. As for you, I'm sorry, but you're just a little bit too clever for us to trust you. I can even believe that you might not say anything back on the ship. But what happens when you get home and reflect on all this? Even though you may think what we're doing is fine, here, now, in the remote jungle of Guinea-Bissau, your conscience will eventually get you. You'll have to turn us in.'

'OK,' said Francis, eyeballing her. 'So what are you going to do? You've got just over an hour before the last Zodiac leaves this island. Even if you managed to clean yourself up, how are you going to explain away a bloodied corpse?'

'Who says we're going to have to explain it away? You might have been attacked by anyone. One of the villagers even. Anyway, who says we're going to use the knife?'

'You brought some spare poison with you, did you, Alyssa?'

'As it happens, she did,' Carmen said. 'The plan was to get rid of it. After they stopped us docking at Freetown, we've got no idea who might come on at Banjul. Or Dakar.'

'So that Ebola story was made up?'

'Didn't you realize that? The captain and first officer are making sure that everyone stays on board.'

Francis wasn't going to admit anything. But it was interesting that both Colonel Joe and old Henry Forbes-Harley had been right about the Ebola. 'So what's your plan?' he asked, trying to keep his cool. 'I don't imagine dry ice would work out here. Another snakebite?'

'It would be, yes,' said Alyssa quietly.

'She will tell them,' said Carmen, 'that the venom is from a local puff adder, though actually it's *deinagkistrodon acutus*, the same that killed poor George, milked from the South East Asian pit viper. You wondered earlier how he'd gone so quickly. The pit viper is known in Asia as "the hundred pacer". Because that's how far you get when you've been bitten by it.'

'I did also, as you guessed,' added Alyssa, 'sedate him first. He was so upset about seeing the MOB he couldn't sleep. He asked for a pill, so I offered an injection.'

'Did he tell you why he was really so upset?'

'Yes. That's how we knew.'

'He confided in you, the doctor?'

'Yes.'

'Ironic.'

'It was, probably, yes.'

Her eyes were full of shame.

'He didn't know it was Carmen?'

'No. He thought it was a man. A blond man. In any case—'

'He didn't know about you two.'

'No.'

'So where did you get the venom?' Francis asked, after a moment.

'Off the Internet,' said Alyssa. 'It gets posted from China. Anybody can buy this stuff. It's terrifying, really.'

'A phial of venom, tucked away with the antivenoms. Who would have thought it? So why did you even have it?'

'We were going to use it . . .'

'On Eve,' Carmen finished. 'She would have been found dead out at the village on that first day.'

'And then you had a better idea?'

'Yes. Alyssa did.'

'Not the nicest of deaths, I imagine?' Despite his best intentions, Francis's voice was cracking.

'Not like propofol or pentobarbital, no,' the doctor replied. 'But it will still finish you off in about fifteen minutes. There is some pain and then you rapidly asphyxiate. But I'll give you a morphine shot first, so you won't suffer.'

'There's nothing else we can do, mate,' Carmen said. 'You will not return to the boat at five. Viktor will be furious, because it means he will miss the tide, and the ship will have to stay anchored here overnight, upsetting the itinerary even further. But he will have no other option. A search party will be sent out. And very soon, one of the dogs will find you. Out here, several hundred yards from the village. How very foolish you were to take a walk against the advice of the expedition team, and go and get yourself bitten by a puff adder.'

Francis's nerve was failing him now. His mouth was dry, his arm was trembling uncontrollably, he could see his heart pounding against his sweat-soaked shirt. He was suddenly so breathless he could hardly speak. 'I've told you . . . I'm happy . . . not to say anything about . . . Rising Star. With one simple . . . understand-able . . . condition . . .'

'Still making conditions,' said Carmen, scornfully. She turned to her companion. 'I'm sorry, Alyssa. We're going to have to do this.'

'Are we?' said the doctor. Now she looked both uncertain and scared.

Carmen turned impatiently. 'Of course we must.'

'Alyssa, please,' said Francis. 'You don't need to. I'll square Ray. I promise I won't say . . .'

He tailed off. Even *in extremis* he was unable to offer his word that he wouldn't turn them in. Because of course he would. If he ever got away from here.

'I give you . . . my *word*,' he managed finally, ends justifying means. But it didn't sound convincing.

The doctor turned to her partner. 'I trust him,' she said. 'We can give him this chance.'

'No.' Carmen shook her head. 'Look in his eyes. He's lying. Surely you can see that?'

From across in the village, the beat of the drums sounded louder. The carnival was reaching a climax.

'It's too much,' the doctor said. 'We should accept his offer. He's right, anyway. Eve didn't deserve that. She was a kind old lady with lots to live for. Who knows how many more years she had?'

'Five at the most,' said Carmen scornfully.

'And Lauren. Lauren was young. Younger than you.'

'A spoilt, depressive alcoholic.'

'And *George*,' the doctor's voice rose to a squeal.

'Stop this, Alyssa! Now is no time for sentimental bullshit. If you want to call a halt to the programme after the cruise, you can.'

'But Francis is giving us a way out. That lets us go on. And he's right. If there's another death, it will be one too many. In any case, it won't be just one. Ray has to go too.'

'We can pay him off. As Francis said.'

'They're bound to investigate, Carmen. We will be found out. Rising Star will be finished. And us too.'

'Of course we won't be found out, darling. Viktor was even warning the guests about snakes as we came up.' Carmen turned towards Francis. 'I'm sorry, mate . . .'

The look in her eyes was both purposeful and contemptuous.

'Come on, Alyssa,' she said. 'Prepare the hit.'

The doctor seemed to have given in. She opened her bag and found a syringe, then looked up at her partner again.

'We don't need to do this.'

'For God's sake, get on with it! We haven't much time. Lie down, please,' she ordered Francis. She was holding her big knife right above him. He did as he was told.

'Put your hands up behind your back. Face on the ground, that's it.' He turned sideways to see her reaching into her bag for a coil of blue nylon twine. She sawed off a length with her knife.

'Face . . . on the ground,' she repeated, resting the sharp point on the back of his neck. Involuntarily he shivered, feeling the steel pricking his skin.

'Are you ready, sweets?'

'OK,' came the doctor's voice.

At the moment before his death, Francis's life didn't flash before him. Instead he was thinking, furiously: how could I have been such an *idiot*, to approach these two here, now. Unprotected and unsupported. If they had been men I would never have dared.

I'd have waited till we were back on the ship, made sure the show-down involved Viktor, the captain, Alexei and a posse of beefy officers. Casual sexism has cost me my life.

Is this really it? he wondered, as his nostrils, pushed against the earth, filled with the scent of dried leaves; no different out here, in Guinea-Bissau, than it was at home. This was the strange thing about the world, wasn't it? You travelled to the farthest corners and found exactly the same familiar things. Fields in India that looked like Berkshire, blackberry-fringed beaches in Tasmania that could be in Cornwall. When had he last smelt this pungent, evocative aroma? As a teenager, at school, playing in the woods at the bottom of the Big Field. With Norman, his bestie of that time. They had gone out there to smoke. On summer afternoons. Players No. 10. And what were those menthol ones called? With the coloured shafts. They had kept those for the girls. Giggly parties, cider, smoky peppermint kisses. So was that it then? An undistinguished end in the jungle of Africa, like some benighted nineteenth-century explorer. A paragraph-long news item in the papers if he was lucky. Absurdly, he found himself wondering whether he would merit an obituary; how long it would be; which photograph it might feature. *Minor Crime Writer Bites The Dust*. Literally.

No, no, no, this was not how he wanted to go. In pain. Gasping for breath. *Oh, God, help him, what a fool he'd been—*

'Step back, please.'

He squinted sideways to see both women spin round. Klaus was on the edge of the clearing, holding a smart little silver pistol.

'It's loaded,' he said; he wasn't smiling.

Carmen froze. 'Where did you get that?'

'Surprising what you can buy in an African village market. I didn't like the idea of being unable to defend my person from pirates.'

'It's illegal to carry a gun on a cruise ship.'

'It's illegal to murder someone. Drop the knife, please.'

Carmen was staring at him now, as if she might be about to risk all with a mad lunge.

'I said, drop the knife. You have five seconds before I shoot. As I'm sure you know, I have military experience. One. Two. Three . . .'

Carmen dropped the knife.

'On your feet, too, please, Doctor.'

Alyssa scrambled up.

'Drop that syringe. Then I'd like you both to unclip your walkie-talkies and put them on the ground. Turn around slowly, kneel down and put your arms up behind you. Francis is going to tie your wrists together with some of that useful nylon twine. And then we can get going.'

Even as the two intercoms were placed on the ground, they crackled into life. The sudden noise startled them all.

'Expedition team, expedition team,' came Viktor's voice. 'Dark Leader here. Start encouraging the guests back towards the Zodiacs now please. The tide is falling rapidly. I repeat, the tide will soon be at a critical state.'

'Dark Leader!' Klaus repeated, shaking his head.

'We have forty-five minutes,' came Viktor's voice, 'until the last Zodiac must leave the island. Alyssa, I've lost sight of you. Please respond. Over and out. Carmen, you too, please. I need you down at the beach for the embarcation right away.'

Francis, standing now, was looking at Klaus.

'How on earth . . .?' he mouthed, shaking his head.

The German smiled.

'Didn't I tell you I always know more than I let on,' he replied.

TWENTY

A s they docked in Dakar two days later, Francis stood by the rail on deck seven, looking down the sheer side of the ship at the quay far below.

'Sad, isn't it?' said Bruce from Chicago, who was next to him, gazing out at the masts and stacks of containers in front of them. 'I don't want to go home now.'

'I *so* don't want to go home now,' chirped Candy. 'I have just loved Africa. Hey, Bruce, look, one last retail opportunity.'

Below them, the hawkers were already out in force, their wares laid flat on the grey concrete, which was stained here and there with ugly dark patches of oil. Scarves, shirts, necklaces, statues, models, paintings – all the brilliantly colourful and inventive art and tat of Africa was on display, available for one last time before the guests made their way by coach or taxi to their transfer hotels ready for their flights out of Senegal later tonight.

'I have ten Mandela shirts and you have a case full of dresses and shawls,' Bruce replied. He turned towards Francis with a smile. 'We have about twenty ebony carvings, ten necklaces and God knows how many bangles. We really don't need more.'

'But this is another country, honey. Who knows when we'll be back? It's all so cheap. And anyway, they'll make fine presents.'

Tonight was the end of the road for Francis too. Goldencruise had not invited him on the next leg, which left Dakar this evening and went up past Cape Verde and the Canary Isles, Madeira and Morocco to dock in Lisbon in fourteen days' time. Once they had checked this lot of passengers out, the staff and crew had a busy day ahead, ending with welcome drinks and dinner this evening for a whole new crowd.

As soon as the guests had left there would be another transfer too: of Carmen and the doctor to the Senegalese authorities, supervised, Francis had been led to understand by the captain, by some operatives from Interpol. The whole operation had been magnificently discreet, from the moment Francis had picked up Carmen's intercom from the dry leaves of the jungle floor and informed Viktor that there was 'a situation' that needed to be dealt with. The expedition leader had waited until the passengers had all left the beach for the *Golden Adventurer*, and then Carmen and the doctor had been taken back to the mother ship on a separate Zodiac, with Klaus, Francis, Viktor, Mike and Leo to guard them.

No announcement had been made. That evening a five-course dinner had been served as usual. The next night, after a day's birdwatching on the lovely River Gambie at Banjul, there had been the Farewell Cocktail party, complete with a full parade of crew and staff in the Panorama Lounge, and loud cheers for Captain Adrushenko.

The prisoners had meanwhile been confined to the ship's jail down on the second deck, while Klaus and Francis had been debriefed by the captain. George's body was due for an autopsy that would confirm his poisoning by a South East Asian pit viper, a snake that could never have made its way to his cabin on the West Coast of Africa. Francis had also made sure that he had picked up the syringe the doctor had prepared for him; now it was isolated for evidence.

Had Klaus not been so sharp, and so resourceful, Francis shuddered to think what might have happened. For as the captain had confided, a negative result had come back from the European Hospital in Takoradi. The autopsy had concluded that there had been nothing suspicious about Eve's death, despite the doctor's 'reservations'. Mrs Bagshawe had reached the end of her natural life and died of old age.

Dr Lagip's bluff had worked. And had Francis not discovered what he had, how might Lauren's death have been presented? A tragic suicide, almost certainly, whatever Don thought; not the first and not the last troubled passenger to have thrown themselves from a cruise ship. Meanwhile, Francis doubted whether any more would have been done to discover how the puff adder had got on board to kill poor George. That would have been another accidental death for the authorities of the Bahamas not to be troubled by. The horrible truth would have been buried at sea, just as many another mysterious death had been over the years. Would that ever change? Francis wondered. Or would the 'high seas' remain like the Wild West, a place where bad things could happen and people could still get away with them?

Francis had not spoken to either Carmen or Alyssa since the showdown in the sun-dappled Bijagos clearing. Presumably, once the case was over, the money that had been left to the Rising Star Trust by Marikit Wyldestone, Mr Krugbender, Major Fisher and Mrs Drew-Higgins would have to be returned to the relevant estates. Though he deplored the murders, Francis couldn't help but have a sneaking admiration for the charity's grand plan. Taking money from the rich and elderly to help orphaned children was an idea of genius; and in an ideal world one that would happen naturally. It was a dreadful shame that Alyssa hadn't just stuck to quiet persuasion, as she had at the start. Though Alyssa had effected the killings, Francis had little doubt that Carmen was the evil, not to say insane, one in the equation. He would never forget that look in her eye as she strode back and forth across the jungle clearing with her glinting knife. Pitiless, was one word for it. Was she actually a psychopath?

As the *Golden Adventurer* was tied up, and the gangway was lowered from the ship's main entrance on deck three, Francis could see a little posse of officials edging forward from a couple of parked minivans. These weighty uniformed gentlemen were doubtless the Senegalese customs people, who would sit upstairs and check guest passports before everyone was allowed to leave. But there was a police van there too, and next to it a couple of suited guys leaning on an unmarked Mercedes. One was black and heavily built, the other white and lean. Interpol?

Behind them, and to one side, was a larger group who clearly weren't police; or if so, extremely convincing in their undercover operation. This latest lot of dancers was highly energetic, arms and legs akimbo, then throwing themselves down to the ground, doing the splits, then up again. The women wore long, low-cut, shiny dresses, rather as if they were heading off for some smart evening function, and hardly what you'd imagine in a Muslim country – but then again, as Viktor liked to say, Africa was always unexpected.

To Francis's right, up on deck, one of the guests had started dancing too. It was Shirley, toyi-toying with husband Gerald, head thrown back in the sunny breeze. She had had some unexpected good news, by email, when they returned from their bird-watching day on the Gambie river. Remission. Francis had toasted her last night, up in the bar with Brad and Damian and Sebastian and Kurt and Sadie and Leo. Shirley would never have come on this cruise, she had told Francis tipsily, squeezing his arm, if she hadn't thought she was going to die. Wasn't it strange, she went on, that it took a threat like that to make you start living; doing the stuff you really wanted to do. But she wasn't going to hold back now. Certainly not. There was nothing like a second chance. She was going to be like one of the beautiful fish eagles she had seen circling above the Gambie river, flying free. She had sounded, he'd thought, rather like Eve, and he'd felt sad for the old widow then, her life taken from her before she was ready, before she had seen Kamchatka or the Komodo dragons.

'*Woezo!*' shouted Shirley now, as she twirled adventurously in the sunlight. Who cared that the Togolese greeting meant nothing in Senegal? She was in a perfect, private moment of happiness, with the rest of her life ahead of her, and her devoted husband beside her.

And this was Africa, after all.

ACKNOWLEDGEMENTS

I am grateful to Tom Robbins, travel editor of the *Financial Times*, who first sent me on a cruise with the wonderful Silversea, and to Silversea and Paul Charles of PCC for arranging a second adventure. What happened on those luxurious and impeccably organized trips bears no relation to the narrative of this book, which is entirely a product of my own fevered imagination. Back home, Roddy Bray gave me helpful insights into the life of a cruise expedition leader; Kendall Carver of www.internationalcruisevictims.org explained about the state of the law at sea; and Captain Michael Lloyd filled me in on some realities of below-decks life. John Honeywell, editor-at-large of *World of Cruising* magazine, shared his expert knowledge of the industry and Dr Roger Stephenson corrected my medical errors. Stephanie Cross offered me encouragement and excellent editorial advice on my first draft, and Sue Cooke, Ben Craib, Linda Hughes, Imelda Dooley Hunter, Katrin MacGibbon, Stephen McCrum and Jo Swinnerton were early and insightful readers. My agent Jamie Maclean sold the book with alacrity, and I am grateful to the fine team at Severn House publishers: Kate Lyall Grant, Sara Porter and Michelle Duff, as well as to copyeditor Anna Harrison. Thanks again to my wife Jo, who would have loved to have come cruising too, but stayed behind to look after our small children: her plot points remain invaluable.